OUT

CARA DEE

Enjoy Nikki!

OUT
CARA DEE

All rights reserved

Copyright © 2017 by Cara Dee

This book is licensed for your personal enjoyment only and may not be reproduced in any way without documented permission of the author, not including brief quotes with links and/or credit to the source. References to ancient or historical events, persons living or dead, locations, and places are used in a fictional manner. Any other names, incidents, and places are derived from the author's imagination. The author acknowledges the trademark status and owners of any wordmarks mentioned in this work.

Edited by Silently Correcting Your Grammar, LLC.
Formatting by Eliza Rae Services.
Proofreading by M.H.

DEDICATION

Lisa, Los Angeles, lipsticks, and loves.

Camassia Cove is a town in northern Washington created to be the home of some exciting love stories. Each novel taking place here is a standalone, and they will vary in genre and pairing. What they all have in common is the town in which they live. Some are friends and family. Others are complete strangers. Some have vastly different backgrounds. Some grew up together. It's a small world, and many characters will cross over and pay a visit or two in several books. But, again, each novel stands on its own, and spoilers will be avoided as much as possible.

***Out** is a novel taking place in Camassia Cove. If you're interested in keeping up with the characters, the town, the timeline, and future novels, check out Camassia Cove's own page at Cara's website.*

www.caradeewrites.com

CHAPTER 1

I HAVE A LIST

Zach Coleman

Quit stalling. You're here for a reason.

Two reasons, actually. I had a list. This was the first item on that list, the priority.

Topaz Pages. What an awful name for a bookstore.

I scratched the side of my head and squinted at the sign above the quaint shop. What color topaz did that even refer to? The sign was black on white, the cursive letters hand-painted on the wood. My mom used to say I had topaz eyes. I called them blue, some called them green. But then there was yellow topaz, so merely saying something was the color topaz was like deliberately screwing with someone. Being all vague and crap.

Gravel crunched under my Chucks as I turned and took in my surroundings, nothing making sense to me. Everything I had read about Malibu seemed wrong, because this wasn't fancy. On the side of the Pacific Coast Highway that slithered up along the coastline, I'd found Topaz Pages sitting here all alone. Actually, there was a pastry shop too. That was it, though. The two businesses shared a two-story building and a small parking lot. Expansive hills were their backdrop, and the ocean was across the road—well, down a cliffside.

It was hot as hell, and cars whooshed by, upsetting the yellow dust. Mansions and beaches weren't far away, maybe a minute or two in each direction, yet this...this looked like a place God had forgotten.

Topaz Pages. I scoffed quietly and walked toward the building. My pale ass needed to get out of the scorching sun before I turned into a poster child for skin cancer. Or an item on the Red Lobster menu.

I gave my armpit a test whiff, satisfied I still smelled the deodorant. Perhaps wearing black jeans and an equally black tee hadn't been the wisest choice, but I was from northern Washington, a place where the sun wasn't outright chasing you or starting wildfires all over.

Why did stars pay millions to live in these mountains?

So far, Malibu wasn't very impressive.

There was a ground-level porch that snaked around the two shops, and someone cared about this place. The stucco building with a flat roof didn't look like much on its own, but with the fresh coat of white paint and all the potted flowers, at least the joint was taken care of. Two Parisian tables and four chairs stood outside the pastry shop. Outside the bookstore was a welcome mat that read "Shhh, I'm reading."

The old-fashioned sign inside the door said, "We're open sometimes."

My mouth quirked up.

A bell clanged as I opened the door. A sigh of contentment escaped me at the first gust of the air conditioner, and I glanced around the modest space, taking in the sight of all the books. Quaint really fucking was the right word for this store. Shelves lined the walls, as well as creating six narrow aisles with books from floor to ceiling.

I ran a hand through my hair and breathed in deep. Old books had a distinctive smell, and it was almost soothing. I wasn't even big on reading, yet it calmed some of my nerves.

I had to wonder, though...how the fuck did a place like this make a profit? A bookstore barely survived in my lumberjack town a couple hours north of Seattle; we had one left, if I wasn't mistaken. And we didn't have Malibu rents.

"I'll be right out," a voice called. A warm, soulful voice. Would this be Henry Bennington, the man I was here for? He was my little brother's best friend's estranged uncle and guardian, and all I had to go on was this address, a phone number I couldn't use, and his name. I also knew Henry had been—at some point—an investment banker.

"No worries," I replied, clearing my throat.

My stomach flipped, and one of the narrow aisles called to me. I'd say it was for the books, but it was only a hiding spot. The nerves were back. Totally unrelated to Mr. Bennington and all about my other reason for being in this state.

Item number two on the list.

I fingered the spines of a few old books. *Stop thinking about that party. Do something about it instead.* I was fucking trying, wasn't I? Los Angeles had a big gay community. Before I left, I'd go to a gay bar and see if I really was into guys. Back home, that wasn't an option the way it was here.

Half the time, I still convinced myself it was in my head. Then I'd pass a guy on the street and find him sexy. Time would fly by, and I'd forget him. Gay porn held no interest whatsoever. Straight porn did, while dating an actual woman didn't—anymore—so one could say I was confused and frustrated.

It summed up the past two years of my life. It all started on my twenty-fifth birthday, when a friend of a friend showed up at my little party, and I couldn't form a word. I hadn't seen him since then. Out-of-towner.

A scowl took over when I suddenly saw the book I was holding in my hands. I instantly put it back and noticed this whole section was about same-sex history, politics, and culture.

Moving on to another aisle, I breathed a sigh of relief. American classics. I could deal with those.

I was right in the beginning of the aisle, so I had a good view of the counter by the door when a man appeared from a back office. I kinda froze, aside from a gulp that tightened my throat. *Don't swallow your tongue.* The man was flipping through the pages of a thick book, and he was fucking gorgeous. In some rugged, strange way. I wasn't sure. Did I find him beautiful? Maybe that was the wrong word. My mouth ran dry.

He looks like how a sucker punch feels.

He looked...charismatic, was the word that came to me.

How tall was he? He probably had a few inches on my six feet. His frame was stockier than mine, though toned and fit, and his T-shirt bordered between loose and hugging his sculpted torso. My eyes fell to his biceps as he closed the book. I could tell he took care of himself. He had a nice tan to go with his brown, sun-kissed hair too. Would my hair look like that if I lived in the sun for a few years?

I shook my head, clearing the fog.

You're here for Ty.

The man looked up from his book, clearly caught off guard, as if he'd already forgotten there was someone else in here. "Oh, I apologize. I assumed you were Martin." Dark hazel, that was the shade of his kind eyes. They exuded as much warmth as his voice did. He had some scruff too. Sharp features to give the warm colors a contrast.

Ty had the same eyes, only brighter.

I can't do this.

"How much for this?" I grabbed the closest book and held it up. My palms became sweaty. I needed to get the fuck out of here, and I didn't even know why.

Mr. Bennington tilted his head, appearing confused. "There should be a price tag by the bar code."

Right. I cleared my throat and lowered the book, sneaking a quick glance at the price. $14.99 was no issue, but what would I do with a copy of *Finding Your Inner Seductress: A Guide to a Lustful Marriage*?

I bought it, though. And told him it was a gift.

He probably didn't believe me.

Then I hightailed it out of there and fled in my truck.

I knew what my problem was. As I paced the floor of my overpriced motel room, it all became clear. This weekend had been too highly anticipated, and the appearance of Henry Bennington had thrown me. There'd been a block caused by information overload. I hadn't registered everything when I saw him; it'd lodged itself somewhere and made me tongue-tied.

I'd known Ty for a few years now. He and my baby brother were best friends, so I already had a perspective on Ty's uncle. The Benningtons were old money—way old—and the banker thing implied there would be an expensive suit and a fancy car. Right there was the first glitch. Because in that little bookstore, he'd been sporting cargo shorts and a T-shirt. His hair, while only a couple inches long, was unkempt, and he was far from clean-shaven. Nothing about him screamed old money. Then, yeah, his looks. Goddamn, I hadn't considered that, 'cause why would I? Why would I head down to California and wonder if my brother's best friend's uncle was handsome to the point where I kind of wanted to come in my jeans?

I'd seen a picture of Ty's dad, to boot. He hadn't been half as attractive.

More than that, though, my main reason for being here—to find Henry—had gotten lost at some point. In my head, I'd focused on exploring myself and clearing some of the confusion. I'd looked up gay bars and clubs, my brain filled with various scenarios and how I'd handle them. Learning that Henry was a man who could make me freeze up like that...it was messing with me. It blurred lines I didn't know were there.

Anyway, I was good now. So Ty's uncle was a smoking hot bookstore owner. It didn't matter. I'd go back to his store tomorrow, and I'd bring my wits this time. I was going to return the stupid book, come clean, and tell him I was here on behalf of his nephew, and then I'd be on my merry way. And with that done, I could finally take a couple days to be someone else—or rather, be myself. The thought of being intimate with a dude was wreaking havoc, and not in an entirely bad way. It was exciting, albeit fucking terrifying. But I'd promised myself this. I was gonna be honest, curious, and open.

After buying a shitty vending machine dinner, I sat down on my bed and scrolled through my messages. I had one waiting from Mattie.

Ty might be getting suspicious. I'm sorry, but you know I can't lie!

True story. My brother had no poker face. I replied.

Just avoid the topic. If he asks, tell him to call me. How's the shop?

Leaving our one and only source of income in the hands of a seventeen-year-old wasn't the best feeling, though Mattie had worked in our corner store since he was fourteen. It was only me and my neuroses that worried.

I doubted anything would go wrong. Mattie was more than capable, and we had Pammie too, our only employee.

Everything's fine. It would take me more than 48 hours to fuck this up.

I laughed under my breath, figuring that was true. I left Camassia Cove Wednesday morning, and it was Thursday evening now. If I got lucky, I'd solve the Henry issue tomorrow, and then…maybe I could get _lucky_. I mean, not with him. I needed that thought to be gone ASAP. I was talking about the people I was hoping to meet this weekend.

I'd heard things could get wild.

It made me slightly anxious, but I was gonna dive in. I couldn't expect anyone to hold my hand.

When I returned home on Monday, I hoped I'd have a better insight into what I wanted.

You could ask Henry…

I shook my head and cursed my brain. Then again…he _was_ gay. It was a huge part of why Ty wasn't living with his uncle. I bet Henry could answer more random questions about the gay life than a man in a club would.

My brief research of the hookup app Grindr had taught me that sex often came before introductions.

I scratched my eyebrow, flicking a glance at my reflection in the window next to the door. I could get laid, couldn't I? I'd never had any issues with women. I didn't work out much; instead, I hiked and climbed often. Was I supposed to style my hair? Shit, I was clueless.

Asking Henry didn't seem like an awful idea anymore. If he could just guide me through some basics, perhaps I wouldn't look like a fool when I entered my first gay bar. Of course, this would be _after_ I explained to Henry that I thought he should return to Camassia Cove and slap some sense into his nephew.

CHAPTER 2

SHACKING UP WITH HENRY WAS NOT ON THE LIST

"Ugh." It was hotter today, and it wasn't even noon. At least I'd gone with a white tee today, but black jeans were kind of standard for me. I didn't own much else, and I hadn't brought shorts.

Locking up my truck, I headed straight for the bookstore, and the bell clanged as I entered.

Again, the former investment banker was nowhere to be seen.

I wandered up and down two aisles while savoring the AC, and I waited for Henry to tell me he'd be right out. I lifted a brow as I stopped at the sci-fi section. It took up the entire back wall of the store, and if one person would lose his shit over this, it would be Henry's own nephew. Ty was a bookworm for all things sci-fi and fantasy. He used to be, anyway.

I hoped there was time to make things right. Being alone with my brother, I'd already made the tough call to decide that if Ty didn't get his shit together, I couldn't allow Mattie to hang out with him anymore. I didn't want my little brother traveling down the same path Ty was currently on. Didn't matter that Mattie would be eighteen soon—old enough to make his own decisions. The shop was in my name, as was our apartment. That meant I could set some rules.

A weird sound caught my attention, and I left the back of the store. The counter at the front still showed no signs of life, but there was the sound again. What the hell? It sounded almost like a sob. A low, muffled one.

"Excuse me?" I set down the book I was returning on the glass top of the counter and leaned forward a bit. The door to the office in the back was ajar, though I couldn't see much. "Is everything okay?"

The sound of a toilet flushing followed.

I braced myself—not really knowing why—as a door opened. One presumably belonging to the bathroom in the back, and then the man appeared from his office. I swallowed hard, having nearly forgotten how goddamn sexy he was. *His eyes.* They won this time, and mostly because they were bloodshot.

"I'm very sorry." He coughed into his fist, keeping his gaze averted, and busied himself with what I had a feeling was a completely random book. "How can I help you?"

I eyed the book he held. Upside down. Next, he grabbed a label maker and began tidying up.

I knew how this was supposed to play out. I knew how humans worked. I was going to ignore that he'd obviously been crying, and he was going to pretend everything was all right. It was how strangers functioned.

"I came to return this." I slid the book on seductresses and lustful marriages across the counter. "I, uh…I didn't really mean to buy it."

He spared me a brief glance, recognizing me from yesterday.

"I figured there was something else going on." He rang up the purchase, and I handed him the receipt. "Don't worry. Bookstores can be intimidating the first time you visit them. You're not the first person to freak out and run away with the wrong title."

Was he making a joke? His mouth twisted slightly, even as he studiously avoided making eye contact, and I grinned. Then it died, and I just couldn't stop staring at him. He looked tired, and not in the "I haven't slept in two days" kind of way. More like life was wearing on him.

He was unhappy.

After completing the return, he gave me back my money before he dumped the book in a bin next to the counter. I peered over to see the box labeled "Donations."

"You can't sell it again?" I questioned.

He shook his head minutely. "Self-help books are ridiculous." He stacked together a pile of papers and opened a drawer. He was back to tidying up, no doubt as a way of keeping busy and not having to face me.

"America disagrees with you," I noted. Self-help books were popular as hell. Even I had a shelf with the latest romance novel and "Be Your Own Dr. Phil" book in my shop.

"I suppose I have no interest in selling books to mainstream America." He bent down to stow away something under the counter.

"Then why would you have the book in your store to begin with?"

"I buy up stock from companies that are going out of business. I don't get to pick the titles. I just wait for the countless boxes to arrive, and then I have to sort through them." He rose again and cleared his throat. His eyes didn't look as red anymore. "I no longer need shelf-fillers."

I guess the one I'd bought had been a shelf-filler.

"Okay." I'd run out of things to say on the topic, yet I couldn't bring myself to wrap it up. I didn't want to be a stranger who ignored that he'd been upset, nor did I want to introduce myself as his nephew's friend's older brother. I wasn't ready. I wanted five minutes in the spotlight before Ty took over. *Here we go.* "Can we skip the part where we pretend this isn't awkward, and I ask you what's wrong? You were upset in there." I pointed toward the office.

Despite that the sharp look he gave me lasted less than a second, I could tell he wasn't happy about my bringing that up.

"Sorry," I said, half embarrassed. It wasn't any of my business. "I'll just..." I jerked a thumb over my shoulder toward the door. "Right. Thanks." I turned and twisted the door handle, wondering how the fuck I was gonna return now to tell him the truth, that I actually had a purpose for coming here. I had to tell him about Ty—

"Wait," he said.

Relief smashed into me, and I glanced at him over my shoulder.

His expression was contrite. "Two days in a row, and I've started each of your visits with an apology. I haven't given you a very good impression of me." He looked out the window, then back to me. "I noticed the Mariners sticker on your truck when you left yesterday. Are you just visiting LA?"

I nodded hesitantly.

He nodded once too. "Please, let me buy you a cup of coffee at Martin's next door and send you off with a slightly better opinion of Topaz Pages."

The *fuckyesokay* was already on the tip of my tongue. Luckily, I managed to hold off an extra second and then say, "Yeah, all right." All cool and shit.

He offered a quick, polite smile and rounded the counter to lead the way. God, the man even wore flip-flops. Had he really been a banker?

"My name is Henry."

"Zach," I replied. Standing next to him, I gave him a discreet once-over as he opened the door and stepped out. He looked comfortable in his army-green cargo shorts, flip-flops, and a tee that was navy blue today. His threads were well-worn and fit his body perfectly, showing a hint of the strength hidden underneath.

I'd never asked Ty how old his uncle was, though I suspected he was in his mid-forties. Henry had faint laugh lines around his eyes and mouth, and some silver strands in his dark hair, all of which I found strangely pornographic.

"So you don't wanna talk about what got you upset, huh?" Me and my stupid mouth.

He gave me a narrow-eyed look, only to sigh and gesture toward the pastry shop next door. "What gave you that idea, young man whom I don't know?" For that one, he only got silence from me, and I stifled a smile. "It was my nephew's birthday last week," he admitted, visibly uncomfortable, and fuck, now so was I. "We are, sadly, not on good terms, so it was upsetting to see the photos he uploaded from his birthday party."

A ripple of pain pummeled through me as I replayed the sounds of his muffled cries from earlier. The man was fucking torn up about not being in Ty's life, and I was being a selfish dick because I wanted five minutes alone with his holy hotness to explore whether or not I was into men? Clearly, I fucking was. On some level, anyway.

"I can't do this," I heard myself say. Yesterday, those words had stayed in my head. Now they were out of my mouth. Along with the truth. "My name is Zachary Coleman. My younger brother—Matthew Coleman—is your nephew's best friend." That had Henry's attention. He went from confused to shocked in an instant. "I'm sorry," I added quickly. "I was gonna tell you this yesterday." *But then I met you, and you were so fucking stunning that I couldn't form words.* "I don't know what happened," I lied. "I chickened out. Guess I was nervous." Great, now I was rambling. Shit, my hands were getting sweaty again. "Anyway, I drove down from Camassia to see you 'cause I think you need to come home and talk to him."

Henry's shock faded slowly, something else taking its place. Resignation, maybe even impatience. Or whatever it was that gave him that stiff, closed-off expression.

"I'm sorry," I said again. Sweat beaded above my upper lip, and I wiped it away. California heat and anxiety didn't go well. No wonder people loved getting stoned here.

"Is there something wrong with him?" he asked tightly.

I frowned. "Well, yeah. He's turning into a douchebag."

I put that mildly too.

Henry scowled. "Excuse me? I don't know what that means. Is Tyler okay?"

"Douchebag means—"

"I know what a douchebag is," he snapped. "I'm sorry." He pinched the bridge of his nose, reining it in, I guessed. "What I meant is, if someone comes from another state to tell me I need to go see my nephew, my initial reaction is to wonder if he's dying, hurt, or otherwise harmed. But he's okay?"

I licked my lips and nodded. "He's fine. But he won't be for long. Can—can we get out of the heat? I'm melting."

He inclined his head and gestured back toward his shop, rather than the other place. "Martin is a queen and a gossip. I don't need his drama for this."

I kinda wanted to meet Martin. That was my first thought. I'd never met a...you know...queen.

On the way inside again, I mulled over the approach I'd take with Henry. I noticed I wasn't as nervous anymore, probably because I'd come clean and was ready to get this over with. And there was a short route to take. There was no need to drag up all the sordid details with Henry. He already knew them.

According to what my brother had shared, Henry and Thorne Bennington had both been perfect sons, and having met their father, I knew they'd been raised to fear rather than respect their parents. Not a hair or a grade out of place. Business majors, then holders of master's degrees from some fancy Ivy League school.

Henry was the bachelor, and Thorne married a woman their folks approved of. Then Henry eventually revealed he was gay. Their parents freaked out and disowned him, and Henry quit everything. He went from living in New York and visiting Camassia on holidays to...this. He moved to California with a hefty inheritance he'd received from his grandparents.

If I wasn't mistaken, he hadn't come out until later in life. Ty had been around, I knew that much. The rest of the details as to how close Henry and Ty had been were fuzzy at best, so I hoped Henry could shed some light on that.

It was clear as day Henry and his brother had been very close, though. Because when Thorne and Shelly died in a car crash, Henry was given custody of Ty, who was twelve at the time. Yet, somehow, Ty ended up living with Henry's parents.

Whoever had made that decision needed to have his kneecaps blown off.

As Henry led the way to his office behind the counter, I stopped short in the doorway. *That's got to be the fattest cat I've ever seen.* The gray, stripey spectacle was sprawled out on his back in an old chair. The room was otherwise fairly empty, except for a corner with a littered desk, another chair, and filing cabinets.

"Did your cat eat another cat?" I blurted out.

Henry's face flashed with amusement. "That's Eagle."

"I don't think anything could make that thing fly."

He waved a hand. "It's a golf term. I found him a couple years ago on a golf course." Then he continued, opening a door that led up a narrow set of stairs.

"Could've named him Double Bogey," I mumbled under my breath.

The second floor opened up to a messy-as-hell apartment. Or maybe it wasn't messy, but there were books everywhere. It wouldn't surprise me if he had more books up here than in his store. The space was open, with only a long bar separating the kitchen from the rest. His coffee table consisted of stacks of books covering a glass top. His burgundy couch housed more books, each one with a bookmark sticking out.

There was no TV. There was one shelving system that was filled with framed pictures instead, and it took me a few seconds to realize they were all Ty's photos. Henry had saved them from Ty's social media, and he'd printed them out. It was the only way he could keep Ty in his life.

Where does he sleep?

As soon as the question entered my head, I saw a nook next to a door I assumed led to a bathroom. The alcove was just big enough to fit a bed and one nightstand.

"Coffee?" Henry went behind the kitchen bar. "There's juice, water, and soda too."

"Juice, thanks." I didn't drink coffee unless I was desperate to stay awake.

While he got started with the coffeemaker and pulled out a

carton of OJ from the fridge, I sat down on a stool on the other side of the bar.

"So tell me what's going on with Tyler," he requested.

"Shouldn't be too hard to figure out," I replied. "Your parents are raising him. Who do you think he's turning into?"

Henry flinched and kept his back to me.

"I know your folks don't accept you 'cause you're gay," I revealed, "and if you don't intervene soon, Ty will be just as ignorant." It was a slippery slope, and I'd heard and seen enough to be concerned. Ty was slowly turning into a guy who measured success in terms of money. A few weeks ago, he casually mentioned that Mattie was lucky to have good grades because they provided him a scholarship to attend the same private academy where Ty was. There wasn't a chance in hell I'd be able to afford private school. It was all Mattie's hard work and straight As. "He uses the word fag like a joke," I added to the list. "He dumped a girl because she drove a shitty car."

"Jesus." Henry had given up on the coffee-making, and now he was standing still with his head hanging low, his hands planted on the counter. "I never wanted that for him."

I believed him, but what did he expect would happen? Henry's parents were...well, *they* certainly screamed of old money. Which came with Jackie O suits, underpaid gardeners, banquets, and bigotry. Next year, they were sending Ty to an Ivy League on the East Coast, something I wouldn't balk at if it weren't for the fact that I remembered Ty's dreams. He'd once said he wanted to get into animation. Now his grandparents were hoping he'd major in business.

One perfect son had died, the other was gay, so they were gonna try with their grandson.

"When was the last time you saw him?" I asked. Ty and Mattie had been friends since they started high school, and I'd known Ty for most of that time. He'd been out of town a handful of times; perhaps he'd seen Henry then, but Henry sure as heck hadn't been in Camassia.

"A little over two years." Henry swallowed, and I saw him scrubbing a hand down his face. "I'm lucky if I get to speak to him on the phone once or twice a year. He wants nothing to do with me." At that, he finally faced me. Looking ten years older all of a sudden, he leaned back against the counter and put his hands down in his pockets. "I send him messages every week. Texts, emails… He rarely responds."

"Because you're giving him too much choice." I tried to stay patient, but it was fucking hard. "Not to sound like a dick, but Ty doesn't know better. He's seventeen—a kid. He's sheltered and easily influenced. He's angry." I stopped there, fully aware that every word I spoke could be a blow to Henry's heart. "I think he needs you. He just won't admit it."

His glare was brief but venomous. "What do you suggest I do if he won't speak to me?"

"Why won't he?" I had too little info there.

He shook his head, his expression grim. "You need to realize that from the time Tyler was six to when my brother and his wife died, I was the uncle he only saw a few times a year. I adore the boy, and he loved visiting me here, but I wasn't there every day like my parents. They lived on the same street."

I could understand that, but Thorne and Shelly must've chosen Henry for a reason.

"I can't defeat my parents," he went on, and the hurt was visible in his eyes. "When my brother died, I moved up to Camassia temporarily. I did everything I could to be there for Ty, but my parents are manipulative people. They made him think I didn't want to look after him. I lived so far away, I never came home, I made poor life choices, I wasn't family-oriented… The accusations rained down, and it got to the point where I had to defend my actions whenever I had Ty. He wasn't necessarily accusing me, but he was questioning. He didn't know what to believe—or whom to believe—and regardless of how I feel about my parents, I refuse to badmouth them in front of Tyler. It's cruel, and the only one who suffers is the child."

So in the end, Ty chose to believe his grandparents. I felt for Henry. Being attacked and worked against, then having to try to explain it to an angry teenager who was still grieving... I couldn't imagine that.

"The biggest mistake I made was when I gave up," he said quietly, gaze downcast. "We had a fight one evening, and it ended with him screaming at me—that I should move back to California and let him live with my parents. I was at my wit's end, and I stupidly let it happen."

Everything made much more sense to me now. I couldn't hold shit against him for moving, either. We all had our limits, and verbal attack was just another term for abuse. Henry's parents needed to be fucking gone.

I stared at him, the entire apartment drenched in his defeat and despair. It was easy to say he simply should've stayed, or that he should've forced Ty's grandparents out of their lives somehow, but then you didn't know the Benningtons. Or Ty, for that matter. If there was something he didn't want, he wasn't gonna do it.

"You still have custody, right?" I asked.

He nodded once. "I don't see how that changes anything. I'll show you." He retrieved his phone from his pocket and showed me the one-sided conversation he had with his nephew. "If he will barely answer my texts, how will he respond if I force him to live with me?"

I scrolled up, up, up. Past messages of Henry telling Ty he loved him, missed him, asked when they could see each other... Last time Ty had replied via text was March. It said, "Happy 46." I assumed that was Henry's birthday.

I lifted a shoulder. "We could do one of those hostile takeover things."

"We?"

"Yes, we." I was stubborn about it. I cared, okay? I'd liked Ty—once. Mattie was crazy about the guy—not to mention upset that Ty was becoming an idiot. "Giving Ty too many choices has obviously not worked. He needs to be made to listen."

Henry didn't answer, though I could tell I had his attention. The man still hoped.

I believed it could work. For some reason, Ty had kept his uncle's address by his desk in his room. That had to mean something, didn't it? I found myself rambling a bit to Henry, telling him what I knew and the conclusions I could draw. If Ty hated Henry so much, why keep the address? Why share bits of information here and there?

"What did he say about you driving all the way down here?" he wondered.

Well... "He doesn't know," I admitted. "I was gonna call you, but Mattie couldn't think of a reason to ask for a number that's stuck in Ty's phone without him getting suspicious. So all I had was that address and your name. I searched for you online, but did you change numbers?" Because there was one number attached to this address, and it didn't work.

"I canceled my private landline since I have a separate one for the store," he confirmed. "I'm sorry you had to come all the way here."

"We've apologized way too much." I only wanted to move forward. "Look, Henry. You have one year before he's legal and can do whatever he wants. You've had a few years to stew in your misery, and shit hasn't gotten better, has it? Giving him space won't make him see the damn light. You gotta fight again, and maybe you gotta fight dirty."

Henry grew even more introspective. As long as I saw

resolve taking over, I was happy. It was better than the suffocating depression. Busying himself with the coffee, he listened as I did my best to explain a bit about Ty, which wasn't easy because I didn't wanna insult Henry. He hadn't missed out on anything good these past couple of years, and some of the bad shit would hopefully work in our favor.

"How would any of this work in our favor?" he asked, baffled.

I scratched my nose. There was no way to put this nicely. "Take this the right way, but your nephew is kinda dumb." I ignored his cocked eyebrow. "He relies heavily on technology and gets everything handed to him. He was driving with Mattie a couple weeks ago, and the car broke down. They had no service, so Ty freaked out, 'cause if he couldn't call AAA, then there was nothing else to do."

"Sweet Jesus," Henry muttered, rubbing his mouth as he cringed. "What happened?"

"They were in that ten-minute strip of forest between the Valley and Camas." I referred to two of the five districts in Camassia. "Mattie walked to the nearest body shop." I shrugged. It had been no issue whatsoever. Yet, Ty had been clueless.

"All right." He got weary. "Where are you going with this?"

"Just sayin'. If you take him to some remote cabin, he won't be able to leave. Hell, you can probably keep him in one place right here. Take his phone and credit card, and he's stranded." Even though there were a hundred ways to get away from Topaz Pages. "What I think you two need is alone time. Away from your folks, away from other shitheads who might influence Ty. There are a few of them at their school."

I could practically see all the issues Henry had with this, though he voiced none of them, instead processing them one by one. It was drastic, I knew. It sounded bad, yeah? Keeping someone against their will. Except, Ty could always wise up and get away. Until then...

Besides, what options did Henry have? If Ty didn't want anything to do with his uncle, and the two old farts who were in control wouldn't give that up, then damn straight, hostile takeover.

Henry placed a glass of OJ in front of me, then sat down on his side of the bar with a cup of coffee.

"I suppose he'd be more stranded here than in Camassia," he murmured pensively. "Turning off the Wi-Fi is no problem, and the cell service here is already horrible." He took a slow sip of his coffee, and I realized I was staring again. "Car keys are easily hidden."

"How will you get him to visit?" I asked.

That made him sigh and frown. "The only leverage I have is a piece of paper that grants me sole custody, and I fear Tyler would listen to my parents more than me."

I liked where his mind was going. With the law on his side, Henry could make his parents convince Ty to come down here for a weekend—in exchange for something.

"If you tell your folks you're willing to give them more power if he visits once...?" I wasn't sure how it would work. I didn't know Henry's parents well. I'd only met them a few times, and that was enough. "It's a shitty situation no matter what. There's a lot of blame games and mistakes to make up for. He won't come easy, I'm guessing."

"He won't, no." He peered down into his mug. "I never should have left him."

"Unlike my old man, you didn't take off because handling kids was an inconvenience," I said.

Henry looked up at that. "That's awful. I'm sorry to hear that, Zachary."

That was weird. My body tingled strangely at the use of my name. My full name, from his lips. That goddamn voice of his.

"When did he leave your family?" he asked.

"I was...eleven, I think?" I nodded, remembering Mattie had been about to turn one. "Anyway. There's time for you and Ty to fix this. My brother and I will be here if you want. Mattie might be a good mediator for you, if you think about it. He could cushion the blow and stuff."

Henry nodded slowly, thinking. "I know who he is now. Mattie—I've seen him on Ty's Instagram." I wasn't surprised. Ty loved to take pictures, and Henry was clearly an avid follower. "I feel terrible this has landed in your lap, though," he continued. "I'd like to reimburse you for anything you've—"

"Dude." I frowned, wondering if I should be insulted. "That's not how family works. We may not be family, but I care about Ty. He used to be a lot different." His anger was new—or rather, different—as was his way of acting out and being a dick. The unsure kid with his nose stuck in a book—unless he was debating something he felt strongly about—was just gone. He'd built up walls now. "Mattie sees Ty as a brother. I'd like to keep it that way."

I didn't know what was going through Henry's thoughts, only that he struggled with something. His brow furrowed, and he took another swig of his coffee.

"What?" I got curious.

He shook his head. "Perhaps one day you can tell me how family works. My experience hasn't taught me anything good." He rose from his seat and poured out the rest of his coffee. "I want nothing more than to reconcile with my nephew, so I will gratefully accept any help I can get. I'm under no illusions—I've missed much, and I won't pretend to know him best." He paused to face me, once again leaning back against the counter.

"Any further expenses are on me, however. Where are you staying?"

"Motel up in Thousand Oaks, but—"

He nodded firmly. "Then you'll either let me put you up in a hotel here in Malibu, or you'll take my place. I can stay at Martin's."

"That's not necessary—"

"It's not up for debate." He was getting a little too good at cutting me off. "You've done so much for Ty—and me—already. Now, you have to decide if you're going to stay another week, or if you want to go home and wait until I can call my parents—"

"*Hold up.*" I took a breath and gathered my thoughts. "Why would I go home? Aren't you calling them now? Or, like, soon?"

"Ah." He cleared his throat, backtracking. "Unless my folks have suffered a dual stroke, they're in southern France right now. As they have been every year for the past forty. The last two weeks in June and the first two of July. They'll be home in a week."

Oh. I didn't know that.

"So, this plan," I started to say.

"Which still needs fine-tuning."

"Right. You'll kick it into motion in a week."

"Yes," he replied.

Okay, then. I had calls to make. I didn't know if I could stay that long. "Do you mind if I call my brother?"

"Of course not. I'll give you some privacy." He moved toward the door. "I have to speak to Martin anyway. I'll be next door."

An errant thought entered my head, and for the first time, it occurred to me that Martin might be Henry's boyfriend.

The door closed, leaving me alone, and I sort of collapsed internally. It'd been so rushed there at the end, making me wonder if Henry had needed the escape. It was a lot to process, a lot that was gonna happen.

My brother was stumped when I'd told him everything, and it took me a minute to figure out that he'd had his own vision of Henry Bennington. I'd shattered it with talk of his bookstore, flip-flops that I may have mentioned randomly, and how much he missed Ty.

For Mattie, the world was fairly black and white. If you missed a person, you went to them. Despite that he had no memories of our dad, he was the one who was angry about it sometimes. I'd moved on quicker, although that was more related to Mom's depression. There'd been no time to wallow or grieve. I'd jumped from one problem to another.

"I don't know how Mr. Bennington is gonna get Ty to visit down there," Mattie said.

I hummed, eyeing the books that filled Henry's place. "He's working on it." I had other things to bring up. "Anyway, I wanted to run things by you. Do you want me to come home?"

"You don't have to." If a shrug had a tone, my brother nailed it. I could picture him. "I did inventory with Pammie all day, and then I went to see Nan."

"How is she?"

"She's good. She said it was about time you took some time for yourself."

I smiled, missing the old bird. Our grandmother was the coolest lady I'd ever met. "Did she curse any?"

Mattie let out a laugh. "Um, yeah, some new nurse gave her tapioca pudding instead of chocolate, so she groused *fuckstick* under her breath."

I laughed too.

Nan stated that her life began when Gramps had died, an old grumpy fool no one missed. Tradition had kept their marriage intact, but once he'd kicked the bucket, she'd started living. Her arthritis and frailty unfortunately didn't allow her to go rock-climbing anymore, but she was inventive. She'd replaced skydiving and treasure hunting on her bucket list with cooking classes, googling curses that made her laugh, and mild sexual harassment.

There was a male nurse a decade or so older than me who worked at the home where she lived, and he brought her crossword puzzles and welcomed butt pinches from Nan and her two girlfriends.

"I've become quite scandalous," she'd told me once with a blush.

Thinking about her made me miss home. I'd never traveled much—and *much* was an understatement. Maybe one day, I could afford it; for now, I was a happy homebody.

One who was going to stay in Los Angeles an extra week, it looked like.

I spoke with Mattie for another few minutes, letting him know that if—*when*, fingers crossed—we got Ty to come down here, my brother was to come with him. Henry was gonna square it somehow. Mattie had no issues getting on a bus, but my impression of Henry made it pretty clear there would be airline tickets.

"I've never flown before," Mattie said with a gulp.

I chuckled, not envying him. The only time I'd been on an airplane, I couldn't really remember. I'd been five or six, so it was before Mattie was born. My parents took me to Orlando, from where I had vague, albeit colorful, memories of Disney.

We wrapped up the call after Mattie proudly told me he'd been able to lie to Ty, telling him I was hiking with a friend in Oregon. As close as those two were, they didn't get in each other's business every day, and up until now, Mattie had shrugged off questions. Either I was busy with work, or I was with a buddy.

So, it was settled. I was staying, and I pocketed my phone as I looked around Henry's apartment. Convenient for him to live right above his shop, though I suspected it was isolating too. I didn't care where I ended up, and I'd saved enough money to extend my stay.

Twenty-seven was gonna be my year. I refused to feel guilty. I'd checked off all my priorities from a too-long list—except for this last one—and it was my turn. I could afford to indulge a little.

It felt weird being up here alone, so I chugged some juice, left the glass in the sink, then trailed down the stairs.

"Oh." I stopped abruptly on the last step, coming face-to-face with Eagle. "Let's face it, you're too fat to attack. Right?"

He flicked his tail, staring. Then he sat down and lazily licked his paw.

"Weirdo," I muttered and walked around him.

I left the store and stepped out into the heat, the blazing sun licking at the edge of the shadows that covered the porch. If someone said, "At least it's a dry heat" one more time... First, the woman at the motel when I'd checked in and complained about the sun, then a chatty guy who sat down next to me when I had lunch yesterday.

Heading to the pastry shop, I peered through the window and cursed under my breath. Henry was standing with a shorter, chubby man, and he was upset again. He looked a bit angry too. I watched as he gestured as he spoke, then how he pinched the bridge of his nose and wiped at his cheeks with the back of his hand.

The other man—Martin, I assumed—rounded the counter to comfort him, and I got uncomfortable. I'd already put Henry on the spot once, and I'd delivered a lot of news that probably took a while to process. I wasn't gonna barge in and catch him crying again.

Looking around me, I spotted my truck. It was parked close, and I walked over and opened the door. Slamming it shut was enough noise, I figured. Then I returned to the porch and fumbled a bit with the door to Martin's shop.

When I entered the establishment, I was satisfied. I'd given Henry time to make an escape out back.

"Hi." I ran a hand through my hair and took in my surroundings. He was going for some countryside style. White-painted wood that looked rough enough to give splinters. Frames with inspirational quotes and famous sayings, and then, of course, two glass counters with baked goods. If he did all those himself, he was a genius. There were cupcakes that sparkled and cannoli with rainbow-colored filling.

"Hello, there." Martin walked over to me and grabbed my hand in both of his. "You must be Zachary. Henry's just in the bathroom."

"Zach." I nodded as he released my hand. "You're Martin, right?"

"Indeed, I am! Lovely to meet you."

He didn't look like a queen, whatever that meant. Maybe he wasn't dressed as casually as Henry, but I'd never seen a queen in slacks and a short-sleeved button-down. And *maybe*...I didn't have a fucking clue how a queen looked.

"Do you make all these?" I gestured at the counters.

"I surely do." The corners of his eyes crinkled with his grin. I couldn't get a grasp on him. Was he feminine or extremely masculine? His voice was pitched higher than Henry's, and he was more...exuberant, for lack of a better word. Yet, he looked every part a man's man. Hell, if his name hadn't been Martin, I would've guessed he was Italian. He had a full head of hair too, not a single gray to be found in the mess of black. Did he dye it? He looked older than Henry by a few years. "I run the most successful business in this building," he added slyly. "Of course, working alongside Henry, that's no difficult feat."

I killed my laugh, though not my grin. "I wondered."

"The internet." He waved a hand with a flourish, returning behind the counter. I noticed he had a tray of cookies there that he was in the process of decorating with icing and sprinkles. "This little shop is mostly for me. The money comes from deliveries, online orders, and my other location. But there's nothing quite like a roadside shop that doesn't look like a truck-stop glory hole, is there?"

I coughed and looked away quickly, and I had to force a laugh. Two minutes with this man and I already knew more about his business than Henry's, and he'd uttered the term glory hole.

I...I kinda loved it.

"Don't scar the young man, please." Henry appeared from the back, eyes recovering. No puffiness, just traces of red. I felt for him. "I see you've met Martin. Don't let his flair for diva antics get to you. Underneath the sparkles, he's a teddy bear."

Just then, as Martin jokingly patted his belly, I saw his nails were painted. They were light blue and glittery.

Interesting.

I was drawn to these two men—in very different ways, no shit—and seriously fascinated. I was sure I could sit down and just listen to them for hours. No clue why I felt that way.

"Has he told you he's the most successful business owner here yet?" Henry asked.

I smirked.

"Oh, you." Martin offered a heavy eye-roll, and Henry chuckled quietly and dipped his hand into a glass jar of what looked like biscotti. "So, Zach. What do you do when you're not reuniting families and dressing like..." He waved a hand at me, and I was quickly learning he used a lot of body language. "Half a goth."

My eyebrows rose before I dropped my chin and glanced at my clothes. What was weird about black jeans and a white tee?

"You don't have to answer him," Henry said around a mouthful of cookie. It was almost adorable. "Martin has two mortal enemies. Artificial sweeteners and the color black."

"It's a pair of jeans," I objected.

Martin frowned. "And your shoes and your hair—"

"My hair's not black." This could very well be the most absurd conversation I'd had. "If anything, your hair is black."

"Therefore, my clothes aren't." He gave a light shrug and decorated a couple cookies. "Henry, I think we need to invite Zach to brunch."

"Here we go," Henry sighed.

"Don't you here-we-go me," Martin griped. "At the very least, we can send him home with some advice that his girlfriend will thank us for."

I don't have a girlfriend, I was ready to say. Instead, the words "I wanna go to brunch" tumbled out of my mouth. And I did. Holy shit, did I ever. My resolve only strengthened as they both looked at me, surprised. So I said, "Count me in."

Here were two gay men I could learn from. Martin seemed charming, funny, and maybe a little silly. Henry was...well, my new hottest fantasy. I saw opportunity everywhere.

They wouldn't understand. They didn't know where I came from. They didn't know how much I wanted to experience something completely new and different.

They didn't know just how much my clothes reflected my life. While I saw shades and gray areas, my existence was dull. Simple.

"Marvelous." Martin beamed at me.

Henry looked wary. "If you're sure... You are most welcome, but—"

"No buts," Martin barked at him. "Don't ruin this for me, Henry Jonathan Bennington. I *swear*..."

"Take it down a notch, princess," Henry drawled.

I grinned, already loving this.

CHAPTER 3

MAYBE HENRY SHOULD GO ON MY TO-DO LIST

Bright and early on Saturday morning, I checked out of my motel room and drove toward Malibu. Henry had given me two options, hotel or his place. I figured staying with him wouldn't cost him as much, and...I wanted to stay there. I wanted to see him and Martin more, while I had the chance.

Brunch was a Sunday thing, so tomorrow, I was going to meet another friend of theirs—a man named Joseph.

He was a makeup artist, Martin had been quick to tell me. He'd continued with complaining that Joseph had a horrible taste in men, and he was always bringing around scholars and young professors. At which Henry had protested, stating that Joseph's partners were perfectly lovely; it was Joseph who couldn't commit.

"No wonder," Martin had muttered. "His boy toys are dreadfully boring."

I got out of my truck and grabbed my duffel bag, ready to test out the life Henry and Martin could give me a glimpse of.

Whoa. As I entered the bookstore, I was surprised to see two customers inside. Quickly looking back before the door closed, I spotted a car. Huh, I'd missed it earlier. Someone was distracted, all right.

Henry smiled politely, then returned his attention to the woman he was speaking to, and I snuck behind the counter to leave my duffel in the back office.

So we meet again.

I narrowed my eyes at Eagle.

The cat my nana used to have had been sleeker, black, and fucking vicious. She'd spoken with her claws and teeth, so excuse me for being a little wary of cats.

"Let's make a deal." I set down my duffel, never taking my eyes off the cat in the middle of the floor. He just sat there on his ass. "You don't scratch my eyes out, and I won't call animal control. Okay?"

The little shit yawned and stretched out, claws digging into the carpet.

A throat clearing behind me made me jump, and I turned around to see the amused expression of Henry. Hands clasped behind his back, one eyebrow arched.

"Making friends?"

"You heard everything, didn't you?"

"'Let's make a deal,'" he quoted.

"Great." I kept my sulking internal and looked around for a place to sit.

"Why don't you get settled upstairs?" he suggested. "I left you some food in the fridge if you're hungry, and Martin's bringing over lunch in a few hours."

That was a good idea. I nodded and grabbed my bag again. "Thanks for letting me stay here."

"My pleasure. I don't have company often. Or ever."

Family. Friends. Lovers.

What was considered company? Henry was so handsome there should be guys lining up. Shit, or not. That thought wasn't very pleasant. Probably because I was officially interested. I just hadn't decided if I should or could do anything about it. He was Ty's uncle, for chrissakes. It wasn't on the list to explore anything with Henry. I was supposed to do that with others, with people I wouldn't have to worry about messes and entanglements.

I had to think about it.

Henry returned to his customers as they were ready to pay, and I went upstairs, grimacing as Eagle followed me. The grimace was wiped off my face, though, when I opened the door to Henry's place. Not only had he tidied up, he had turned the sleeping nook into a slice of hotel heaven.

Something twisted inside me. I walked closer and brushed my fingers over the neatly folded bundle of two towels. There was a satin ribbon around it, and a new toothbrush was tucked underneath it, along with a note.

Zachary,
Make yourself comfortable. I've changed the sheets, there are shower products in the bathroom, and help yourself to the food and snacks in the kitchen. If there's anything you need, don't hesitate.
-Henry

Damn. Merely picturing him putting this bundle together for me was giving me all kinds of fuzzy, warm feelings. How fucking sweet was he?

Eagle came sniffing around my bag, and I sat down on the foot of the bed.

"I think it's safe to say I'm not straight," I told him.

He turned, dismissive, and sauntered over to the couch.

The bed looked too inviting to resist. Too bad Henry had changed the sheets. I wouldn't have minded being surrounded by his scent. For now, his apartment would have to do, and I did like the smell of whatever soap he used. There was a hint of manly scents, whether it was cologne or aftershave. Coffee too. And something edible. I'd have to check out the fridge later.

For now? For *now*, his apartment would have to do?

I caught myself, thinking back on that. As if there would be a *later* that looked different? At this point, I couldn't imagine it. I'd never so much as kissed another guy. I touched my lips, wondering what it'd be like to kiss *him*. He was larger than me. Would I feel surrounded? Enveloped?

I gusted out a breath as a rush of arousal flooded south. Oh boy. Definitely not straight, though I'd suspected that for a while. Now to find out how far I wanted to go with a man.

I wanted to talk to Martin.

I glanced at the pillows. Okay, maybe I could talk to him after a quick nap.

I woke up slowly, and to the sound of whispers.

"I mean it, Martin. Let him sleep."

"He needs to eat. He's so cute, I just want to keep him as a pet. A pet that's *fed*."

I smiled into the pillow.

"What the hell is wrong with you?" There was no heat in Henry's voice. "Do I need to push you down the stairs? He'll come down when he's hungry. Let's go."

"Can I at least buy him new pants?"

"For God's sake," Henry grated. *Don't laugh*, I told myself. *Don't fucking laugh*. There was some shuffling, and their voices moved farther away. "*Go*, you old fool."

"I'm going! One observation, though." Martin was moving down the stairs. "This is the most action your bed has seen since you moved in and Joseph's ex passed out drunk."

Henry sighed heavily. "Wait, which ex? Tommy?"

"No, the twink in pharmaceutical sales."

"Samuel."

"That's the one. He wore way too much black too."

My snicker was muffled by the pillow, and once the room was silent, I flopped onto my back and stared at the ceiling. I felt refreshed, and I was in a good mood. At the growl of my stomach, I noted I was starving too. Martin could feed his pet, I guessed.

Dragging my lazy butt out of bed, I straightened my clothes and shook my head in amusement. I was really getting a kick out of their dynamic. I wanted friends like that. I'd worked basically all my life, even when I was in school, so I only had a few people I called friends. One was recent, to boot. Dominic was even gay, but we weren't close enough yet that I could feel comfortable discussing any of that with him. Meghan was a no-go too. There was no way I could talk about this with my ex.

After a trip to the bathroom, I was ready to face the men downstairs, and with a disgruntled look, I acknowledged Eagle as he mirrored every step I took.

"Did your daddy tell you to keep an eye on me?" I scowled.

The fur ball ignored me, and he didn't walk past the threshold of the office behind the store. Almost as if he knew the bookstore and beyond were off-limits. While I continued, Eagle heaved himself up into the cushy chair in the corner for a nap.

I found Henry and Martin outside—in the blistering heat. Henry was setting one of the little tables there, fishing things out of a takeout bag, and Martin had just fetched a bottle of wine from his own shop.

He was the first one to spot me. "Well, good morning, sunshine." He smiled.

I mustered a small one, widening it when Henry faced me.

"Have a seat." Henry got an extra chair from the other table. "Did you sleep well?"

I nodded slowly. "Can I ask why we're sitting out here? It's gotta be a hundred degrees."

"Have some faith, handsome." Martin crooked a finger. *Come here.* "The middle seat should work for your northern self." He grabbed my arm gently as I reached them, and my attention was split in two. A nice, cold breeze was flowing out of the window outside Martin's pastry shop, and I spotted a fan right inside. They came prepared. At the same time, it was impossible not to register his fingers brushing my arm. "My, my. You do have a beautiful complexion. Fair and smooth."

I wrinkled my nose and eyed my arm. Sure, I was pale. I lived in Washington. The fine hairs were dark, probably making me look even paler.

"Are you done groping the boy?" Henry asked, his features drawn tight.

I didn't know what sucked more, being called boy by a man I was all but lusting after, or the possibility of being the reason he suddenly sounded irritated.

I sat down between them and gawked at the Styrofoam boxes that revealed fancy-looking rolls with creamy filling. After Martin had tutted at Henry and called him a testy bore, he told me they were fresh lobster rolls.

"This looks so good." I nodded in thanks as Henry slid me a container, and I lifted the heavy roll and took a big bite. "And expensive." The addition came out muffled by food, and Martin merely beamed at me. Because his pet was getting fed?

"Nothing I do can repay you for what you've done for me,"

Henry told me. "While you're here, you're my guest. Please don't worry about costs. I want you to enjoy yourself."

I swallowed and nodded once. "Thank you." It was easier to accept when he put it like that, like I had helped him out. Perhaps I had, though I could probably get a full tank of gas for this lobster roll. A few more meals, and my trip—motel included—would be compensated for.

"With that out of the way..." Martin picked the decorative piece of lettuce from his roll. "I have a question, Zach."

"You can't buy me new pants, man," I said.

The two men shared a stunned expression before amusement took over, and I felt bold. Comfortable, most of all. I smirked and shifted in my seat, then dug back into my food.

After the chuckles had died down, Martin faced Henry with a serious look. "I want to keep him. Don't tell me I can't."

Even Henry smiled at that.

"But no, you rascal, that wasn't what I wanted to ask," Martin told me. "Although, I'll certainly try again later. My question is about next week. Will you be doing any sightseeing?"

I hadn't really thought about that. I was here to explore something else. That said, it would be cool to see some of the stuff I'd watched on TV. The Hollywood sign, Santa Monica Pier, and Venice.

"Maybe some." I chewed slowly, guessing this was an opportunity to try some of that honesty. My stomach did a somersault, and my hunger faded momentarily. I had to jump, though. I'd regret it if I didn't. "Ehm, the thing is..." I cleared my throat and reached for a wineglass. Condensation had fogged the surface, and I took a big gulp of it. I wasn't much of a wine drinker, but it did the trick. "I was wondering...um, what's West Hollywood like?"

I'd heard it was a neighborhood with a strong gay culture. A gayborhood, if you will.

You learned the weirdest terms online. I still wasn't sure what the difference was between twinks and twunks.

Henry had grown still, and he put down his lobster roll and wiped his mouth with a napkin. He didn't look super comfortable.

Martin eyed me up and down, a small smirk playing on his lips. "So perhaps you don't have a girlfriend at home."

I shook my head no.

Looked like all I had to do was mention West Hollywood and they knew where I was going with this.

Martin patted my hand. "Hon, is this new to you?"

"Very." I managed a weak smile, and my heart pounded. "I don't want to suppress it, though. I've had these thoughts for two years. I wanna find out."

If I didn't know any better, I'd say he looked proud. It didn't make sense. With their obvious surprise settling, they started eating again. At least Martin did. Henry seemed more interested in his wine.

My guess was it was a sensitive topic for him because of how he'd been treated when he came out.

I didn't know Martin's history.

"How old are you?" Martin asked. "Twenty-two, twenty-three?"

I nearly balked. I didn't look that fucking young, did I? "I'm twenty-seven!"

He waved a hand. "Semantics for me." Thoughtful and chewing, he looked at his friend. "What do you think, Henry? We can't in good conscience send him to WeHo clubs."

"Definitely not." Henry's voice was quiet yet firm. As if the idea were ludicrous. "They'll eat him alive."

"Do you go there? To the clubs there, I mean." I glanced between the two.

Henry's mouth twisted up.

Martin laughed outright. "Oh no, dear. We've aged out of the system."

I wanted Henry's take on things. Despite his evident discomfort, I looked at him in question. *Teach me. Or hell, kiss me if you won't tell me where to go.* Okay, perhaps that would make him more uncomfortable.

He surrendered with a sigh, and he put down his food once more. "West Hollywood's clubs might be too much if you're just testing the waters and want to take things slowly. Their scene is a meat market. Not that I've been there in ages. As Martin pointed out, we're not part of the demographic anymore."

"We're too old," Martin supplied.

Henry shot him a frustrated look. "Thank you for reminding me."

"You're very welcome," he replied, and I couldn't help but grin. "Henry's right, Zach. If you want sexy go-go boys and a round of *Dude, Where's My Car* when you wake up not knowing where you are, the clubs there are perfect." He made a dismissive gesture with his hand. "Of course, you can find low-key bars there as well, and many of my friends have settled down in domesticated gay heaven in the neighborhood, but we can probably find you a nice gay bar on the westside too."

West Hollywood wasn't west enough?

Henry inclined his head. "There's no need to dive straight into the club scene." He paused. "You haven't visited any gay-friendly bars at home?"

I shook my head. "I'm not...hiding, per se. But I haven't been comfortable yet."

If I came home with a boyfriend, I didn't believe I'd face

many problems. My nana was open-minded and accepting, and Mattie had friends who were already out. I just...I guessed I was one of those guys who liked to process things on his own first, and this was the option with which I was most at ease. I wouldn't be on my own, but I would be away from everyone I knew.

"What's the scene like in Camassia Cove?" Martin asked.

Henry tipped his head from side to side, weighing his answer. "There are a few places in Cedar Valley, but it's no Silver Lake."

"Where's that?" I'd never heard of Silver Lake. We had a Silver Beach. Maybe it was close?

"Not far from Hollywood," Martin answered. Oh, so it was a neighborhood here in LA. "I grew up there. It's very gay-friendly. And full of special people." The way he said special... "Hipsters, artists, snowflakes who burst up in flames if you're not politically correct."

Henry snorted.

Okay, so I wouldn't visit Silver Lake. I didn't wanna step on any toes and offend someone. It was practically a given, with how new I was to this.

"So, a chill bar or something," I said, getting us back on track. "Will you guys go with me?"

"Abso-fucking-lutely, darling." Martin nodded and licked filling off his finger.

"Thank you." I was relieved.

"Wait for it," Henry muttered.

I frowned in confusion, and Martin's eyes landed on me, his expression gleeful.

"You can't go to a gay bar like that," he said.

Goddammit.

"You're talking about shopping, aren't you?" My shoulders slumped. I didn't know squat about fashion, and I wasn't very interested.

"I am, yes, and it's nonnegotiable." He was too smug.

I agreed to his terms, though. I wanted to experience as much as possible. Even if it meant shopping.

"Can we go today?" I asked.

Martin laughed softly. "Boy's eager, Henry."

Henry merely hummed and took a swig of his wine.

Shortly after, a truck rolled up, and I looked over my shoulder to see a woman my age stepping out. The white vehicle had Martin's shop's cupcake logo on the side.

"Oh, here comes the boss." Martin smiled widely and rose from his seat. "How are you, my darling?"

The curvy brunette grinned right back and got out of the sun. "All good, Uncle M. Deliveries to Calabasas and Topanga. Hi, Henry."

"Hello, dear." Henry smiled.

"Orders are packed and ready to go." Martin kissed her cheek, then put his arm around her waist. "Mariella, I want you to meet Zach. He's visiting from Washington. Zach, this is my niece and ballbuster, Mariella. She handles all the boring stuff so I can make pretty treats all day long."

She laughed at him and stuck out her hand. "Nice to meet you, Zach."

"You too." I shook her hand. "So it's just you two taking care of everything?"

"Oh, no." Mariella pointed toward the truck. "He has another location in Santa Monica. I come here once a day to pick up the goods, that's all. He only takes care of a small portion of the orders here too."

"Sometimes you have to come up twice," Martin corrected with a sniff. "We're getting more deliveries every day." He looked at me seriously. "You *must* like my Facebook page."

I didn't dare tell him I wasn't on Facebook. So I just nodded.

CHAPTER 4

FUCK THE LIST. I NEED A COMING-OUT DIARY

Five hours later, I was stepping out of Martin's Mercedes that he parked behind the building. I assumed the black Lexus belonged to Henry. Bookstores sure raked it in.

"Don't look so glum," Martin chided.

I'd use the term shell-shocked.

I had a serving of petulant anger reserved for Henry too. Because the bastard had bowed out of shopping, and I was sure he could've saved me more than once. Shopping with Martin was *awful*.

Other than spending way too much money on me, which made me highly uncomfortable, his generosity had extended to not pushing me into more than one dressing room. But God, once he'd figured out my sizes and measurements, he'd been a hurricane. He'd held up item after item in front of me, hemming and hawing, never once listening to what I said.

Our three-hour outing resulted in five shopping bags, and I wasn't sure I had the energy to go to a bar anymore.

"If there's anything that doesn't fit, leave it in a bag, and I'll return it next week." He stopped outside of the bookstore and handed me the two bags he'd been carrying. "Tonight is a test. I will let you dress yourself, but if it's an utter disaster, expect me to stop by before brunch tomorrow."

He didn't wait for a response. After a swift peck on my cheek, he returned to his own shop.

My brain was tired. I had a snarky joke on the tip of my tongue but bit it back. I bit back another thank-you too. In the car, he'd told me if I thanked him for everything one more time, he'd spank me.

I didn't think I was ready for spankings.

Henry looked up from where he stood behind the counter as I entered, and it was like he just knew the hell I'd been through.

I scowled at him and dropped all the bags. "You *left* me."

He was trying not to laugh.

Make no mistake, I understood now why he'd bailed and blamed it on work he probably didn't have. Shopping with Martin couldn't happen again. And it wouldn't surprise me if Henry had been subjected to this in the past. Maybe he'd made himself the same promise. Never again.

"That bad, huh?" His eyes gave away the mirth.

I could only huff. *Bad* didn't come close. Being as crappy as I was when it came to picking clothes, I didn't know what colors I liked, much less what cuts and fabrics I preferred. Somehow, that'd given Martin carte blanche.

"There's one shirt I already know I wanna return," I said. 'Cause I didn't do shiny, and the button-down I was talking about was green and shiny. So, so shiny.

Henry found that funny, and he couldn't contain the chuckles anymore. I huffed again and snatched up all the bags, ready to dump it all downstairs and weed out the crazy threads.

It hadn't escaped me that Martin had slipped a lot of shit into the carts when he thought I wasn't looking.

"Five stores," I stated. "If I fall asleep on my feet tonight, it's your friend's fault."

"Noted." He smirked faintly, though the humor faded when I opened the door to the back office. "One thing, Zach. I have suffered through one shopping spree too many with Martin. And yes, there is, without a doubt, much you'll end up returning. But keep this in mind: he doesn't shop for your body. He shops for your personality." His next smile held traces of fondness—the affection he carried for Martin. "Even if a shirt looks ridiculous, please try it on. You might surprise yourself with what you see in the mirror."

I furrowed my brow, unsure of what he meant, but I nodded. "Okay."

"Okay," he echoed. "The upstairs is yours—I won't disturb you. But if my computer goes off, would you mind letting me know? I get notifications when Ty makes posts on social media."

"Of course," I replied automatically. His words rummaged around in my head as I went up the stairs. Again, it was easy to forget the main reason I was here. For Henry, it was probably impossible to forget.

I had to give Martin credit for allowing two pairs of black jeans to leave the store. They were skinny and tighter than what I was used to, but I liked them.

The rest was...new.

There was a full-length mirror on the wall between the bathroom and the sleeping nook, and I stood there while I tried on the new outfits. Eagle was watching me, and I didn't know why I kept talking to him.

"This is too much." I grimaced at my reflection. "Too ridiculous. I tried it." I couldn't do pastel colors. The light green belonged to babies, possibly as wallpaper in a nursery. I pulled it off and tossed it in the return pile on the bed. Next was a dark blue tee, and at first, it looked good enough. "Oh God." Then, not so much. The V-neck was too much V. It was practically plunging. I shook my head quickly.

Before I picked up another shirt, I caught myself in the reflection. I straightened and cocked my head. The skinny jeans rode low and hugged my form like a second skin. My exposed torso... I splayed my hand across my stomach. I was skinny, wasn't I? I had muscle definition. Sliding my hand higher, I ghosted it over my chest. No hair. Did I want more definition? Maybe. I couldn't tell. However, I shouldn't drop a single pound. My hips were narrow, and I couldn't help but wonder what it would look like—what it would *feel* like—to have Henry behind me. His hands traveling up my sides.

I closed my eyes and tried to imagine what I wanted from him. He seemed careful, kind, and gentle in nature. There was definitely an air of caution to him. Like he was holding back and didn't say what was on his mind.

I liked the kindness. If I concentrated really hard, I could picture a warm kiss on my neck. His breath gliding over my skin, lips soft yet demanding. I swallowed hard, the image too enticing.

If he cupped my junk, I'd blow in a minute.

"Shit." I stared into the mirror again. My eyes looked darker, wilder. I liked it. I wanted to see the same indecency in his. Because I didn't only want it kind and gentle. I fantasized about filth that made me flush. I wanted to be exposed and revealed and vulnerable and, and, and fucking taken. Swept off my feet, out of control, *ravaged*.

There were fantasies locked inside me. I couldn't tell what

they were of; I just had this feeling. With an ordinary and mundane life like mine, I craved emotions that were foreign to me. I wanted to be pushed, I realized. Out of my comfort zone, away from the conventional.

I wanted to try something weird.

Weird for me, anyway, which wouldn't take much.

I needed a new list. A list for coming out as…whoever I was. A list of things to explore and discover. Or, fuck that, I needed a diary where I could gush about all the new things. Not that I'd gush about shopping.

Grabbing another shirt, I held it up for inspection. It was another V-neck tee, this one less showy. It was soft and the darkest purple, and it felt good on my skin once it was on.

This one was a winner, though I could see what Martin spoke about now. I wore a lot of dark colors. Sifting through the pants he'd bought for me, I found another pair of skinny jeans. They were faded gray and almost threadbare. If they didn't still have the tag on them, I would've thought they were old.

Fuck, I liked these. I was wearing this tonight.

"Henry, you downstairs?" I called from the stairs. I'd just come out of the shower when his computer dinged next to the couch.

"Just about to close up. Something wrong?" His voice was far away.

"You got an alert." I waited for him to acknowledge he'd heard me, and then I returned to the bathroom. I left the door open so the fog would clear from the mirror in there.

I had twenty minutes to get ready. Martin and I had exchanged numbers during the hellish shopping trip, and he'd texted to tell me he was calling an Uber at eight.

The fifth shopping bag was the most intimidating one, I was

learning. Not only had he neglected to tell me he'd bought some accessories, but he'd bought hair products and a lotion too. I'd never used lotion before, though it was easy enough to apply. Plus, it smelled good.

The accessories were next level. I picked out a leather cuff and decided to leave the rest for another time.

A shadow flashed by; Henry had come up, and he headed for the computer. I tightened the towel around my hips and ran my fingers through my damp hair. Clueless here too. What the fuck was I supposed to do? My hair had a life of its own. Unless there was a funeral, I didn't mess with it.

I gave up. The clothes and the cuff would work for tonight. It was my first time.

Boxers on, deodorant on, new jeans on, then the tee. Reminded how soft and comfortable the formfitting clothes were, I made a mental note to bug Martin about paying for my own shit. I'd tried and failed a dozen times, but it didn't feel right that he was footing the bill. He'd said it was partly for him; he hadn't been able to do this for someone in a long time. Even so...we'd just met, and I was a grown man.

I slapped on the leather cuff and exited the bathroom, nearly stumbling into Henry on the way.

"Sorry." I sidestepped before I could make impact.

"No worries—" He stopped short and looked down at me, at my clothes, and he cleared his throat and averted his gaze.

"Is it not okay?" If I'd fucked up, I was gonna need some serious help. "I thought it looked all right."

"No, no, it's..." He shook his head, only to let out a low laugh and scrub a hand over his jaw. His laugh wasn't necessarily humorous. It was the kind of laugh I exhaled when it was either that or crying. Henry gave me a small smile. "You look very handsome, Zach."

"Oh. Good." The relief was immense. "You had me worried."

He laughed a little again, and there was another head shake. "I doubt you'll be paying for your own drinks tonight." He checked his watch while I savored my ego boost. Fuckin' A. "Speaking of, I should get showered and dressed. Martin texted you, yes?"

I nodded.

"Great. I'll be down soon."

"Okay." I moved out of the way and grabbed my wallet and phone before heading downstairs. Since I had some time to kill, I thought I'd make an effort to see if Eagle was good or evil. Not for the first time, he'd followed me down the stairs, and I just barely beat him to the chair in the corner. He sat down in front of me, observing and flicking his tail.

"I know this is usually your seat." I leaned back and clasped my hands over my stomach. "Henry thinks I won't pay for my drinks. Any comments?"

Eagle chose that moment to leave. Great. He snuck into the bathroom; maybe he had his litter box there. I'd get to know him some other time, then. I had other things to consider, anyway. Namely, about the drinks. Wasn't that something the aggressor, for lack of a better word, did? I'd only had a couple relationships, and I'd been the one paying. Same for the handful of hookups I'd had. I was the one walking up to someone and offering them a drink.

I hoped it was okay to enjoy both. When I tried watching gay porn, the bottom role appealed to me the most, but not exclusively. Far from it.

Did Henry see me as a bottom? I pinched my lips, slightly worried I'd make a fool of myself. I was going into this blind, with no clue of the protocol. I didn't even know what to expect.

Having no desire to overthink it, I pulled out my phone and distracted myself by sending Mattie a text.

Hope everything is okay. If you're going out tonight, remember to be careful and text me before you go to bed. Look after Ty too, please?

I sent a message to Nan too.

Sending hugs from a scorching hot LA. (Saw this curse online and thought you'd like it: twatnozzle.)

I snickered to myself, then saw Mattie had responded.

Ty's grandparents are out of town. He's having some people over. Nothing big. Will be careful.

Knowing I could trust him made it easy. He was no saint. He'd come home plastered a few times, and I'd lectured him once or twice about safe sex when he pulled the stupid excuse, "But she's on birth control!" Didn't fucking matter. Other than that, though, he was a good kid.

It was almost eight o'clock, so I stood up as Eagle left the bathroom.

"Thanks for the chat," I said dryly and left the store. Martin was locking up his shop as I stepped outside, and he was certainly dressed for a night out. He wore a navy-blue three-piece, sans jacket, and looked damn nice. I liked the vest thing.

He evidently approved of my outfit too, judging by the wide smile. "Look at you, honey. This is promising for brunch tomorrow." He winked, then checked his watch. "Car will be here in two. Is Henry about done?"

"I think so."

He nodded. "Have you eaten?"

"Yes." I'd gotten that twisty stomach feeling again when I'd opened the fridge to see a prepared meal for me. Henry had made lasagna at some point, and I'd only needed to reheat it.

There'd been a note with my name and everything. "So, where are we going?"

"A friend recommended a new place on Fourth Street," he answered. "It's in Santa Monica."

That didn't tell me much. LA was a confusing city, but I was ready to have some fun and see what was out there. Though, to be honest, I had a hard time believing anyone would catch my attention more than Henry had.

The man in question appeared a few seconds later, and I nearly swallowed my tongue. Again. Sweet Jesus on a pogo stick. Flip-flops and cargos had been replaced by charcoal dress pants and a simple white button-down. And, as he locked the door, fuck me if I couldn't see how nicely he filled those pants. His *ass*... Ha. Good luck, Santa Monica men.

"Are we ready?" Henry walked over, hands in his pockets.

Oh, I'm ready.

CHAPTER 5

I WANT TO MARRY THIS PURPLE DRINK

It was gonna take a while to get used to the distances between everything in LA. It was a quarter to nine by the time we arrived, and the bar was packed. A Rhianna remix blared from the speakers, seductive and heavy, and I barely heard Martin when he said he'd found us a table.

Holy shit. I was struggling to take it all in. The crowd seemed to be around my age, with some older and some younger. The ceiling was high, and everything was painted black. Except for the accents. Multicolored shards, bulbs, and other glass shapes hung from the ceiling and cast a spectrum of colored shadows in the spotlights, catching in the smoke that poured out from somewhere. There was a dance floor, albeit a small one, and the rest of the floor was filled with round tables—no barstools. People weren't here to sit around. Except for those who'd managed to snag a booth along the western wall.

I had no clue how Martin had done it.

The music pumped through my system, causing my pulse to speed up.

The sleek leather booths varied in all colors, and I slid in next to Henry.

"You like this?" Martin leaned forward over the table to be heard.

I nodded and realized I was grinning.

There were mostly men in here, though plenty of women too. Martin had explained in the car that gay men and straight women tended to share the same space.

"Thank you for bringing me here." I leaned forward a bit too.

He waved me off with a smile, and then a waiter arrived. I eyed the blond up and down, only to check out other guys nearby. I wanted to get a sense of what people wore on a night out. And they were making it difficult for me. I saw ratty jeans and suits, slacks and glitter, makeup and ruggedness. All walks of life, I guessed, as long as they could pay fifteen bucks for a drink.

The waiter and Martin exchanged words, and then he took our orders. Martin ordered for me, Henry went for an Old Fashioned—explaining in detail how he wanted it made, which I thought was funny—and Martin got something with tequila. Most of all, I enjoyed how Henry had to lean into me to be heard by the waiter.

The two top buttons had been left undone on the crisp shirt that hugged his torso so well, and I bit my lip. I wanted to touch his chest hair that teased the top of the opening.

Once the waiter left, Martin explained to us that the last drink from the wait staff was ordered at nine, so after that, we'd order at the bar. Then he continued with, "That's where you're heading soon, Zach. With us around, no one will approach you."

So?

I looked over at the bar. Could I even get there? There were people everywhere.

"I can pay for my own drinks, Martin," I said.

He chuckled, the sound drowned out by the music. "But you want pretty things to notice you, don't you?"

I wanted *Henry* to notice me. Glancing up at the man next to me, I tried to gauge his mood and opinion on the whole thing, and he merely smiled encouragingly. Well, then.

On the other hand, he had no idea I'd jacked off thinking about him in the shower today. I needed to learn how to flirt with a man. He'd told me I was handsome; couldn't I pay him a compliment too?

I faced Martin again. "How do I show my interest?"

"Now we're talking!" He clapped his hands together once. "This part's easy. *Men* are easy."

"A smile and eye contact will be enough for you," Henry told me. "You'll be fine."

Yeah, for some reason, I didn't think that would be enough for him. He was beginning to strike me as a man I'd have to beat over the head with my advances before he got it. I hoped I was wrong.

"A hand on the leg works too," Martin said with another hand gesture of his. It was always the same little wave, dismissive and regal. "There's no mistaking the intentions."

Perfect.

My heart jackhammered in my rib cage before I summoned the courage to slide a hand onto Henry's thigh. "Like this?" My mouth ran dry.

Henry tensed at the contact, his eyes flashing with disbelief and something dark, but it was gone in a second. He nodded stiffly, his smile equally forced.

I narrowed my eyes and huffed internally. He didn't get it.

He thought I was demonstrating. So I left my hand there while the waiter returned with our drinks.

"What is this?" I laughed and stared at my concoction, served in a tall glass with two thin straws. It was purple—not burgundy or dark like my shirt, but light purple.

"Try it," Martin encouraged and took a sip of his own drink.

I took a tentative taste and felt the flavors of violet and raspberry and vodka exploding in my mouth. It was fucking delicious. I'd dump beer for this treat. I'd marry it. The aftertaste of ice cream made me register vanilla too.

"Good, yes?" Martin grinned. "Now, show us your type. There's eye candy everywhere. Who catches your eye?"

Besides the obvious, the hunk next to me? All right, I could do this. Taking another swallow of my drink, I craned my neck and peered out over the crowd. Of course, with my sitting down and most people standing, I only saw those close to us.

There was one guy my age who had bedroom eyes. My mouth quirked up when his gaze met mine, but I continued looking. *There.* A man in a suit. He and his companions had a bar table, all of them having a good time. His smile was sexy and reached his eyes. He was tall too. Perhaps a little slimmer than Henry.

"Him." I nodded at him. "Black suit, blue shirt."

It hit me that I wouldn't have looked at him twice if I saw him on the street at home. He was handsome, sure, yet I'd somehow ignored everyone who didn't stand out. I'd only paid attention to the bolts of lightning, mainly because they'd stolen it. But there was something to be said about thunder too. They rolled in slowly and took over the skies.

"Oh, really." Martin looked away from the man and back to me, one brow arched. "A little old for you, no?"

Bingo.

My thumb traced the muscle in Henry's thigh, and I shook

my head. "Nope." I wished I had the guts to look up at Henry right now. I felt a tremor going through his leg before he made an effort to relax.

"Well, this is interesting." Martin took a slow sip of his drink, whereas Henry downed half of his.

"Excuse me for a moment," Henry said. "I need to go to the bathroom."

Dammit. I slid out of the booth but didn't offer him too much space. Actually, there wasn't much space to give to begin with. He followed smoothly and stood up, and I finally mustered up the courage to look him in the eye. There was definitely heat in them this time, and my cheeks felt warmer. Tension ticked in his jaw. His brows drew together, and I disliked the confusion mingling with the heat. He couldn't believe it, huh?

His chest brushed mine on the way out, and then he broke the gaze and disappeared.

I exhaled heavily and slumped down in my seat to finish my drink.

"Oh, my." At Martin's comment, I feared he'd caught me, though when I followed his stare, I had to smirk. He'd found a Latino ass to gawk at.

"Smooth, Martin."

He shot me a playful glare.

I people watched for a while, hoping to get another drink soon. I asked Martin for the name of the drink so I could order another, and he told me it was called Violet Haze. I repeated the name to myself to remember it and checked out some more guys.

Henry returned but didn't want a seat. He suggested we move to the bar instead, while he was giving me something new to fantasize about—his arms. Forearm porn was happening as he folded up the sleeves of his button-down. How had I not noticed them when he was wearing T-shirts?

The bar was more packed than before, and sadly it was Martin that Henry and I had sandwiched between us as we made our way over there. Although, Martin had a pretty fucking nice ass too. He just wasn't Henry.

"You continue along, young grasshopper," Martin called over the music. "Henry and I will be here."

"You're serious?" I threw him an incredulous look.

It was darker in this area, so I couldn't get a good read on Henry's face. Martin was insistent, though. He wanted me to spread my wings, and that was the point of this, wasn't it? Fucking hell. All right, I'd check shit out, maybe buy someone a drink, maybe get a drink in return, and then I'd be back.

It took me five or six steps into the crowd to lose sight of the men. I came to a stop in the dark and looked around me. Completely alone in a gay bar slash club, literally surrounded by moving bodies. Laughter pierced through the pumping music, a P!nk song this time, drinks sloshing, women dancing, men dancing, smoke billowing, rainbows from the spotlights jumping.

A hand on my ass made me turn around so fast that my neck hurt. There was a murmured, "Gorgeous" in my ear. Then a hand on my abs. No one stuck. I didn't see faces. They kept moving. My chest and stomach twisted with nerves and the slowly building excitement, and the grin on my face was next. This was fucking wild—for me, anyway.

I walked at snail's pace to the other end of the bar, and it didn't take more than half a minute before a man offered to buy me a drink. This was it, I was gonna try. I nodded and thanked him, telling him what I wanted. While he leaned over the bar, I couldn't *not* check him out, and he was...he was okay. To others, he was probably smoking hot. To me, he was Abercrombie forgettable. Nice body, nice face, nice hair, whatever. If he were a few years younger, I could picture him working in a Hollister.

"What's your name?" I asked over the music.

He smiled curiously and handed me my drink. "Rick. You?"

"Zach."

Well, this was going *great*. I snorted to myself and took a big drink, fucking in love with this cocktail, and it wasn't weak, either. Between this one and the first, I already had a buzz setting in.

Rick got close and spoke in my ear. "You from here?"

I shook my head, and we kinda got pushed together in between two barstools. "Washington. What about you?"

"Born and raised in Glendale, then went AWOL a few years ago and never looked back."

"AWOL?" I cocked my head, wondering if I'd heard that right.

Rick and I were the same height, and this time when he leaned in, his hand went to my hip. "Always West of Lincoln—you know Lincoln Boulevard?" I shrugged. He laughed. "Just how new are you to LA, Zach?" My name rolled off his tongue with amusement in his tone.

I chuckled. "Brand new. Got here Wednesday."

I couldn't tell what color his eyes were, but they sparked with interest.

"If you're only here for a good time, count me in," he said.

Oh boy. Okay, so he wanted a quick fuck. Sometimes, that was what we wanted. He wouldn't get anything from me, though, so when he suggested we hit the dance floor, I lost him there.

LA was doing something to me. I got careless. I lost track of time too, and the atmosphere kept me energized and ready to go. I paid for my next three drinks myself, and I danced for the first time since junior high. The music never stopped, people came and went, some paused and tried to hit on me, and I flirted a bit as well. It was all in good fun, though I ended up having the most fun when I stumbled into a bachelorette party in the corner of the dance floor. Surrounded by drunk, giggly women, I could relax and spread those wings Martin had talked about.

I acknowledged some of the women were pretty—beautiful, even—but it ended there. I wasn't in the mood for any kind of meat market, regardless of gender. I wanted to drink, dance, and find out who I was.

It was me and another guy—a stranger—who'd almost literally landed in the laps of these ladies. He and I exchanged brief greetings. "Mario," he said, and I returned with, "Zach." I was nursing the last of my drink, my mind starting to swim, and he disappeared to buy a beer.

"I gotta pee!" one of the girls exclaimed.

I had to go too, and that was how I ended up in line for the bathrooms with tipsy Teresa and shit-faced Sharon. The line to the men's room was, perhaps not strangely—though it was still weird—longer than the line to the ladies' room, so the chicks dragged me with them. I was too drunk to protest.

I blinked at the harsh light inside.

I got into an empty stall and rested one hand on the wall to steady myself. Women seriously talked in here. I thought that was a myth. Not here; Sharon and Teresa discussed their friend's wedding, and another party of women was chattering about guys and appointments.

Once I was done, I zipped up and left the stall to wash my hands. That was where Teresa met up with me, and she opened her clutch, makeup falling out along with two condoms and a phone.

She found that hysterical.

"You okay?" I chuckled.

"Oh, I'm more than okay, sweetie." She grinned and touched up her lipstick. "Are you here with a boyfriend?"

I shook my head and dried my hands.

"Trying to find one?" She faced me with a tube of something. I couldn't tell what it was, even as she opened the cap.

"Not really," I answered. My tongue felt weird. Thicker. I grinned for no reason, still tasting the violet ice cream and blackberry from my new favorite drink. "There's a man I find really fucking hot, though."

Teresa's eyes lit up. "Tell me about him." Stepping closer, she stroked the fabric of my V-neck. "So soft. Where did you buy this shirt? Um, and so ripped." She quirked an eyebrow. She was nutty. I sure as heck wasn't ripped. "You talk, I make pretty."

I didn't know what that meant, nor did I give a shit. What I did care about was rambling when the topic was Henry Bennington. Mostly, I gushed about how fucking hot he was. I wanted him in that dance crowd with me, sweaty bodies pressed together—and what was she doing? I jerked as she brushed her thumb over my cheek, leaving the spot wet.

I peered into the mirror, then squinted to see better. My vision was blurring around the edges. "What the..." I laughed and leaned closer. If it'd been black and I'd been wearing a football helmet, I'd call it war paint. As it was, it was only a streak of glitter. "Did you just put glitter on my face?"

She waggled her eyebrows. "Fabulous, isn't it?"

I lifted a shoulder and looked again.

"Come on, let's take a picture," she suggested.

I groaned. Even in my drunken stupor, bathroom selfies were stupid. *But you want to see the glitter on your face.* I hesitated, which Teresa took advantage of. She told me to show the camera *attitude* and then puckered her lips in a kiss to the phone. My mouth twisted up, and before I knew what I was doing, I raised my chin, offered a cocky expression, and smirked a little. With a streak of glitter gel on my cheek.

What had happened to me?

"Give me your Insta handle. I'll tag you," she said.

I actually did have an Instagram, although I never used it. Maybe I should start.

Maybe I really fucking dug this scene.

Just one...more...drink.

Parched and hot, I tried to escape the dance floor and bumped into more people than I could count on the way to the bar. I'd left the bachelorette party with cheek kisses and social media promises, and then I'd found myself dancing with Mario.

A slight annoyance had pierced my buzz because I couldn't truly enjoy him. Henry was on my mind. I'd caught sight of him a couple times, always by the bar—never alone. He'd bought someone a drink, I was pretty sure. Once, I'd seen him pocketing a slip of paper. Did people still give out their numbers, or was everyone tagged on Facebook or Instagram?

"Violet Haze!" I hollered to a bartender.

And where was Martin? I hadn't seen him even once.

"I'll take care of that," a man said, motioning for the receipt.

"No, it's fine. Thanks." I didn't look at him. Ready to find Henry, I slid a sticky twenty across the bar, and then I gulped down some Violet Haze and searched for my fantasy.

The drink was gone by the time I found him, thankfully alone. He stood by the end of the bar, and in my unreliable state, I thought I detected relief in his eyes. For me, no relief. Just want. He looked too fucking good for words.

I got a little close, not that he seemed to mind, and he dipped down to speak in my ear.

"Are you all right? I sent you a message."

Shit, I'd missed that. I pulled out my phone and checked it.

I hope you're being careful. Don't leave your drink, please. Martin left, but I'll wait for you.

He knew how to twist my stomach. I wondered if I'd ever met someone as sweet and considerate as he was.

The text was sent twenty minutes ago, and I was stunned to see it was already two in the morning.

"I didn't know it was that late," I said.

Henry's eyes crinkled at the corners. "Time flies when you have fun, doesn't it?"

Evidently. "Did you have fun?" I wanted to get closer and fucking closer. The crowd helped. I didn't have a choice but to press up against him as people passed behind me. "I saw you weren't alone."

A heavily remixed version of a Katy Perry song started, and I inched in farther so I could hear Henry's reply.

"I had to occupy my time while waiting for you, didn't I?"

The way he phrased himself had me snapping my gaze upward to meet his. He'd had a few drinks, and I could tell his tongue was a little looser. Did that mean there was a possibility he was interested in me too? If there'd been any indication before, he wouldn't have had to wait at all.

He grinned softly at my cheek of all places, but then I remembered the glitter. He ghosted a finger over it.

I couldn't suppress the shudder. The tingles traveled across my cheek.

"I'm glad you had fun, Zachary."

Katy Perry was singing about aliens ki-ki-kissing and ta-ta-taking her, and it catapulted me into a territory I guess I didn't have the balls to enter when I was sober. Not without some insurance. Now, it wasn't an issue.

I blurted out, "Can I buy you a drink?"

As his eyebrows went up, someone bumped into me from behind, sending me straight where I wanted to be, chest-to-chest with Henry.

We stared at each other in the darkness of the club, and I curled my fingers into his shirt along his sides. Henry swallowed hard enough for me to catch his Adam's apple wobble.

"You gotta know I'm flirting with you." I grinned, nervous and exhilarated.

He cleared his throat and nodded once, then murmured in my ear. "What I don't know is why. You can have virtually anyone in here."

Oh God, I wasn't sure I could explain when I was two-and-a-half sheets to the wind.

I clutched the front of his shirt, keeping him where he was. "Is it welcome? The flirting." Because that was all that mattered at the moment.

His hands finally traveled up my sides, and I shivered harder than the first time. His cheek touched mine, and I wanted that kiss so fucking bad.

Henry wasn't having it. "You've had a lot to drink." That was a no, except he kept me close and didn't remove his hands from me. "I should get you home."

Man, I loved that idea. "So take me home with you."

"Jesus." He swallowed hard once more, then took out his phone to get an Uber.

"Did Martin meet someone?" I asked.

He nodded.

All right, then.

CHAPTER 6

HNNNGHH...

"Zachary."

Only one person used my name like that. I snuggled closer to Henry's warmth and slid a hand up his chest. It was so firm and masculine and sexy and perfect.

"Wake up, darling boy. We're here."

I grunted and forced one eye to open. The world was spinning, and I thanked whatever higher deity one could believe in that I wasn't feeling sick. In fact, I felt good. And horny. Horny for Henry. Ha! I giggled and groaned at the same time and let him help me out of the car.

Everything was pitch black. One lamp glowed in the bookstore, one in the window of Martin's shop. The rest was like... like...like outer space. Except, it was hot here. *At least it's a dry heat*, I mimicked the motel chick in a lady voice. In my head, it sounded lady-like, anyway.

"You called me handsome earlier," I slurred. "Very handsome, even."

"I did." He guided me across the dusty, gravelly parking lot and dug out his keys.

"I'm calling you sexy," I said. "Very sexy."

He rumbled a low laugh, the sound husky and arousing. "Now I know you're wasted."

"But it's true!" I exclaimed. Out here in the wilderness, my voice sounded too loud. Too hoarse. "You didn't get it when I put my hand on your thigh. I was all...disgruntled."

Henry cursed under his breath, and I heard him unlocking a door. We were already there, huh? I hadn't noticed. Would Eagle greet me in the office? Would Henry lead me up the stairs? I wanted him to. I could trip him and get him into bed that way, maybe.

"Ugh." I rubbed my eyes with the heels of my palms. My thoughts were fucked up. If I'd been with a woman, people would've called me a predator. It wasn't any different with a man. "I'm horrified by my thoughts. I thought I would let you know."

"What's horrifying about your thoughts?"

"I was thinking...I could trip you and land on top of you in your bed."

"Good lord, Zach." He sounded hoarse too. Raspy, almost. "Is that really what you're thinking?"

"Yeah, I'm sorry." I squinted in the low light, and I was glad he was leading the way. I would've fallen here. Or there, over that stack of books. So many books. "I had a really good time tonight. A woman put glitter on my face, and a guy who wanted to fuck me bought me a drink. But I kept thinking about you. I'm sorry," I repeated. "Is it because I'm too young? Not hot enough? Inappropriate 'cause of the Ty stuff?"

"Please stop speaking," he commanded. It came out almost in a growl, and it sent a ripple of lust through me. "I've had one drink too many to make responsible decisions."

Fuck responsible. Fuck *me*.

If Eagle was around, I didn't see him.

Through the office, up the stairs. I leaned heavily on Henry to savor the feel of his chest while I could. He was a good man; he wouldn't shove me off while I was lit.

"You didn't answer—" Before I could finish my sentence, I was pushed up against the wall in the stairway. Shock flooded me and caused me to gasp. Then I had Henry looming over me, and he grabbed my hand and put it over his crotch.

I whimpered.

He's so fucking hard.

"This is on you, boy," he whispered angrily. "You better behave, or I'll—"

I reached up and slanted my mouth over his, kissing him firmly. He let out another growl, one of defeat and frustration, and then he was kissing me back hard. Deep. I tasted him on my tongue, whiskey and orange and Bailey's. My first kiss with a man, an incredibly sexy man.

He made my head spin and swim more than a hundred Violet Hazes could.

I squeezed his hard cock instinctively, and that alone was enough to set me on fire. He grunted into the messy kiss and moved his fingers into my hair. He controlled the kiss. I was along for the ride, and I couldn't be happier. It was two years of curiosity and pent-up excitement of which Henry was getting the brunt. My dick responded quickly, filling with blood and arousal. For the first time, I cursed the tight jeans. They were in the way.

"Oh, fuck." I pushed my hips against his and felt his erection tight with mine. And it was everything I craved. Cocks together, male musk, muscles, all things firm and masculine. It was the headiest moment I'd lived through, not to mention dizzying and electrifying.

"Zach." His whisper was rough, and I could tell he was warring with himself.

"Don't stop. Please." I kissed him deeper, if that was possible. "Whatever you do, don't stop. I know I'm drunk, but this is what I want. I'm fucking desperate for it. For *you*. You're so goddamn hot." I sucked in a breath, the desire spearing me in half. It was sharp and demanding, and if he didn't give me what I wanted, I'd lose my ever-loving mind. "I can finally do what I want," I panted. "Fuck, you feel good. I want you so much."

Henry didn't say anything, but when I caught a glimpse of his eyes, I saw the wild and crazed need I'd wished to see all night. It evened the score, if only a little. To see him desire me...I needed it. It set me loose, in a way. I didn't hold anything back. I dragged his bottom lip between my teeth, then kissed my way down his neck. I fell in love with his scruff and his manly scent, the spices and the faint taste and smell of fresh perspiration.

He was the epitome of a man, and I wanted to inhale him. Swallow him whole, consume him.

"Oh God..." I threw my head back as he nipped at my jaw. I wanted to feel him at my neck and my throat. "More, Henry. Please..."

He hummed and pushed up my shirt. "Let me see this perfect body of yours. It's been haunting me since you walked into my life."

I shuddered and grabbed at the hem, quick to yank it over my head. He had to be next. Our mouths collided with lips, teeth, and tongues, and I started unbuttoning his shirt. When I got my hands on his chest, my knees about gave out. I was pretty sure another desperate sound escaped me.

"I'll take care of you," he murmured, breathing heavily. I moaned the second his hand covered my dick, and pleasure exploded behind my closed eyelids. "Let me suck you off, sweet boy. I'll make it good for you. So good." He spoke in between dizzying kisses, and I could only groan in response. "Use your words, Zachary. Do you want me to swallow your cock and suck the come from you?" He cupped my junk firmly, the tips of his fingers gentler on my balls. *Oh Christ*, I heard myself breathe out, though I could've imagined it. "Tell me. I have to hear you say it."

"I want it." Shit, did I just whine like a goddamn kid? I unzipped my pants, fumbling like a fool, and pushed them past my hips. "I want you. I want it all. Just take me."

He cursed and sank to his knees, and a beat later I felt his fingers wrapping around my cock. I was fucking leaking at this point. He didn't wait, not even for an extra breath. My cock was engulfed in warm, wet heat. I cried out hoarsely and collapsed against the wall. My hips bucked into him, and he swallowed me on every thrust.

I worked my hands into his hair. It was soft to my touch, silky and perfect. He encouraged me to fuck his face, and I did it without thinking twice. There was no thinking whatsoever, only feelings and desires, and I preferred it. Perhaps I would regret the amount of alcohol tomorrow, but I didn't think so. The only thing that could make me regret this was if I didn't remember it. That'd be a crying shame. For now, this was everything. There were no inhibitions, effectively turning my first sexual experience with a man into a glorious one.

"Fuck...amazing..." I moaned and forced myself to open my eyes. I had to see him. The way he worked my cock, his mouth taking me in so greedily. Teeth grazing gently, teasingly, and his tongue... "Shit," I choked. One shudder set off another. "Suck my cock. Suck it."

He hummed around me.

He stole my breath when he cupped my balls and rolled them in his hand. His touch was warm and comfortable, but I wasn't fooled. I wasn't too drunk to feel the dark promise behind every action. He had more in him. He was doing this for me, making sure my first blow job by a dude was mind-blowing. The way I wanted it. If he—and I—got another chance, and fuck, I hoped we did, then I had no doubt he'd go by his own rules and show me what was up.

Henry swirled his tongue around me and sucked hard at the slit, then took me deep, down his throat where his muscles contracted around me. Again, he made my knees buckle. I could only take it—accept it. I stared hungrily through hooded eyes how he left my cock glistening with his spit. He sucked cock like he loved it. Maybe he did.

"I wanna try." I was struggling to withhold my orgasm. "I wanna suck you too."

Other than a smirk while he kissed the tip of my cock, there was no response. He went back to deep-throating me, and I was losing it. Fast. The pleasure built up. My muscles tensed, I trembled and shuddered, my breathing got choppy.

It was only then I noticed he was stroking his cock. Those sexy charcoal dress pants unzipped, belt unfastened, a hint of a V that pointed to his long, hard, thick cock. My mouth watered, a bead of pre-come trickled down his shaft, and I was done for.

"Oh, *fuuuck*." I fisted his hair and fucked his throat hard once, twice, and a third time. I screwed my eyes shut, and then I shot in several ropes down his throat. He didn't miss a drop.

I lost my strength. While riding the high of the most intense climax I could remember, my legs gave out. I sagged against the wall, needing to sit down. His mouth had disappeared from my dick, but I felt it against my lips instead. His drinks mixed with my come, and it sparked a second's worth of hunger for me. I kissed him deeply and passionately, for the first time tasting myself on another person.

The fucker managed to steal my air once again, because a heartbeat later, he covered my spent dick with his load. Hot spurts of come splattered against my softening junk, and I did what any horny guy with a newfound love for men would do. I rubbed the fluid over my cock, down my balls, as he kissed the breath out of me.

"You have no idea how mouthwateringly sexy you are." He breathed heavily into the sloppy kiss and collapsed against me until we were a heap of listless limbs on the stairs. "I can't think near you."

"If this is the result of that, I don't mind." I crawled into his embrace, unable to stop kissing him. "I want to sleep with you. Wake up next to you."

He exhaled a lazy chuckle, his voice scratchy and husky. "I don't think I'm capable of saying no to you."

"Good. Fuck." I swallowed dryly, still needy. The hard-on was gone, as was the ache to come, but the cravings for him were hanging on in the best ways. I brought two wet fingers to his lips and coated them with his orgasm before I dove for a hard kiss. "Oh my God...tonight just went from amazing to out of this motherfucking world." I closed my lips over his and licked up the saltiness with one swipe of my tongue.

"Jesus, Zachary," he whispered into the kiss. "Let me drag you to bed before you pass out on me. And before I take advantage again."

"Tempting." I grinned, seeing two of him for a second as I lost my focus.

I was a stumbling mess while he got us upright. He managed to straighten our clothes. In the meantime, I was groping him and telling him more about my night.

"We have to go again." I didn't bother correcting my slurred speech. My body was powering down. "You have to dance with me and get glitter on your face, because this is what life is about. I missed out on it, I guess. Sitting behind that damn register after school and doing inventory on the weekends...burying my mother. That part sucked the most, but I've waited long enough now. I need to live. I need glitter nights and purple drinks and more of you."

Henry held me close for the last steps up the stairs, and he pressed a lingering kiss to my temple. Then we were in his bathroom. I was glad he didn't turn on the light, 'cause I wasn't sure I'd be able to handle it. He cleaned us up a bit and offered me a glass of water and two painkillers.

I gulped them down.

Next thing I knew was my face landing on a pillow.

I woke up tangled in Henry and the biggest fucking hangover the day after.

It was the first time I felt miserable and ecstatic at once.

He was still asleep, though I could tell it wouldn't be long before he rose. He shifted and seemed half aware of my hand on his chest and my leg between his. When he frowned in his sleep, I reached up to smooth it out with a finger.

Don't regret it, don't regret it. If he regretted last night, I'd be the puppy he kicked. It hurt to move, yet I couldn't quit touching him. It was an amazing feeling. His chest hair underneath my fingers, the hard planes of his torso, his warm skin. I'd open my mouth and say something—or kiss him—if it wasn't so dry I feared it'd been pasted shut. The taste wasn't awesome either.

Henry grunted and stretched his arm over his head. "Did..." That didn't work, so he tried again. "Did last night happen?"

"Um-hum." I pressed a closemouthed kiss to his shoulder before my bladder demanded I leave the bed. "Don't regret it, please. I'll be right back." Now more than ever, I needed a shower and my beloved toothbrush.

"We need to talk about it later, though," he murmured drowsily.

As I scooted down, I bit his hipbone gently. "Did you just ask to join me in the shower? I think you did."

His sleepy smile relaxed me this fine, brutal morning.

I escaped as quickly as I could manage, and I relieved myself and brought my toothbrush with me into the shower. Henry walked in as the water was turning hot, and I...well, I gawked. Toothpaste foaming and dribbling down my chin, I stared as he dropped his boxer briefs and gave me a glimpse of his fuckable ass.

"It's not polite to stare, my dear," he drawled, flipping up the lid to the toilet.

"How can I not?" I, for one, was thankful the glass in the shower hadn't fogged up yet. "Your ass is incredible. And your thighs..." I spat toothpaste down the drain, and he flushed the toilet, temporarily turning the water colder. It was almost refreshing.

He shook his head, amused, and looked at me in the mirror while he grabbed his own toothbrush. "Where the hell did you come from, Zach?" He didn't sound like he expected an answer, so I just lifted a shoulder and stole some of his body wash.

He joined me shortly after, and he replaced my toothbrush with his mouth in a tentative kiss. Screw tentative; I locked my arms around his neck and went all in. He shuddered under the hot spray and pressed me closer to him, one of his hands sliding down to squeeze my ass. My turn to shudder.

It was a lazy shower. I wasn't sure we could manage any other pace. In between slow kisses and languid gropes, we washed each other and exchanged murmured words about last night.

"You still have some glitter here." He cupped my cheek and brushed a soapy thumb over the streak of sparkles. "I watched you last night. You were amazing out there on the dance floor. Carefree and so alive."

That's what it'd felt like. Hell, I was still riding that wave. It started with those lobster rolls, when I fessed up about what I wanted.

"It's freeing. Like something's been unlocked." I squinted up at him, the water beating down on us. "I guess I always figured coming out was something you did for friends and family, and maybe it is, but it's personal too, you know? The person I was last night is new. I wanna get to know him."

He smiled and kissed me softly.

The silence that stretched between us was comfortable, yet filled with words left unsaid.

I was getting to know him a little by now, through him and through Martin, and I could guess some of his answers to my questions. *Will you explore with me*, I wanted to ask. *You'll find many to explore with*, he'd probably say. Henry Bennington had all the hotness and none of the confidence. Not about his own appeal, anyway.

No worries. You didn't live the life I'd lived and quit as soon as the going got rough.

Martin had bought me shorts. Two pairs. One pair of trunks or board shorts and one pair of slightly baggy cargo shorts. The latter came with a matching belt, both beige, and I picked a simple white T-shirt. It wouldn't attract the sun as much.

Um. "I guess Martin does nothing simple," I muttered. In a glance in the mirror, I'd caught the print on the back of my shirt. In subtle gold, it said, "Let Me Be Perfectly Queer."

I burst out a laugh, which caused a headache from hell, and Henry walked out of the bathroom, fully dressed and with a curious expression. I showed him the back of my tee, and he chuckled.

"Return pile?" he guessed.

"Nah." I kinda dug it.

Henry seemed to dig my response.

I pocketed my phone and wallet, then stuck my feet into my Chucks.

"We'll have to get you some flip-flops," he said. "Paradise Cove is on the beach."

"Paradise Cove?" Bending over to where the bags were next to the bed, I rummaged through them, and would ya look at that, Martin had bought me a pair of shoes. They weren't flip-flops, but Vans were easier to get in and out of.

"The brunch place we're going to." Henry came up behind me, a sharp jolt of shock and lust shooting through me as he grabbed my hips and pressed his crotch to my ass. Sweet Jesus. "You can't bend over like this and expect me to stay away."

"Aye-aye, Captain," I choked out. Fuck, could he continue? The biggest surprise was him taking initiative like that—kinda bold, wasn't it?—and the second biggest thing would be his cock. "You might wanna step back, though. I'm getting hard."

He gave my ass a thorough groping, and he groaned under his breath before backing away.

Then, Henry was gonna be Henry. As soon as I had straightened, he looked half embarrassed, and he started apologizing.

"Dude." I shook my head at him. "I liked it, okay?"

"Even so..." He made a gesture, all Martin-like. "I apologize. You fluster me, and it's been a long time since I felt so—" He stopped and gave my hand a gentle squeeze. "I'm incredibly attracted to you, and it's difficult to remember you're new to this."

"Don't treat me like I'm new." Maybe I was naïve, but I

wanted this. "If I can explore myself and this—" I gestured between us "—with you and not some random stranger, I'm all in. I feel safe with you."

"I'm flattered," he murmured and dipped down for a quick kiss. "You truly don't regret anything from last night?"

"The opposite. I want a repeat as soon as possible." I smirked at the obvious direction of his thoughts, and I grabbed my shades. "Let's go to brunch."

CHAPTER 7

HASHTAG BRUNCH

This life was a bit dangerous. Henry and Martin were clearly well-off, and I was acquiring a taste for their lifestyle. As I sat next to Henry in his fancy Lexus while he drove along the coastline toward the restaurant, I warred between feeling guilty and wondering if it was superficial of me to want more. I'd worked hard all my life, never got squat for free, and I valued my high morals.

Being some kept boy held zero appeal for me, and I remained uncomfortable with the purchases Martin had made. I guess the notion was new to me too. It wasn't only uncomfortable, it was also foreign. The concept of gifts and indulgences hadn't really existed in my life. They were reserved for birthdays and Christmas and were always modest. But now... There was envy. What I wanted was to be able to afford this on my own, and I didn't see that happening ever.

The convenience store supported my brother and me, and I had cut some things out in favor of setting a little bit of money aside every month. In short, I had enough to live like Henry and Martin for perhaps a month. Then my years of meager savings would be gone. While I wouldn't necessarily regret giving myself this gift, it wasn't real. I would prefer to spend it on something lasting, or something that would give more in return, no matter how much I would cherish the memory of my time in LA.

I'd considered investing in myself—possibly a higher education—but I had no ambitions or career goals. Couldn't say I wanted to go to school again either. The option hadn't existed for me. When Mattie was grown and on his own, maybe.

I shook the thoughts for now and looked out over the mountains to my right. These mountains had nothing on the ranges we had at home, but they were pretty nonetheless.

"Tell me about Paradise Cove?" I asked. "Sounds all secretive and private."

Henry smirked faintly, looking sexy in his own sunglasses. His Ray-Bans were probably not rip-offs. "I don't think any place with valet is secret, but it's certainly beautiful—right on the beach, cliffs all around. It's a popular place. Martin and I go every Sunday." Of course they did. "You'll have to try their Bloody Mary. I've never had a hangover it couldn't cure."

I made a face and side-eyed him. The last thing I wanted to cure a hangover was the poison that'd gotten me in that state.

Henry slowed down and eventually turned left, leaving the main road for a narrower one that went down the mountainside.

"Do you go out often?" I wondered. "I'm curious about your and Martin's social life."

He hummed. "Martin goes out more than I do, perhaps once or twice a month. I tag along sometimes. I suppose I prefer quieter evenings more often than not."

I liked that. I wanted a truckload more of yesterdays, but in the end, I knew in my gut I was always gonna prefer my small-town life.

"Do you ever miss Camassia?" I asked next.

His smile was gentler this time, almost wistful. Before answering, we came to a stop as we neared the end of the road, and he pushed down his window to grab a ticket. He explained that there were still available self-parking spaces; if we'd arrived later, it'd be all valet. It was such an LA thing. Or a major city thing.

He cleared his throat, and I watched his forearms flex as he steered the wheel and circled the parking lot. "I do miss Camassia Cove—especially lately. For years and years, I had this vision of buying a cabin up in Westslope." He spoke of one of our northern districts, where it was all forest and rivers and wilderness. "At the same time, I've grown to love my life here. Did Martin tell you how we met?"

"No."

He grinned, pulling into a spot. "I should let him tell the story. He uses it as a conversation starter or icebreaker sometimes."

"Who made a fool of himself?" I chuckled. "That's usually how it goes."

"Oh, it was me. Otherwise, he wouldn't be so quick to share it." He killed the engine, and we stepped out where there was no central air. Jesus. "We went to college together at Columbia. He was pre-law and a lot different from the man you met this week." That was hard to imagine. Going from pre-law to decorating cupcakes? Jeesh. "He was still very much out and proud, whereas I couldn't have been shoved farther into the back of the closet. Being who he was—and is—he vowed to take me under his wing and get me to come out. I actually denied being homosexual. He didn't believe me for a second."

I wondered what had given Henry away.

81

Looking around the parking lot, I followed Henry toward a glorified beach hut. Of course, it was a hell of a lot bigger than a hut, but the flip-flop certainly fit. It was decorated to be a diver's hangout.

"Did Martin start college later?" I asked. I remembered he was a few years older than Henry.

Henry nodded, leading the way to the hostess's corner right on the edge by the beach. "He'd spent some time traveling Europe and Asia before starting school." He paused to greet the hostess, and I guess I shouldn't have been surprised she knew him by name. She even indicated that Henry and Martin had a standing reservation and private table. On the way to the outdoor patio, which was literally canvases and clinging greenery over beach sand, Henry put his hand on the small of my back. "Anyway." He lowered his voice slightly. "I was late for my first class, not to mention completely lost, and I wasn't watching where I was going." Now I could see where he was heading, and I grinned. "I slammed into him and dropped my books, simultaneously cursing 'Fuck me' in a loud voice."

"What did he say?" I laughed.

There was another pause as we reached our table. Martin and the Joseph guy weren't here yet, so the round corner table that seated four was all for us. Henry pulled out a chair for me, which was fucking sweet. Then he sat down next to me, and the hostess said a waiter would be with us shortly.

I placed my sunglasses on the table.

"He said, 'Name a time and a place, but for God's sake, don't announce it in front of the entire class.' That was when I noticed I'd stumbled into him right outside a lecture hall full of students, and of course, they'd all heard me."

Elbow on the table, chin resting in my palm, I laughed behind my fingers and admitted that would've made me turn a hundred shades of red.

"Oh, believe me," he chuckled, "I was beyond mortified." He smiled and tucked his shades into the chest pocket of his T-shirt. "That's Martin for you. It took him eight months to get me to admit I was into men, and the following summer, he brought me home with him to his parents in Silver Lake. It was the first time I visited Los Angeles."

I watched him—more like gazed at him—and realized I was head over heels in crush with him. It only made me smile, and I wouldn't change a thing. He was in my head and definitely crawling his way under my skin, and I fucking loved it. He was a great man to be infatuated with, wasn't he? He'd had his own little smile playing on his perfect lips since we woke up, and the hazel in his eyes seemed almost brighter. Out in broad daylight and sitting so close, I detected flecks of gold and green, and the hints of silver in his scruff were so sexy.

I couldn't wait to get to know him better.

Our waiter arrived at the same time as Martin did, and another man followed. Joseph was around Martin's height and dark-blondish, had a great build, and the most charming grin. It was dimpled and everything. His eyes were blue and framed by lashes long enough for me to pay extra notice.

"You must be Zach." He extended his hand, and as I shook it, he leaned down and kissed my cheek. Well, all right, then. "Martin wouldn't shut up about you in the car."

"Oh," was my dumbfounded response.

He moved on to exchange a hug with Henry while Martin prattled off drink orders to the waiter.

"Um, orange juice for me, please," I cut in.

Martin raised a brow and sat down. "Dear, you really need to try the Bloody Mary here. At the very least, their mimosa."

"I already tried," Henry said with a wink my way. Then he faced Martin and Joseph. "If you arrived together, it means you stayed in Santa Monica last night, Martin."

"He called me at ten and told me to *fetch* him." Joseph smirked wryly and unbuttoned the top button of his dark blue shirt. I'd spotted black slacks on him, making me wonder where Martin had gone wrong. Joseph's blue gaze landed on me next. "How was your first night out? I would've joined you guys if someone had bothered calling me." I could only describe the look he sent Martin and Henry as bitchy.

"Won't happen again." Henry patted Joseph's hand on the table.

"It was good," I said.

"Good?" Martin looked at me in disbelief. "Honey, you were on fire on the dance floor. I had to fan myself more than once watching you. You have moves."

My face felt hotter.

"Then you found comfort in the arms of...what was his name?" Henry leaned back, amused, and draped an arm along the back of my chair. I sure liked that bit.

"Michael," Martin sighed dreamily. "Precious cub, that one."

While he went on about Michael's attributes and stamina, Henry silently slid me a menu, reminding me we were here to eat. I flipped it open and swallowed at the sight of the prices. *Stop it. Enjoy yourself. It's vacation.* And that salmon sounded so good with eggs Benedict...

"You won't regret that one." Henry's murmur was followed by his chin resting on my shoulder, though it lasted only a second or two, as if he caught himself. We were in public and hadn't discussed our status, no matter how temporary it was. And shit, that was the last thing I wanted to think about.

"What're you getting?" I kept my voice down and scratched my neck.

"I woke up with a sweet tooth. Waffles for me." He sent me a predatory look and a knowing little smirk. He was saying it was my fault he wanted something sweet. "The energy will do me good too."

I coughed lightly and looked away, over my shoulder, to hide my grin. The beach was right there, past a few rows of beach chairs.

"Martin, what on earth are you doing?" Henry's question made me face the table again. My brows shot up, 'cause Martin was holding his hands apart, clearly demonstrating the length and girth of something.

In the meantime, Joseph was watching me. His calculating gaze had me sitting straighter. What was he doing? Did I have something on my face? No, he was observing. His mouth twitched, and I lowered my eyes. Had he caught on? Could he tell there was something between Henry and me?

My buzzing phone saved me from the strange tension, and I checked it while Henry and Martin bickered the way they did. It wasn't a message as I'd expected, though. It was an alert telling me I'd been tagged in something on Instagram.

Then my face was split in half by my half-embarrassed smile. It was the woman from last night, Teresa. She'd uploaded the selfie of the two of us, captioning a series of pictures "Wild Bachelorettes and Bitches." Shit, I really was giving that camera attitude. I didn't look like myself, or like anything I'd ever felt. My eyes flashed with heat, alcohol, and joy in the photo, and my smirk was cocky. With glitter streaking my cheek.

I brushed my fingers over my cheek and clicked the love button. Next, I screencapped the photo so I could save it.

"What has you blushing?" Henry murmured as our drinks arrived.

I showed him the screen. The first picture in the series was of her dancing with her friends, the second was of her and me, and a few more followed. Champagne, wide smiles, laughter, and kisses with her girlfriends.

"My God, you belong in a magazine." Henry's quiet words caused my face to flame even hotter.

"What're you looking at?" Martin demanded. "Don't hold out on me."

He and Joseph had my phone for a minute after that, and I grabbed Henry's hand under the table and put it on my thigh. I just needed some contact. Actually, I needed a whole lot more than that, but a hand on my leg would suffice for now. My blood was rushing in my veins from seeing that photo, and I wondered if they'd understand. This was huge for me. The man in the picture was so new; he was brazen, cool, and ready to live life.

"You're coming out with a bang, darling." Martin fanned himself and flashed me a wink.

I chuckled self-consciously.

"Gorgeous," Joseph agreed.

Under the table, Henry's hand traveled higher until he stroked my junk and applied enough pressure for me to gulp. I pocketed my phone again and did my best not to let my eyes flutter closed. His hand was gone—or in a more brunch-appropriate location on my knee, but the lust wouldn't fade.

That morning, I had brunch on a beach in Malibu with three beautiful gay men and a fucking hard-on.

"You're a horrible business owner." I stretched out on the bed and exhaled a clever *unff* as Henry dropped a kiss to my happy trail. "God..." As glorious as brunch had been, this was better. This was how I cured my hangover. With naps and cuddles.

"I'm not arguing, but what makes you say that?" He hooked two fingers into my boxer briefs and pulled them down.

I lolled my head along the pillow, lazy and full, and wove my fingers into his hair. "Your store is open, but here you are, almost naked in bed with me. And about that, you should lose the underwear."

He kneeled between my legs, his sculpted thighs calling my name. They were just so damn perfect.

"The bookstore isn't my income. It's my hobby—and my accountant's migraine." He lost the boxers, and I wet my bottom lip as I stared at his cock. Last night, I hadn't really gotten a good look. "I invest."

I should've known. He'd been an investment banker and all.

"In what?" I sat up and trailed my hands up his thighs. "Can you lie down? I wanna touch you."

He let out a breath, his semi-erection thickening. Staring at him made my mouth water. Then I had him on his back in the middle of the bed, and I repeated my question about investing. Even his spectacular body couldn't distract me from getting to know him.

"Real estate and small-business ventures." He placed one arm under his head and eyed me with a deep-seated hunger. "You are a beautiful man, Zachary."

"So are you." I grinned and swung a leg over him, my hands landing on his chest for support. "If I were to invest in something, what should I go with?"

He lifted his brows, then hummed and thought about it. "What do you do?"

"Nothing worth anything." I freely admitted to myself that I felt lacking. "I have a corner store in Camas." Mentioning that part of Camassia was all that was needed for him to understand my financial situation. Working class would've been an upgrade. "I want more," I said, exploring his chest with my fingertips. "What you and Martin have built, I want that—"

"Do keep in mind I'm almost twenty years your senior," he pointed out. "I was also born into wealth."

Maybe I was a little impatient now that I was finally getting a taste of something else.

His expression softened. "Tell me about your family. You mentioned your father left you."

"Not much to tell." I lifted a shoulder and half regretted bringing this up. "It's me, my brother, and my grandmother."

"What happened to your mother?"

Now I definitely regretted it. "Suicide." Lowering my head, I pressed a kiss to his sternum and breathed him in. There was an undercurrent of excitement that'd been pulsing through me since leaving the bar last night, each pulse whispering *you're with a man, you're with a man, you're with a man.* I wanted to explore sex and Henry's body until it bordered on worship. Actually, worship sounded great too.

"I'm sorry." Henry cupped the back of my neck and lifted his head to kiss my hair. "How old were you?"

When I found my mother's body hanging from a rope in the ceiling in the garage? "Eighteen." The week after my birthday, to be exact. "She'd been waiting until I was legal so I could take care of Mattie."

"Jesus," he whispered. "Come here."

He turned us on our sides, and I grew uncomfortable. Irritated. I didn't need the consoling, but most of all, I cursed my stupid mouth. I should've kept it shut. The life I'd known for twenty-seven years had no business intruding on my vacation.

When Henry asked careful questions about my past, I answered on autopilot in a monotone voice. *Why did she...?* Because she was sick. She'd battled depression for as long as I could remember. *You were so young.* Meh. I'd been taking care of Mattie for years already. My childhood had consisted of the highest highs and lowest lows. I'd lived the meaning of walking on eggshells, never knowing when I woke up in the morning what state I'd find Mom in. *Did she not get help?* I guess...it just never worked for long. She'd self-medicated for most of it. Booze, uppers, downers.

"I have some amazing memories too." I looked up, searching his eyes. Relief hit me when I didn't see pity. If anything, he radiated compassion and empathy. "My grandfather on my mom's side was pretty well-off. He used to own a chain of stores, and sometimes, Nan and Mom would sneak us out on adventures." Mattie probably didn't remember those. "We'd go camping or go to a hotel in Vancouver or Seattle and eat our body weight in dessert before dinner."

Henry said nothing. He only stroked my cheek and pressed soft kisses to my face every now and then.

"He was grumpy as fuck," I said. "My gramps, I mean. We lived in the same town and rarely saw each other. Nan would flip him off behind his back."

He chuckled quietly.

Henry had more questions, and I resigned myself to ramble just to get it out of the way. My whole point of this trip—uh, other than finding Henry for Ty's sake—was to get away. Start fresh, see what was out there, and explore. So dragging up my past was no fun. However, I wanted the same from Henry, so I suffered through my own shit first.

Did okay in school but couldn't afford college—plus I had Mattie. Didn't date a whole lot but got on the girl wagon when I was around nineteen. It was easy, and to this day, I was sure I'd loved my first girlfriend, Meghan. Then she moved to Seattle for college. When she returned, friendship felt more natural.

When he asked about Nan, it got marginally easier. She was a hoot, and she'd always done as much as she could for Mattie and me. She moved in with us after Mom killed herself, though it was cramped. Her health was getting poor too, so it didn't last long. Gramps had kicked the bucket years prior, and all stores but one had been sold off. It left us enough money to get her into a decent home, and we could afford to let Mattie play lacrosse until he got bored with that.

"Nan's the loudest cheerer," I said. "He was good when he played, and not even osteoporosis could keep her from attending games." At Henry's slight confusion, I explained bone frailty. He nodded. "Mattie's not interested in sports anymore, though. I think he's gonna get into engineering or something with cars."

"Hm." His mouth tugged up at the corners. "And what about you, Zach? What do you want to do?"

Good question. "I'll let you know when I figure it out. I have some savings, but..." It wasn't enough to get me far. "The thought of going to school makes me shudder."

He kissed me, lingering. "Of course it does. You've been self-reliant from an early age, and school would feel like a step back. It wouldn't be, mind you, but I understand four years is too much for someone who's been waiting so long to get somewhere."

Jesus, in one sentence, he summed it all up perfectly.

I kissed him back and deepened it. It'd been a while since I tasted him, and he had wicked skills with his tongue. It seduced me with each stroke.

"Is this a hint for us to change the topic?" He smiled into the kiss.

I nodded once and crawled on top of him.

CHAPTER 8

THERE'S A TONGUE IN MY ASS

We met up with Martin downstairs for an early dinner. He'd made chicken parm and picked up a bottle of wine, and it wasn't until I sat down on the porch that I realized how hungry I was. Napping with Henry entailed orgasms that left me flushed and starving, and I was pretty sure the flush hadn't left me. The mere memory of our cocks sliding together was giving me shivers.

He'd also made me jerk off on his chest while he squeezed and groped my ass.

I'd been so close to begging for more. Not fucking once had he pushed a finger inside, and it bugged me. Next time, I'd ask.

"I have to head out soon again," Martin said as he fanned out a napkin on his lap. "Tanya's going on vacation. Can you believe that? It messes with my schedule."

"You poor baby," Henry mocked.

"Who's Tanya?" I asked. "Shit, this is delicious." Martin

could cook. The spaghetti, the cheese, the breaded chicken, the…spinach, I think—all of it, fucking amazing.

"She's the only person allowed to touch my hair," Martin replied. "I'm glad you like it, dear."

"When's your appointment?" Henry wondered. "Zach, you should go with him."

"What's wrong with my hair?" I frowned.

"Don't get me started," Martin muttered. "But yes, brilliant idea, Henry. Zach, you're coming with me."

Henry gave my leg a gentle squeeze. "Try something new. It's what you're here for, remember? It's our duty to make sure you experience as much as possible."

"Uh, something new? We have hairdressers in Washington too, believe it or not." I found them both a little crazy. "For the record, the kitchen shears work fine."

Martin feigned a heart attack at that, and even Henry looked dismayed.

When Martin had recovered, he launched into a tirade about his stylist—not a hairdresser—and her excellent scalp massages. It made me laugh and scrunch my nose. I knew I was gonna agree, 'cause when push came to shove, I wanted to experience things Henry and Martin's way, but that didn't mean it wasn't nuts. I wasn't completely foreign to luxury, either. Another ex-girlfriend of mine used to get her hair done for over a hundred dollars.

"Fine," I griped. "But I draw the line at manicures and shit."

Henry found that very reasonable and said he didn't like those either, whereas Martin called us both heathens.

"Zach," Tanya sang.

"Mmph." I peeled my eyes open, her fingers in my hair

having been too much for me to handle. She'd almost put me to sleep during the shampoo session. "Holy shit." My gaze landed on my reflection in the mirror in front of me. Her latest magic had included dragging her long nails along my scalp while styling my hair. "I look almost cool." I turned my head to check it out, and damn if I didn't love it. She'd kept most of my hair as it was but cut it really fucking short on the sides.

"Almost?" She cocked a delicate brow in the mirror, coming off as anything but delicate in that moment. "You take that back right this second." The blonde was tall and statuesque, with lips as red as her nail polish.

"I look utterly and completely cool?" I guessed.

She nodded firmly, lips pursed. "If Martin doesn't approve, I'm dropping him as a client."

She'd already finished him before it was my turn, and now he was—not too surprisingly—enjoying a pedicure next door.

"I love it," I said sincerely.

"I'm glad." Her expression warmed up. "Come with me, I have some products for you to bring home."

I followed her to the register and pulled out my wallet, prepared for anything. I'd known the second I stepped foot inside this place—called The Cut—that I'd be paying the big bucks. Everything was white and stainless steel, the only colors courtesy of the shelves of fancy shampoos and conditioners that were for sale.

"These are the two I've used for you today." She set two small bottles on the counter and went on to explain about some fucking oil and refreshing gel. She described how I was supposed to use them too.

"I'll do my best." I accepted a small paper bag with my new products and peered inside. I could do this. Maybe. "How much do I owe you?"

"Not a dime. Martin's got it covered. Products and tip too."

"Motherfucker," I blurted out in a moment of annoyance. "I'm sorry, but he and Henry need to quit fucking paying for me."

Of course, Tanya didn't have a reply for that, so I thanked her and walked out.

The sun was setting over Malibu as we drove back to the apartment. It should've been peaceful; instead, I was having my first real argument with Martin.

"Don't you understand it makes me uncomfortable as fuck?" It was impossible to keep the irritation out of my voice because he was so goddamn dismissive about it. "I'm here to enjoy myself, not be some pet project. I already feel bad—"

"Okay, that's enough, Zach." He threw me an angry look. "Could it be that you're seeing this the wrong way? Henry and I love having you with us, but we are not completely selfless. Between his jaded, lonely ass and my inability to stick to one partner, we're doing this as much for us. We didn't pay for all your drinks last night, did we? No, because you wanted to go there. It was your request. But damn right, I will pay for whatever *I* want you to experience. Same for Henry. If there's something he wants you to do, expect him to assume he's paying."

Well, fuck him and that fucking logic. I hated that he made sense. At the same time, it was their generosity that made me enjoy myself even more, so the problem didn't disappear. And that was my problem, not theirs. I had to make a decision; either I let them drag me out on shopping sprees and hair appointments and thanked them like a good boy, or I had to say no and keep my dignity. A dignity they had no interest in robbing me of. It was all me.

"You didn't let me pay for brunch," I pointed out.

"Hmm. Oopsie?"

Oop—? I glowered at him, and he only smiled.

"Cut us some slack, please." He flourished that dismissive hand. "Let us enjoy the doting before you leave us behind for greener pastures."

Wow, that was heavy on the guilt.

I took comfort in the fact that they didn't seem to think less of me because I couldn't live the way they did. As for the rest... I'd work on it.

"Why can't you stick to one partner?" I asked, making a reluctant topic change.

"Ah. Well, I see a twenty-five-year-old dick and automatically want to suck it."

I spluttered a laugh.

Henry did a double take when I entered the bookstore with a smirk playing on my lips, and then he cursed and rounded the counter. Fully expecting a kiss and maybe a compliment, I frowned as he walked past me. The hell? Oh. Never mind. He was locking the door.

"Come here." He yanked me into his arms and kissed me hard.

"Umph." I sucked in a breath and fisted his shirt. "Want—oh, fuck...wanna take me right here?"

"Don't tempt me." He gave me another drugging kiss, his tongue invading my mouth, then smacked my ass and let go. "Get upstairs."

I grinned, victorious, jogged past a cat with a staring problem, and hurried up to Henry's place.

"What're you thinking about?" I kept my tone casual. "What we should do tomorrow? Dinner plans?"

"No." He trailed after me, and the huskiness of his voice sent a shudder through me. "I'm thinking about my tongue fucking your sweet little asshole."

Fuck me! I stopped short with eyes wider than saucers and spun around on him.

He wanted his what where?

He pointed at the bed and began unzipping his shorts. "Lose your clothes and lie down on your stomach."

"Is this because of my hair?" My grin turned wobbly. I couldn't make sense of the storm of feelings surging inside me. Most of all, I liked the shock. Being caught off guard. And he was usually so fucking kind that his dirty side was a surprise. That was after he made me come three times already.

"Tip of the iceberg." He moved closer and pulled at my tee. "I've spent the two hours you were gone fantasizing about what I want to do to you."

My heart pounded, and I rushed to get all the clothes off me. After setting the pace in our so-far very brief relationship—or whatever the hell I was supposed to call it—I couldn't wait for him to take charge and hopefully be a demanding fucker.

Feeling emboldened for a moment, I hit the bed stark naked and on all fours, and I glanced at him over my shoulder. *Take me.* I swallowed and pushed my ass toward him, and he narrowed his eyes at me.

"Be careful with what you offer, darling." He joined me on the mattress, stroking his cock lazily.

"I trust you." I was honest. Honest and goddamn excited.

"I make mistakes too." It wasn't a warning, just a quiet statement as he caressed my buttocks. "We were reckless last night."

"How so?"

"Protection." He smiled ruefully, then dipped down to kiss

my spine. Goose bumps rose across my back, and I shivered. "You're not a stranger from a bar, so I'll trust you, but we should have had this discussion before our clothes came off."

"I'm clean." I'd be embarrassed if he knew just how clean. I hadn't touched another woman since my fantasies about being with men had started occupying my thoughts two years ago.

"Me too. Very much so." He grinned faintly into the next kiss, this one closer to where my ass cheeks parted. "Promise me you'll be careful with others, though?"

"Buzzkill," I accused. "The fuck would I think about others when I'm with you?"

He had no answer for that. Instead, he rested his forehead along my lower back and reached for my cock. I startled, only to let out a heavy breath and face forward. My head hung, my eyes fluttered closed. His fingers worked me teasingly, stroking the soft skin stretching around my hardening cock. At the same time, his kisses traveled lower.

The anticipation made me shake. Rim jobs were something I saw in porn, and it hadn't really appealed. With Henry, it seemed all bets were off.

"You have the most beautiful tight little ass," he murmured. "Just soft and round enough to squeeze and sink my teeth into." He nibbled at one cheek, and I laughed breathily. "I can see when you tense up." When he slid a finger over my opening, I did tense up.

"Christ." I gulped. He'd barely started, and I was already losing control. I took a deep breath, but I fucking lost it. An explosion set off inside me as he tightened his grip on my cock and licked the length of my ass. "God-fucking-damn, Henry," I growled. He hadn't given me any warning!

"Drop to your stomach and form a fist around your cock," he commanded quietly. "You'll fuck it slowly."

My body obeyed him without hesitation. Pushing away the

pillows, I gripped my cock and felt him grabbing two fistfuls of my ass. Heat rose to my face, and it wasn't all arousal. There was a trickle of embarrassment and a whole lot of vulnerability. I couldn't *not* wonder how the fuck he found this sexy, but his lustful groan settled most of my nerves.

Henry licked me firmly, softly, teasingly, so fucking sensually, and greedily.

A choked gasp escaped me, and my eyes flew open. He blew out a gentle breath right across my asshole, then rubbed his thumb over the skin. I clenched and trembled.

"So responsive," he whispered. "Tell me you want me to prepare your ass for my cock."

Those words triggered me to push my cock into my fist, and I moaned against the mattress. "I want it." I couldn't imagine he'd ever *fit*...but God, I wanted it.

"Good boy."

"Hnngh." My intelligent reply had to mean I was loving the *good boy*.

He went back to driving me crazy with his tongue. Each wet pass over my opening made me thrust into my hand, and more than that, I pushed back against him when he didn't give me enough.

"You're turning me into a damn slut," I muttered, out of breath.

"Good. I think the slut needs to spread his legs for me some more."

I groaned and forced my knees apart, and then we found our rhythm. It was fucking hypnotizing; I succumbed to it, the desperate rocking, the push and pull. Henry tongue-fucked me sensually and deeply until I was begging like the slut he was turning me into. His hands squeezed and abused my cheeks, and I found myself hoping my flesh would be red after this.

"Fingers," I panted. "Fuck me, Henry—oh God."

As if he'd been waiting for me to give the green light, he immediately wriggled the pad of his thumb inside me, and my automatic response was to clench down.

"Relax, Zachary," he murmured huskily. "Otherwise, I can't fuck you one day." A few deep breaths got me there. "Perfect. Fucking beautiful. Bear down on me, okay?"

"Uh-huh." I squeezed my cock, face buried in the mattress, and breathed through the sharp sting of his finger. He must've replaced it with his middle finger, because he went deeper. "Oh Jesus." I was panting again and swallowing dryly. "More." I couldn't fucking believe what I just said. The pain hadn't faded, and I was asking for more?

Henry complied, coating two fingers in spit and tonguing me expertly before forcing them inside me. The sound of my cry was muffled by the bed and my gnashed teeth, but what shocked me the most was the ball of pleasure that exploded inside me. I met his thrusts instinctively as my body heated up and flushed.

It was like being drunk. I threw myself into the moment recklessly and chased the crest, the rush that would send me flying.

Henry fucked me without mercy. Harder whenever he wanted me to fuck my fist faster, slower when he wanted to be a teasing bastard. I groaned unintelligibly and then gasped as he brushed against something. Oh God, was that what I'd read about? Holy fuck, I needed more.

"Please," I whimpered hoarsely. Sweat began to bead on my forehead, and the sheet was getting damp where I muffled my sounds. "Please—*fuck*, Henry."

His breathing was getting heavier, his kisses wet and sharp along my spine and cheeks. It hit me with another jolt of excitement that he was stroking himself, and I blurted out the first thing that came to mind.

"Don't come on the sheets."

He nipped at my ass. "Why?"

I swallowed. "I wanna feel it," I whispered.

There was no forgetting when he stroked himself off over my cock on the stairs. I wanted to feel it again. It was the fantasy that drove me closer to the brink, and I almost missed Henry's curse.

Clutching the sheet with my free hand, I pushed back harder and jerked my dick impatiently. My balls ached, my ass clenched. It sent ricochets of pain up my body, but the pleasure won. I panted and screwed my eyes shut, getting closer. *Closer, closer.*

"Please come," I bit out.

Henry grunted and hauled in a breath. I felt him straining, his legs tensing up wherever they touched me.

Moments later, the first hot splash of his release coated the crease of my ass, and I lost it. I spiraled, my mind swimming, and started coming. It was too much, at the same time as it wasn't enough. With his fingers buried deep in my ass, his come running down my thighs, my cock spurting in my hand, and the sensations pummeling through me, there was nothing to do but take it. Processing would come way later.

I forgot to breathe. Black spots filled my vision, and I white-knuckled the sheets so hard that my hand hurt.

When I finally collapsed, I didn't know whether to laugh or cry. It was overwhelming to have both your head and body in the game. Sex hadn't been this intense for me in the past.

"Get—get your fingers outta my ass and come snuggle," I croaked.

He chuckled, as out of breath as I was. "They've gotten attached." He slipped them out slowly, and I shook. He did seem awfully into my ass, especially because he couldn't help himself; he brushed his thumb over my opening and rubbed in the come. "Such an exquisite sight."

I squirmed and grinned sleepily.

"I'll be right back." He literally kissed my ass. "Just getting a towel."

I zonked out.

CHAPTER 9

I'M NOT PREGNANT, I JUST HAVE THAT GAY GLOW

Put it in your mouth, dammit.

I glanced up at Henry's face. His light snores meant he was asleep and that I could stare unabashedly. Thing was, I itched to blow him. I'd spent the past ten minutes creeping on him while he slept, and I didn't even feel bad. With all that sexiness on display, he needed to be ogled.

Watching him got me hard. Thinking about sucking his cock had me needy, yet something held me back. I guess I was afraid I'd be awful at it. After the pleasure he'd given me, I wanted it to be good.

Quit overthinking, idiot.

Carefully shifting the covers away completely, I leaned over him and kissed the top of his thigh.

It was admittedly a turn-on that he was asleep. It was dirtier, and I'd watched porn where the sleep thing was part of role-play.

I gently gripped his semihard cock and gave him a slow

stroke. Goddamn gorgeous. His cock, I loved just staring at it. It was soft and smooth. Warm. Long and thick.

He shifted in his sleep, and I inched closer, breathing in the scent of him. The tip of my tongue darted out to lick the vein that traveled up the underside. He was growing harder, and his breathing pattern changed. It wouldn't be long before he woke up.

Before I could overthink it—uh, further—I lifted his cock and wrapped my lips around the blunt head. The softness of the skin did it for me, and I swirled my tongue around him as I took him deeper. Ugh, I could've been doing this since I started dating.

I remembered once...a boy in my class, I couldn't have been more than fourteen. Blow jobs were kinda always on my mind at that age, and sometimes, possibly, I thought about a classmate doing it. A guy. Over the years, there'd been a few of those errant thoughts. Still, it wasn't until I was twenty-five that it really hit me, and now I had a *lot* to make up for.

Since I was new, I did what I liked. I tightened my lips on the upstroke, simultaneously using my hand to stroke down his smooth skin. He was uncut like me, and once he was fully hard, the skin wouldn't stretch over the head. I sucked harder, tasting him at the slit.

He shifted a little again, and he exhaled a heavy breath. Then his hand was in my hair.

"So good... Fuck." His whispered groan made my cock throb, and my breath stuttered. "That's it, baby boy...keep sucking me like that."

I didn't know something had been missing until he spoke. Now I wanted more of his filthy words.

Call me baby boy again.

I used more tongue, and I tightened my grip at the root. I

could take little more than half of him, so I used my hand for the rest. He would have to teach me how to suck him deeper.

A bead of salt exploded on my tongue. I hummed and swiped it over the slit, tasting more. Then I sucked him in again and breathed deeply through my nose. Fuck yes, got another inch. Or maybe a half inch. Whatever. I was in love with giving head now too.

"I can tell you like it," he rasped. "God." He swallowed audibly and shuddered. "My gorgeous cocksucker."

"Mmph." I pressed my dick hard against the mattress and closed my eyes. Saliva trickled over my fingers, and I used it to slick up the rest of him. Needing a quick break to breathe, I licked and kissed and nibbled at the skin while I stroked him faster.

Henry gasped and fisted my hair firmly.

It wasn't the perfect position. I couldn't reach everything I wanted to explore, so I pushed myself up on all fours and figured he wouldn't mind having my ass close. This angle was better. I kissed my way down past his balls and licked them.

"Jesus Christ," he panted.

His thighs went rock solid as I sucked on his balls. Shit, my mouth fucking itched to suck harder. I became frenzied, and it was possible it made me sloppy. I couldn't help it. I had to have more. Back to his cock, I took a bit more than I could handle, and I choked.

That made him groan my name.

So I did it again and again. My eyes watered. I gave no fucks. Next, his rough hand was on my ass, and he was as grabby as ever. I loved it. He squeezed and stroked, fingering me lightly. It only spurred me on.

"Close, baby," he moaned.

I wrenched away, panting. "I wanna try swallowing, but you gotta—gotta keep my head in place."

He cursed viciously and pushed me down on him. I grunted, my dick weeping at this stage. After he came, I had to get off quickly.

"Perfect," he gritted out. A beat later, he tensed up and started coming.

The wet heat flooded my mouth, sending my thoughts in two different directions. Taking a whole load was fucking different than small tastes, and I wasn't a huge fan. But damn... the entire situation—and the fact that I was doing this to him—had me ready to burst.

What I didn't manage to swallow dribbled down the corners of my mouth, and there was no time to lick it up before Henry yanked me to him forcefully and kissed the breath out of me. My stomach flipped as I landed awkwardly, though it didn't stop me from moaning into the kiss and diving in for more.

"Hi," I laugh-croaked.

He let out a breathless chuckle and merely shook his head.

I think I did okay.

It was a grumpy Martin we met up for breakfast around ten, coincidentally the same time Henry opened up his very popular bookstore for the day.

"Can't be easy being a baker and getting up at four, can it?" Henry was amused as he sat down on the porch and dug out bagels from a bag.

"Call me a baker one more time," Martin threatened. Next, he sniffed. "I'm a renowned pastry artist."

I chuckled and poured OJ for myself. The men already had their coffee.

"What are your plans for the day?" Martin asked. With a wave of his hand, he added, "Other than screwing each other's brains out." At that, I froze. Henry grew still too, and Martin rolled his eyes. "Good God, we share a wall, Henry."

Shit.

I cleared my throat and focused intently on spreading cream cheese on my bagel.

"No wonder you told me he was off-limits." Now Martin was all sly, his smirk directed at Henry.

This was interesting information for me.

"Oh, really?" I smiled at Henry.

If I didn't know better, I'd say he was feeling a little flushed himself. It didn't show, but he sure looked a bit embarrassed.

"It's not what you think," he told me. "Martin's always on the prowl, so I told him to back off. This was before I even knew you were gay. Or bisexual. Or whatever you kids label yourselves these days."

I burst out a laugh, finding his stiff ramble cute as fuck.

"That's the only reason, though?" I wondered.

He inclined his head. "At first—"

"But then," Martin interjected, "I do recall him saying you were sex on legs with the most beautiful eyes he'd ever seen."

Was I glowing? I was glowing.

"Thank you for recalling that so well." Henry glared.

"Simmer down, boys," I said mildly. Then I propped my elbow on the table and rested my chin in my palm. I blinked innocently at Henry. "My eyes, huh?"

He tried to hold that glare with me too, tried and failed. "You're bad news." He leaned in and kissed me quickly. "A man doesn't stand a chance."

Good.

"You can flirt later," Martin said. "Joseph called earlier. We're invited to a work event of his this Wednesday."

"Work event?" I cocked my head. Work sounded like work.

If I couldn't stay in bed with Henry, the very least I could do was head out and do some sightseeing.

Henry explained, brushing some crumbs off his tee. "In Joseph's industry, that means a party at some swanky club."

It sounded more fun, suddenly.

"The company where he works," Martin continued, "they signed with Sony last week."

"I thought he was a makeup artist," I said.

Martin nodded. "He is, and ShadowLight now has a contract with Sony for in-house productions. Bastard got a promotion too."

"I would assume so." Henry took a sip of his coffee. "They have to expand quickly, don't they? I thought they were a small company."

I tuned out while they talked about Sony, Joseph, some studio lot in Culver City, and expansions. The bagel was delicious, and Nan had messaged me four new curses she'd learned that made me grin.

I don't know what a fuckwhizz would even be.

Martha's grandson taught me "bitchflaps" today.

I won at bingo night and accidentally hollered out, "Take that, dick wipes!" I was horribly embarrassed.

Hope you're having fun in LA, honey. I googled "twat wizard" today, which, to be honest, sounds more like something to brag about. Love you bunches.

I shook my head, snickering.

"Where the hell did he find these?" I was baffled, remembering the stores Martin had taken me to. Sure, there were graphic tees in most of them, but... Anyway, I sure hadn't seen him throw in a washed-out blue one with the front logo saying, "Straight Outta The Closet."

I put it on and smirked at the mirror, brushing a hand over the yellow block letters. Jeans, Chucks, and shades followed, and then I was ready to meet Henry downstairs.

He laughed when he spotted the shirt.

"Let's go, you lousy store owner." I smacked a kiss at him, and he pinched my ass on the way out.

I'd told him I could go alone, but he wasn't having it. He closed his shop for the day, and then we left Malibu in my truck.

As sexy as he was behind the wheel of his Lexus, I thought he fit in here too. Window rolled down, arm resting there, and the wind catching in his hair, he looked damn good in an old truck. It helped that he tended to dress a lot more comfortably than Martin. Henry, despite the finer things in his life, was rougher around the edges.

Unbidden, I pictured the scenery changing. From the hills and beaches of Malibu to the mountain ranges and forests surrounding Camassia. He'd mentioned wanting a cabin up in Westslope, so I assumed he liked nature. Did he like working with his hands? Imagining him chopping wood and wearing an open flannel shirt sat extremely well with me.

It was a world away from this.

"So tell me about yourself." I sent him a sideways smile and obeyed the GPS when it told me to take the next exit. I'd given up on finding my own way the first day I arrived in the LA area. "I told you my story."

He chuckled quietly and drummed his fingers along the door. "To quote you, there isn't much to tell." Somehow, I doubted that. "If you've met my parents, you probably know how I grew up."

True. I'd only been at the elder Benningtons' estate once, and that'd been enough. They had art everywhere, where others would have family portraits. Other than seeing a couple pictures of Henry and Thorne as young boys—posing with formal smiles with the family dog—there wasn't much warmth in that house. And I already knew Henry had been rejected by his family when he came out. So, no, I didn't care much about the Henry he'd been around his folks 'cause it had been a fake version of him.

"I wanna know about your life here," I said. In LA, he'd been himself for far longer. "How long have you had the bookstore?"

"Only a couple years," he replied. "When my brother turned sixteen, he told me running a bookstore was his dream. He wanted shelves filled with science fiction and fantasy." Just like Ty. Ty used to love those books. "Losing Thorne wrecked me. Because of our family situation, I didn't see him often enough. He flew down a few times a year, and I visited in Chicago where he'd met Shelly, but..." He looked out the window, rubbing his scruffy jaw absently. "When they returned to Camassia, I feared our parents were going to turn him against me, which was foolish of me. Thorne was always protective of me."

"He was older?"

Henry nodded once. "By two years."

He'd opened that store in memory of his brother. That, and unfulfilled dreams, maybe. It angered me when shitty parents stood in the way of their children's dreams, even if it meant running a bookstore that wouldn't rake in millions.

"You're turning the store into a sci-fi heaven, aren't you?" I remembered the back wall being all science fiction, and how he was getting rid of what he called shelf-fillers.

"I am," he chuckled. "I didn't plan for it at first, but then I found Tyler's blog. He hasn't written anything in ages. It used to be full of his recommendations for science fiction novels."

So, it was for both Thorne and Ty, that store.

"Yeah, he's a bit busy banging cheerleaders these days," I mumbled, ignoring Henry's wince. "What did you do before you opened Topaz Pages? For the record, it's not an awesome name."

"What's wrong with Topaz Pages?" He got a little defensive. "It's my favorite color and books."

I grinned. "Topaz like my eyes?"

He scoffed under his breath and turned his head to the window. Too adorable. "After leaving JPMorgan, I got into real estate. It's an exciting market." His definition of exciting was different from mine. "I lived near Echo Park back then—close to Silver Lake and where Martin had his house. I'd say he lived there, but he spent most nights with other men."

We'd landed in the heart of Venice now, but after today, I wanted to know everything there was to know about his history with Martin. Featuring Joseph too. He'd watched me weirdly during that brunch.

CHAPTER 10
DAMN YOU, JOSEPH

So...Monday nights were apparently reserved for playing cards on the porch. I had no interest in joining, opting to veg out in bed with a bag of M&Ms and a Coke. With the window open, I could hear Henry and Martin when they bickered.

They acted like an old married couple.

I texted with Mattie while I gave Instagram a go too. It was a decent distraction, and the filters were fun.

Ty and I had a huge fight today. I hope his uncle will help.

I responded, asking what it was this time, and then returned to Instagram. I'd uploaded photos of Venice Beach, the pier in Santa Monica, the Hollywood sign, and a couple randoms of palm trees so far. A picture of downtown LA's skyscrapers was next, but first, I read Mattie's answer.

We went to Silver Beach, and he told a girl in our class she couldn't tag along because she was fat.

"Jesus Christ," I growled. The guilt hit me hard; I'd been having a fucking amazing day with Henry, and this was going on while we were kissing and holding hands and going out for brunch and dinner together like an actual couple. Scrubbing a hand over my face, I was hit with a dose of reality. And reality was, this LA glitz didn't belong to me. In real life, I was a pseudoparent with responsibilities that went beyond clubs and funny tees.

After telling Mattie I was calling Ty, I uploaded the last picture and found Ty's cell number.

He answered on the third ring. "Bennington, who's this?"

"What the fuck is wrong with you, Ty?" I got out of bed, the hardwood floor creaking under my feet. "Did you really tell a girl she couldn't go with you to the beach because of her weight?"

There was a pause before Ty replied. "I should've known Mattie was gonna snitch to his big brother. How are you, Zach?"

"I'll be good once I get my hands around your ne—" Shit. Not the best approach. I could be mature for this. Maybe. "Look. Do you not see what an ass you're turning into? What you said to that girl is straight-up bullying."

He had the nerve to laugh. "You're not my father, man. Where do you get off telling me what to do? You're nothing but a glorified babysitter." He hung up on me.

Eyes wide, I stared at the screen.

"That little shit." I ran a hand through my hair and looked around me, then headed straight for the stairs. Fuck the fucking Benningtons and their vacation in southern France. Henry had said he didn't have the number, but how hard was it to track down?

As I reached the store's exit, I paused upon hearing Martin saying, "You know he's interested."

The window was open a sliver here too. Stay or go? Tell Henry about Ty, or...eavesdrop?

Yeah, like there was any contest. I had the darkness of the shop to keep me hidden as I walked closer to the window.

"I'm aware," was Henry's muttered reply. "He sent me a message after brunch."

"Have you discussed it with Zach?" Martin wondered.

I'm wondering too. Discuss what, Henry?

"I'm hoping to avoid it," he said. "Zachary is...different. It's not just fun and games."

That boded well, at least.

"It is for Joseph," Martin pointed out, his tone patient. Almost gentle. "This is what he does. Hell, it's what both of you do—usually."

"That's hardly the case anymore," Henry argued. "You of all people should know I've been a goddamn monk for years."

"Four years and two months. Should I count the days too?"

I narrowed my eyes at nothing. I couldn't see either of them, the table outside Martin's shop a few feet too far to the left, and now I desperately wanted to know what they were talking about. I wanted to read their expressions. Joseph and I were clearly involved in whatever they were discussing, and there was a rock in the pit of my stomach telling me it wasn't awesome news.

"I suggest you talk to Joseph," Martin said. "Zach is the first man you've shown interest in since Oliver, and that was a shit-show. Joseph might be under the impression you'll pick up where you left off."

Henry sighed heavily. "And what if Zach is interested? He *just* started exploring men. I'd feel awful standing in the way—"

"For fuck's sake, Henry," Martin interrupted irritably. I caught myself nodding, agreeing. It wasn't fucking up to Henry to make decisions for me, nor did he know how I felt. "Zach is a sweetheart. He doesn't strike me as one who needs to play the field for the sake of it."

My affection for Martin grew tenfold.

"I'd feel even worse if he *wanted—*" Whatever Henry was going to say was lost as a phone rang.

It was Martin's. "Sorry, I'll be right back. It's my niece. You deal the next hand."

If I walked out there now, Henry would know I'd overheard them.

Returning upstairs, I was accompanied by Eagle lugging his big butt up the stairs, and I only had one question for him.

"Who's Oliver?" I whispered.

An hour later when I heard Henry coming up, I'd built a mountain of questions. I didn't care if he knew I'd listened in either. If it was about me, I had a right to know.

I'd kept my underwear on after climbing into bed so I wouldn't get distracted, which I thought was pretty mature thinking on my part.

"Did you have a nice game?" I asked.

He looked too troubled to pull off a lie, and I was glad he didn't try. "For a while, perhaps. I had a conversation with Martin that I could've lived without."

"Oh?" I pushed myself up to sit, the covers pooling around my waist.

Henry left his clothes on and sat down on the foot of the bed.

Not a good sign, was it?

"I need to tell you a bit about Joseph and me," he said,

visibly uncomfortable. When that happened, he became more formal, rigid in his posture, and he struggled with eye contact. I gave him bonus points for bringing this up with me, though. He could've easily kept his mouth shut.

"I'm listening." It was possible I had some jealousy rearing its ugly head too.

He scratched his jaw, thinking. "Before I begin, I should tell you that I've always had a habit of either hesitating too much or not enough. Hiding who I was for so many years left its mark, and it's followed me into relationships." He paused. "My love life has essentially consisted of brief periods of casual encounters and long dry spells. Once I jump into something, I ride it out until my uneasiness—originally, fear—catches up to me. You see, casual encounters were all I had until I finally found the courage to come out to my parents. I was constantly looking over my shoulder, even here in LA."

Since I didn't know if he wanted me to be close, I stayed put, though my entire being shouted at me to scoot down and grab his hand or something.

"I've been in a couple loving relationships since then, but I couldn't shake the depression for a long time after my mother and father told me I was no longer their son." He fidgeted absently with a side pocket in his shorts, tracing the button. "It made me feel like I was still living a lie. Every time I met a man, I had my parents in my head looking at me in disgust."

"That's a heavy burden," I murmured.

He nodded with a dip of his chin. "Joseph has a similar story. He and I met through friends about ten years ago, and he's the one who helped me put my parents behind me."

Ugh, nothing worse than being jealous of a good guy.

I sucked.

"How did he do that?" I wondered.

"His father was ten times worse," he sighed. "Joseph's a few years younger than me, but if you keep our generation in mind, maybe you can guess that a big issue for many of us was HIV and AIDS. I've lived in both New York and LA, and I don't know anyone in our community who escaped the eighties and nineties unaffected one way or another."

Of course, I'd known about the epidemic. "Did you lose anyone?"

"A couple college friends," he replied. "In many ways, I'm lucky. Families and relationships were shattered everywhere, not only because people fell ill, but because it became that much harder to come out." He met my gaze briefly and put his hand on my foot through the covers. "Joseph's father was convinced that he was going to drag the 'gay plague' home with him. For two weeks, during a school break, he kept Joseph locked up and beat him within an inch of his life." Jesus fucking Christ. "When Joseph managed to escape, he came out here to live with an aunt who accepted him for who he is."

"I'm glad he got away." I couldn't imagine that pain. I'd lost both my parents, but that was different. My dad didn't bail because he found me disgusting. He was just a loser deadbeat. And my mom... Her problems had been personal.

"Me too." Henry mustered a small smile. "He'd been in LA several years when I met him, but I didn't need to see the fresh wounds. The scars were enough to infuriate me. I told him I couldn't believe a parent would do that to their child. Of course, disowning me wasn't as bad—"

"They did more than disown you," I interjected. "The shit they did to turn Ty against you...? Abuse is abuse, verbal or physical or emotional."

He nodded, the minuscule smile reappearing for a second. "That's what Joseph made me realize. Same principle. Mind you, it took him a couple years before I believed it, but eventually, it was easier to put them behind me. For once, I could start living my life the way I wanted to."

With Joseph, I added internally. I didn't know how, though I was sure he fit in here somewhere. Henry and Joseph had more than a little history.

"It wasn't until then I considered myself truly *out*," he said. "You told me it was personal, remember?" I nodded, and he nodded once too. "I think many of us can relate to that. Being out is more than just telling friends and family. It's a feeling."

"Yeah." Like a weight off one's shoulders.

I wasn't sure I was there yet—with that feeling—but I was going in the right direction.

"So you and Joseph got together, right?" I hoped I sounded casual.

Henry chuckled under his breath. "We started sleeping together, yes. We were never an item, and I only ever viewed him as a friend. We're also almost exclusively tops, so we had more fun together when there was someone between us."

My jaw dropped an inch before I firmly smashed my lips together. They shared guys together. And just like that, it all made sense. What Martin and Henry had talked about downstairs. Joseph was interested in having *me* between him and Henry.

I squirmed, unsure how to feel. It was unsettling.

"I don't want you to think of me as some Casanova," Henry said. "It couldn't be further from the truth."

"Right. You still had your long dry spells, or however you put it, but then when you didn't, you and Joseph were bagging twinks left and right."

"Well," he coughed, "something like that, sans the bagging. A couple here and there. No need for bags."

"You know what I mean." I rolled my eyes. "Move along. Who's Oliver?"

"I didn't mention—" As he narrowed his eyes at me, it hit me that I'd given myself away. Aw, shit. Now he knew I'd been downstairs. "How much did you hear, Zachary?"

Fuck me if I didn't blush. Thankfully, there were only a couple lamps in the windows, so the place wasn't too bright.

"Enough to now realize that Joseph might want a threesome with us."

He wasn't fast enough to hide his grimace. Little things like that, I took comfort in. And it was kinda obvious to me now that I wanted Henry to myself, for however long we lasted. I hoped it was long. Did that make me naïve?

"I wanna hear about Oliver," I said.

He released a breath, some of the tension leaving him. "Oliver was a big mistake. A guy in his early thirties—Joseph was dating him. And our, how shall I say... Our modus operandi for when we played with others was to introduce them over a drink and then take it from there. If there was someone I'd met, I would invite Joseph over to meet him and vice versa. And he invited me out for dinner to meet Oliver, his new boyfriend." It was getting less hot for me. "We had fun a few times before I got suspicious of Oliver. He had mood swings that rivaled my mother's when she was out of Prozac. My feelings for him were also entirely wrong. I didn't want to sleep with him. I wanted to make sure he ate right and went back to school."

I snorted softly.

"After knowing Joseph for so long, though, I'd come to rely on his judgment," he went on, quieter now. "We learned that Oliver struggled with depression." That made me stiffen. "Joseph wanted to help him, and Oliver grew attached to us both quickly. For all intents and purposes, we were in a relationship, the three of us. All for the wrong reasons. We were babysitters more than anything, but it was the easiest way to make sure Oliver didn't do anything stupid."

I swallowed. "He was suicidal?"

"Oh. No, darling." He shook his head and squeezed my foot affectionately. "Oliver is fine and well today." I was relieved. "He did self-medicate, though. Unlike your mother, he'd started using cocaine. We couldn't be there all hours of the day, and someone who doesn't want help…"

Won't accept it.

Henry continued. "Oliver and I were alone one day, and he told me his parents wanted him home so they could help him get better. I thought it was a wonderful idea and promised I'd be there in whatever capacity he wished. He's from Denver," he elaborated. "Then Joseph came home from work, and I expected he would be as relieved as I was."

"He wasn't," I guessed.

"No. He was furious. He claimed we should work this out together, just us three." The tension made a return. "See, Joseph had made me think it was Oliver who needed us. It turned out it was Joseph who wanted us together." He sighed. "Once Oliver returned home, it took Joseph quite a while to get over him."

I tilted my head. "Um, what about getting over you?"

"Me?" He frowned. "It wasn't me he'd fallen for."

Oh, really… Then why insist on having Henry be part of the relationship?

"How can you be sure?" I eyed him dubiously.

"Because he told me, and I trust him. Besides, we never made sense. He's a control freak and bitched like a little queen every time he bottomed. Between you and me, I think he's irritated because he liked it so much."

I spluttered. "I don't think I want details about you and Joseph, but I'm sure he gave you rave reviews."

"Your reviews are the only ones I care about." Henry finally left the foot of the bed and crawled over to me. I smiled. He did too. "My beautiful lover."

Funny how I'd never been much of a blusher before him.

He dropped a quick kiss to my forehead, then landed next to me on the mattress, sadly overdressed. "About Wednesday when we meet Joseph..." He raised a brow.

"First things first," I said. "You never bottom?" I wouldn't call it a compatibility issue, though I did want to fuck him.

His brow furrowed. "Of course I do."

"But you said exclusively tops earlier..."

"*Almost.*" He stifled a yawn and unbuttoned his shorts. "Call me old-fashioned, but it's a relationship thing for me. Too intimate to share with someone I wouldn't consider being with long term."

Of fucking course I had to wonder if that included me.

"Now, about Wednesday," he said. "I need to know your thoughts—"

"I don't wanna be fucking shared with Joseph," I replied bluntly, annoyed.

Either Henry didn't notice I was irritated, or he didn't care. He exhaled, and an "Oh, thank God" gusted out of him. He reached for my hand and brought my knuckles to his lips. "I haven't met many men who've turned him down. Forgive me for worrying."

His words melted away most of my annoyance, and his kisses took care of the rest.

"Martin was right, by the way," I murmured. "I have no interest in playing the field. Whatever this is between you and me is just ours for as long as it lasts."

He caressed my cheek, gaze flicking to mine. "I might need you to remind me of that from time to time. I'm a jaded old man—"

"You're not that old." I rolled my eyes.

"—and despite that, the intensity of these past few days has gotten my hopes up." He tapped my nose as I grinned. "I told you you're bad news, Zachary."

"Bad or dangerous?" I waggled my brows.

He laughed and conceded. "Dangerous. Definitely dangerous."

He was wrong, though dangerous was better than bad.

CHAPTER 11
MOM AND DAD ARE FIGHTING

Tuesday was weird.

Around five in the afternoon, I found myself standing on a beach alone with my feet sinking down into the sand with each wave.

I scratched my head and squinted at the sun. The cliffs around me changed colors depending on the time of day. They'd been brighter when I got here. Now, as the sun crept closer to the horizon, they shifted to orange.

Checking my phone again, I wasn't too surprised to see I had no service. Malibu needed to get on that.

Was it safe to return to the war zone yet?

If Martin and Henry were crazy when they bickered, they were downright certifiable when they argued. Apparently, an old ex of Martin's was back in town, and he was planning on seeing him. Henry called him an idiot because this other dude had stolen Martin's car... So now they were yelling at each other.

I hoped they were done. I'd escaped with a "Fuck no, don't drag me into this, you crazy old birds" when Martin had tried to explain how *this time was different*.

I checked the time and sighed. After I spent the morning in bed with Henry, he'd gone down to open the shop, and I had run out and bought breakfast for the three of us. It'd been enough alone time to process everything I'd learned last night, and I'd arrived with the intention of telling Henry about Ty. But Mattie called with a work problem, so I had to spend two hours on the phone because we'd gotten a double shipment of dairy products to the store. If it'd been soda, I would've let it slide. We sold that without ever having to worry about expiration dates.

It wasn't until after noon I'd been able to tell Henry about his nephew, and I was thankful he'd immediately started his search for a number to use to track down his parents. The family lawyer might have it, and he was gonna call back in the morning.

"Fuck it." I peered down and hauled my feet up from the soft sand. Henry and Martin better fucking be done by now.

It was the first time I'd found Henry sitting with Eagle. They were both cuddled up on the couch upstairs, and I couldn't help but laugh. They were just so *cute*. Henry looked like he was fresh out of the shower. Nothing on top, though I suspected he wore sweats or boxers underneath the blanket.

There was a box of assorted chocolates next to Henry. A glass of red wine on the table.

"I've been waiting for you." The only thing missing in his tone was an actual pout. I wasn't sure I'd be capable of handling that without breaking out in hysterics.

"How's your other half? I don't like it when Mom and Dad

fight." I set the box of chocolate on the table, where he'd pressed pause on something on his tablet. I supposed for someone who rarely watched TV, a tablet was enough.

"We're not on speaking terms." The man was testy.

"You're adorable, you know that?" I leaned forward, checking out the selection of chocolates. They looked awfully extravagant, usually meaning pricey-as-fuck, so I wouldn't be gorging. Popping one into my mouth, I mmmph'd at the deliciousness and leaned back against the cushions. "I don't know who this Jacques Torres guy is, but he knows his chocolate."

"I have a dealer in New York," he said. "By dealer, I mean a dear friend I went to college with. I order them through her whenever she's heading out here for work because I don't trust regular shipping."

I hope she comes around a lot, I almost said.

I was going home sooner rather than later, though.

"Whatever makes you less cranky, lover," I replied cheekily and patted his arm. Eagle fucking hissed at me. Was I getting too close to Daddy? "I thought we were making progress." I stared at the cat.

"Perhaps he'll give you less attitude if you call me lover without sarcasm," Henry suggested. "I know one person who'd certainly like it."

I smiled and leaned closer, ignoring Eagle's bitchy glare.

"My lover." I pressed my lips to his, kissing him softly in several pecks. "My handsome, drop-dead gorgeous lover. Better?"

It took me off guard how much I enjoyed saying it. Cheesy as hell or not... Henry was my lover, and there wasn't a word in that sentence I didn't get a thrill from.

He sighed and nodded, then stole another smooch. "Much. Where did you go when World War III broke out? I apologize for that, by the way. I didn't want you to get involved."

I shrugged, placing an arm along the back of the couch. I was sitting higher while he was all but lounging, so in a rare switch, I got to be the top for a change. I enjoyed it a shitload. "Drove around for a bit. I bought a donut in town—don't tell Martin—then went to the beach for a while."

"Zuma?"

"No, too crowded." Zuma Beach was closest, huge and full of people. I didn't know which one I'd ended up at.

He hummed and lolled his head toward my shoulder, and my fingers found his hair. "I'm going to tell Martin. I'll also mention you liked it more than his."

I laughed silently, my shoulders shaking. "Your dynamic is nuts."

"You're not wrong," he chuckled drowsily. "We've been best friends for twenty-five years. We've been each other's parents, brothers, and therapists." They'd been through a lot together.

"Were you two ever...?"

He shook his head. "Entirely different tastes and preferences. No, we clicked right away, but strictly as friends and brothers."

I wanted something like that for myself. It wasn't only my love life that'd been put on hold while growing up. It was everything. Friends, hobbies, education...

"What about Joseph and Martin?" I asked.

"Ha," he huffed, amused. "Those two—that's another dysfunctional relationship. When I introduced the two, it was almost as if they made a conscious effort to hate one another. It's a struggle to this day. Sometimes, they're very close. Other times, they're constantly fighting."

Tomorrow would be interesting, then. With Henry and Martin not speaking, Joseph evidently wanting a three-way with Henry and me, and that shit not happening...I just hoped there wouldn't be any drama.

"Speaking of dysfunctional relationships..." Henry leaned forward with a grunt, Eagle jumping down, and grabbed his tablet. "It goes without saying that Tyler and I will have a rocky relaunch, so I was wondering if you could go through this list for me. I've been thinking about punishments—especially after what you told me he said to that poor girl. But without established trust, I fear punishments will only divide us further."

He showed me the document he'd been working on, and a weight I hadn't known existed was lifted off my shoulders. He was right; they'd have a rough go at first, but I had no doubt Henry would be good for Ty. The remaining concern was whether or not Ty would snap out of his dickishness.

The first item on the list read "Volunteer," followed by an additional list of places. Soup kitchens and LGBTQ+ centers, and addresses for them. He'd jotted down notes about a place called Second Family as if he knew it well. "Talk to Marisol, bring Tyler to a group session," it said.

Speaking to a counselor was next, which gave me a slight pause.

"He shouldn't view any of these as punishments," I noted.

Henry inclined his head. "But he will."

The following four items were more classic punishments for teenagers. Revoked privileges, like his cell phone, no car, no going out, et cetera.

"He probably won't have access to any of that when he arrives," Henry added. "I have a feeling he'll leave, given the chance."

I nodded. "You should add cleaning Eagle's litter box. That shit's nasty."

Henry smiled. "Aw, he's my cuddle monster."

"His shit still stinks."

"It's because of his food. It's supposed to help him lose weight."

Sure, sure.

The humor faded as I read the rest of the list, approving of the whole thing. For not being a parent, he was going into this as prepared as he could be. I shared his views on what was structure and good values.

"Are you ready for this?" I had to ask anyway.

"I'm determined," he replied honestly. "I wish I'd been stronger before—for him and myself—but I can't dwell on that anymore."

"Nor should you," I muttered. "You had too much working against you. Now it'll be just you and him. And Mattie and I will be here for as long as we can." About that... I looked around the apartment, perfectly suited for one person. It worked great for us too. Four would be a stretch. "What're you gonna do about space? Mattie and I have no issues going to a motel—"

"Nonsense." He was dismissive. "I'm renting a house for us. Lord, I don't think even Ty and I could share this apartment. Imagine the head-butting we'll do?" He had a point. Ty wasn't a stranger to slamming doors, and Henry would need some privacy at the end of the day to regroup. "How long do you think you and your brother can stay?"

Huh. It was surprisingly easy to tackle this topic when it wasn't about Henry and me. I was already dreading the day, but this was about Henry and Ty. I was here to help, not share his bed. Well, mainly.

The concern was Pammie. She'd be alone with the store at home, and there came a time where simply a bonus wouldn't cut it. We were open from seven in the morning to ten at night, and the mere thought made me wince. Unlike Henry's bookstore, we actually had customers.

"You're worried about something." He reached up and smoothed out the crease between my brows. "What's the concern?"

I explained it to him, about Pammie being our only employee. When Mattie was home, there was no issue. They split the hours and were like any other full-time workers.

"Would you lose business if you closed for vacation?" Henry asked.

"Yes, when the door is locked, it does pose a problem for customers to get in—"

He pinched my side, and I laughed.

"I mean, would you lose them to any competition?" he clarified. "Smartass."

"Nah. It's called a convenience store for a reason. They go where it's convenient. Those who live nearby come to us."

"So," he went on, "theoretically, if I were to compensate you for lost income—since I truly need help here—you'd return to Camassia later on, and the customers would be back."

Tempting bastard. He phrased himself that way on purpose too. That he needed help, that it wasn't me freeloading.

"Theoretically," I agreed. There was one problem, though. "Here's the thing, Henry. I wanna stay, and I have no doubt Mattie's gonna love it here."

"But," he hedged.

"But we can't put our lives on hold forever." Mostly because what was going to hurt now was going to fucking shatter me later. Here, I was living in a fantasy. A dream. It just wasn't real. "Once Ty gets here, I can stay another week or maybe ten days. Mattie doesn't have anything until school starts, so that's between you guys. I gotta get back to work and Nan."

He hummed. "Well, if you're going to be all reasonable about things..."

I chuckled and pressed a kiss to his temple.

He was gonna have to make a lot of decisions in the near future. Unless Ty changed schools, Henry might have to move to Camassia by the end of the summer. Ty still had his senior year of high school to get through before he was off to college. For now, I told myself to be satisfied with what we'd discussed. I'd have a few more weeks with Henry.

There was one worry, having spent time in LA now. What if Ty did want to move here?

The following late afternoon, Henry and Martin's stony silence remained in effect.

"What about this?" I held up a shirt and showed it to Martin. Their ongoing war of not speaking was even worse when they were in the same room. Lunch had been horrific. I'd ended up telling knock-knock jokes to see if they would crack.

They didn't.

Martin pursed his lips and tapped his chin thoughtfully.

Henry was on the couch with Eagle again. He was taking a vacation day from his store… Though, in his defense, he was still working. I just didn't know with what. The table was strewn with finance stuff. He was wearing *glasses*. Hot. As. Fuck.

"No, I want to see you in something tighter," Martin said. "What pants are you wearing?"

"The slacks," I told him. They resembled the charcoal dress pants Henry had worn the other day. He'd said my ass looked delectable in them.

"Then, no." He took the shirt from me and started sifting through the clothes in the closet space Henry had given me. "Try this one."

Jesus. When Martin said tight, he meant it. The light blue button-down hugged my torso and biceps to the point where it almost strained. "Maybe it's—"

"Perfect." Martin clasped his hands together under his chin. "Every man in the club will want you. All of them."

I lifted a brow, then narrowed my eyes at him. He was a shit. He was doing this to rile up Henry.

"Only one of them matters." I winked.

I didn't need to look over my shoulder to sense Henry relaxing.

Martin waved a hand and asked where I kept my accessories.

He picked out a cuff and some leather cords to attach around my wrist, all while muttering about getting me more stuff.

"Okay, you're free to go," he told me. "I'm heading out quickly. We have—" he checked his watch "—three hours. I can bring back dinner—"

"Tell Martin I've got dinner handled," Henry said.

"Oh my God, you two," I groaned.

Dinner was awesome. Something must've happened while I was in the shower, 'cause now they were silently seething.

"Should we discuss how smoking hot we all are tonight?" I suggested innocuously. While certainly true, I had a feeling they weren't chatty this evening. So I ate my delicious pasta dish from some Italian place in not-silence. I hummed appreciatively and made yummy noises.

I'd gotten a slight tan, which made me happy. It made my arms look better, and Martin had insisted I neatly fold the sleeves to my elbows. The party we were going to was upscale, hence the button-down and slacks. To be honest, I was digging the fashion stuff. I didn't understand much of it, but I enjoyed the results. Having never paid attention to what I wore and how I looked before, it was a nice change.

I even tucked a napkin into my shirt so I wouldn't spill.

To fuck with Martin, no doubt, Henry was going with all black. Black dress pants, black button-down, black shoes, black leather belt. He looked like a god. Add a nice watch to that…? Goddamn. I wanted to jump his bones.

"Will there be dancing tonight?" I asked.

Martin nodded stiffly.

"Awesome." I took a sip of my wine and eyed the grouches. "What else can I expect?"

"Makeup." Martin so wanted to ramble. He was excited about tonight. He just couldn't bring himself to show it when he was fighting with Henry. "Have you heard of Brooklyn Wright?"

I shook my head.

"She's amazing. One of the best makeup artists in the business," he went on. "She's the owner of ShadowLight, and they're launching their own makeup brand. Tonight, they will give us a glimpse."

I wasn't particularly interested in makeup, though. "Will they know what a Violet Haze is at the bar?"

His mouth twitched. "Yes, dear."

Henry cleared his throat. "You've probably heard of Tennyson Wright."

Well, sure. Famous director.

"He's Brooklyn's brother-in-law," Henry finished.

"Oh. Cool." I took another bite of my food, hoping I'd thawed them out a little. "So…does this mean it's some celebrity event?" Nan would get a kick out of this. She was a film buff.

"There will probably be a few," Martin answered. "Brooklyn is close friends with Tennyson's wife—Sophie Pierce?"

"Oh, she's good." I nodded. She was an A-lister. I'd seen a few of her movies. My grandmother adored her.

Would I break some code if I asked Sophie for an autograph? I hoped she showed up.

"Noah Collins might show up," Henry pondered out loud. "Given he's worked closely with both Wright brothers..."

I didn't know who the Noah dude was, but I was getting increasingly enthusiastic about this party. It was part of the fantasy, things I'd seen on TV but never thought I'd be part of. LA was a heady drug that sucked you in, wasn't it?

"Did you read the article about Noah and his husband?" Martin asked Henry. My head snapped up; they were fucking talking. Or would be, if Henry responded.

And he did, nodding. "It was good. Julian's such a gifted composer too."

I grinned.

They offered looks of confusion, after which it dawned on them.

So they went back to glaring at each other.

I sighed.

CHAPTER 12
IS IT OKAY TO FANGIRL?

I was starstruck. We'd only just entered the club—somewhere in Hollywood—and I was already losing my composure. There was a real red carpet outside, reserved for famous people who were arriving later. The club was decorated as a fancy studio, albeit with a lot less light. The spotlights were mounted on big stands, the bar was built to look like a makeup artist's station, the back wall complete with a huge mirror and light bulbs framing it. High chairs, like director's chairs, instead of barstools.

Low couches and tables took up the space along the walls, and the rest was one big open area. If the building was an old warehouse, I wouldn't be surprised. Except, the ceiling wasn't as high.

It was already packed with people. They were mainly industry people, Martin explained to me. As in, they were—in one way or another—involved in film, music, or anything surrounding it.

"I'm not including the caterers and bar staff," he said.

I chuckled, and we passed a guy carrying a tray of champagne flutes.

There were fancy snacks too.

I tentatively grabbed Henry's hand, something that earned me a smile from him, and then we sort of walked around for a while. Martin knew several people here. Henry knew a handful. I was introduced to people I'd never meet again.

The venue was big, and it took us some time to cover the whole place. I noticed there was more than one bar too.

"I wonder where Joseph is," Martin said. "Let me know if you see him."

I guess. I wasn't too thrilled about that part, although I was stoked he'd invited us.

Martin wandered off to socialize.

"Let's get a drink and find a place to sit." Henry gave my hand a squeeze, and I followed him.

He ordered for me, making sure they got my drink right. He was too sweet. In the meantime, I was staring at everyone, taking it all in. The dresses and suits these people wore...I didn't wanna know what they'd cost.

Again, I remembered my ex, Meghan. She'd been good at putting together cheaper things and making it look extravagant.

There were photos on display here and there, pictures of models with heavy makeup. I spotted a few women by one display, their phones up. Selfie-time, huh?

I smiled and shook my head in wonder.

Henry inched closer, handing me my cocktail, and he spoke in my ear. "I love watching you. How you process."

"Thanks for making me self-conscious about it." I let out a laugh and clinked my glass to his whiskey. Violet Haze was served in a martini glass here, instead of a tall glass. It meant I'd need more of them. "This place is insane."

Henry looked out over the floor, pensive. Had they dimmed

the lights further? It appeared darker suddenly, and the music a little louder.

"If you were to show them the mountains around your town, they'd call that insane too."

Maybe. Some of them, sure. I got his point, though. I also heard him say *your town*, as if Camassia wasn't his anymore.

I'd need a dozen Violet Hazes to forget that.

I took a big gulp of my drink.

It did get louder. And darker. It hadn't been in my head. As the club filled to the brim, the party came to life. Henry pointed out a few minor celebrities, famous for being famous but good to have around because they were whores on social media and knew how to spread the word.

When Martin found us on a couch in the seating area, he had Joseph with him. It made me straighten up, and I linked my fingers with Henry's.

"Hello there, my gorgeous lovebirds." Joseph smiled and sat down next to me, his hand on my thigh as he leaned over to kiss Henry's cheek. "No more sneaking around for you, huh? Not that you were subtle last Sunday."

"Play nice, Joseph." Henry's warning held no warning whatsoever, though his eyes tightened at the corners.

"Yes, yes, no extra fun for you." Joseph waved it off. So Henry had already told him there'd be no, um, threesome. "I have the evening to change your minds." I grew uncomfortable as he placed a finger under my chin and leaned closer to my ear. "Henry and I can make you see stars, Zachy boy."

I stiffened and inched away. I didn't make it a habit to jump into bed with complete strangers, and his advances were anything but sexy.

Joseph rose from the couch before I could respond, though I had no clue what I would've said, and he smirked at us. "You do make a cute couple. I'll have to buy you guys a drink later. Work calls."

He left, taking a silent Martin with him.

Henry had been tense, something I didn't notice until his shoulders relaxed. "What did he say to you?"

I shook my head and finished my drink. The jealousy lingered, and it bothered me. They'd been friends for years, had a lot of history, a sexual one included. The day I went home, Joseph would still be here.

"Let's get another drink." I kissed his jaw. "Then you're gonna ask me to dance."

He tilted his head and captured my mouth with his. "You got it."

"You gotta stop doing that," I laughed and panted, fearing the music had drowned out my voice. Holy shit, he was indecent. I groaned and turned my head to nuzzle his jaw. With him behind me and dancing bodies all around us, nobody could see him cupping my crotch, fondling it sensually.

"I'll do no such thing." He kissed my neck as a new song poured out. It was slower, like the foreplay of music. The bass reverberated through me, and Henry's cock against my ass didn't exactly improve my situation. A few more songs like this and I'd come in my pants like a teenager.

I shuddered, moving against him. It was getting all kinds of hot, and I wiped at my forehead. The third drink had given me a slight buzz too. And I was learning that my favorite Haze made me bolder.

Maybe it was a good thing we were interrupted.

I blinked dazedly, then grinned when I saw my favorite Martin. He appeared in the crowd, yelled something over the music, then gestured for us to follow him. I couldn't very well protest and say one more song; he was already disappearing again.

"There's probably someone he wants you to meet," Henry said in my ear.

He took my hand, and I followed after adjusting my dick. The bastard had gotten me hot and bothered.

"Martin!" Henry called. "Where are you going?"

That was my question too, 'cause he was leading the way out of the club. We left the main area, and Martin continued to a sealed-off hallway where a security guy waited. He let us through, and Martin finally slowed enough to tell us what was going on.

"This is called networking, dear," he told me. "When you get the chance to meet higher-ups in the industry, you go with it. You never know what connections you'll make."

Henry narrowed his eyes. "You're up to something."

Martin waved a hand. "Of course I am, but even if I weren't, networking is always good. I already booked a work event—a charity thing. My pretty pastries will get more publicity."

That was great and all, but I didn't see how this concerned Henry and me. There was no reason for us to network. No cupcakes to sell.

We came to a stop outside of a door, and Martin opened it. Inside was a mini version of a club, a dark room with a small bar. The low couches and tables in the main club were here too, just fewer of them. Twenty people would fill the room.

"Oh, shit, that's..." Not only was Sophie Pierce in here, but the music was low enough that I heard myself being un-cool. Thankfully, no one else seemed to hear it, and my being tipsy made it easier to unclench.

Did Joseph have to be here, though?

He stood up when he spotted us, and he smiled warmly. "Get over here, gentlemen. Let me introduce you to my gorgeous boss."

A beautiful woman with dark skin and a gold dress that made even me perk up tinkered a laugh and slapped Joseph's thigh. "You already got your promotion, hon. You can stop flattering me now."

He chuckled and winked at her. "Never, my love." As we reached their table, Joseph cupped my elbow and encouraged me closer to him. "This is Zach Coleman, a sexy little thing visiting from Smalltown, America."

I gave him a WTF look, then plastered a polite smile on my face as he introduced me to Brooklyn Wright, the owner of ShadowLight. I shook her hand, blurting out a compliment about her dress that made her beam, and others followed. Others whose names I wasn't sure I'd remember. Her husband was sitting next to her, then Tennyson Wright—and I had to admit he was hot as fuck, something I hadn't considered before. Now, being here, a whole lot of doors had opened. I was seeing men everywhere.

"You directed *A Killer's Walk* and *Fallen*." I was all about blurting shit out, and as if he didn't know the films he'd made? Christ. "I loved *Unrecovered* too."

He smiled and shook my hand firmly. "I appreciate it."

"The lovely Sophie Pierce, of course," Joseph went on.

She rose with a stunning smile and extended her hand so I could greet her. "It's nice to meet you, Zach. Are you enjoying LA?"

"Very much, thank you." I had to lean over the table a bit to grasp her hand. And I kind of didn't want to let her go, 'cause I was shaking hands with a Hollywood actress who'd been nominated for an Oscar *twice*. "I love your work, and my grandmother will be jealous when I tell her I met you. You were awesome in *A Killer's Walk*. Oh, and *Beneath the Scars*."

She seriously blushed. How adorable was she? She didn't look too many years older than me. Her sexy husband was a lot older, I remembered that much.

"Look alive, Noah." Tennyson leaned back and slapped the arm of a man on the other side of Sophie. He was another hot one. Bearded, tall.

He resurfaced with a "What? I'm alive" after shaking hands with Henry.

Sophie laughed. "You should meet Noah, Zach." She gestured at the man to her left. "He directed *Beneath the Scars*."

He inclined his head. "Good to meet you."

"You too." I shook his hand eagerly—shit. I was forgetting to play it cool. "The last scene sort of slayed me, when the mom was in the mental ward and her son came in."

He grinned. "One of my favorite scenes too. I'm glad you liked it."

Okay, I was more than a little starstruck.

Sophie sat down again, cuddling up with her husband, and she shared a joke with her brother-in-law. I wanted to say his name was…Asher? It was a lot to take in, and I was still being introduced to people. At least Henry was back to my side, my hand in his again.

The last person I shook hands with was Julian, Noah's husband. Martin informed me he was a composer and had done the music for *Beneath the Scars*.

"If you'll excuse me, I have to show my face at the party," Brooklyn said. She was bringing two women with her, along with Joseph and her husband. "Please have a seat, Henry. Joseph told me you're the one I need to talk to about Second Family. If you have time, I'd love to set up a meeting."

I whipped my head in Henry's direction, surprised. Was he

involved in that company? I remembered it was on the list of LGBTQ+ centers he was taking Ty to.

"I'll look forward to it, dear." Henry nodded.

Sophie piped up. "Oh, was that for the boys' dog ranch?"

"I just love it when you call us boys, princess," Tennyson drawled.

In the mix of chuckles and laughter, Brooklyn clarified to Henry, "Asher and Tennyson run an organization called Fight for Fighters. Have you heard of it?"

"Of course," Henry replied. "Rescue dogs and rehabilitation, right?"

They continued talking about some collaboration, and I snuck past them to sit down next to Tennyson. A guy came over with a tray of drinks, and he took my order for a Violet Haze too. Then Martin joined me with a tipsy smile and a kiss to my cheek.

"You belong here in LA, darling," he told me.

I grinned. "How much have you had to drink?"

"Not nearly enough! I need champagne."

The following hour was an overwhelming experience for me. While Martin moved from seat to seat to socialize with everyone, Henry spent two whiskey drinks talking to Tennyson, both them kind of resembling one another in the tall, dark, and handsome category. They shared the same mild manners too and were closer in age.

I chatted a bit with Noah and Julian, and I smiled widely when I got Julian hooked on Violet Haze.

By the time Henry wanted my attention, I'd made tentative plans to meet up with Julian for coffee, but I wasn't sure if this was one of those things people said and didn't mean. I liked Julian; we were the same-ish age and not originally from this town. He seemed a bit more cautious than I was, though he was outgoing enough to suggest the coffee. I hoped he meant it. He'd mentioned growing up in Germany, and I wanted to hear more about him and how he ended up in LA, married to a director.

"Are you having a nice time?" Henry murmured, kissing my temple.

"Very. You?" I tilted my head and got his mouth. "You somehow forgot to tell me you're the owner of Second Family."

He chuckled quietly. "I'm not. Just one of the co-founders. I'm not actively involved in the daily operations, although Tennyson's proposal is a great one. I'll have to bring it up to the board."

"And Brooklyn is involved in this?" I asked.

"It's her idea." He nodded and took a sip of his drink. "She and Sophie seem to be in charge of the storyboarding for their husbands' charity's projects."

Well, all right, then. I guess networking had worked for Henry too. The envy in me burned hotter, and I was getting sick of not going places. I'd put myself on hold for too fucking long.

"Sophie!" Brooklyn poked her head into the room. "Time for you to show your face too. The photographer is here for the shoot."

There was going to be a shoot?

"On my way." Sophie drained her champagne glass, kissed her husband, and stood up. "I take it you're staying here?"

"Well, yes, there are people out there." Tennyson flashed her a wry smirk. "I can check in on the kids."

She giggled and was off with an, "I'll be back soon, my hermit."

Henry and I weren't far behind her. I thought it was best to go to the bathroom before my next drink, and then I wanted to dance some more. I hoped it would lift my spirits, and if dancing didn't work, having Henry's hands on me would.

The rush hit me when I got up from my seat, and it threw me. "Shit." I grinned and grabbed on to Henry's arm. Having three cocktails while sitting down was catching up with me now.

"Steady, boy." Henry's eyes lit up with amusement.

"Before you go, Zach…" Julian walked over to me, his smile gentle. He was a cutie. "Here's my number."

"Oh. Thank you." I smiled back, hopeful. This meant he was serious about the coffee, right? I was suddenly itching to make friends, and he seemed like a nice guy. A nice guy with his own business card. It just said his name on it. His number and email were listed on the back. The buzz and his business card brightened my mood.

CHAPTER 13
I, UH...LIPSTICK

Henry had to lead the way back to the club, 'cause I would've taken a wrong turn or two. There were more than a few private rooms, not to mention doors leading to storage and supply closets. Then we were smack-dab in the middle of madness once more, the music pumping and the crowd drunker.

"We're going that way." Henry pointed straight ahead.

So we crossed the dance floor, and the atmosphere got to me. I crept up behind Henry and snaked a hand up his chest. He covered my hand with his, only to reposition us so I walked in front of him. Then I had his perfect mouth pressing sensual kisses along my neck, making me wanna stay right here and do a little bump and grind with him.

"Where are we going?" I asked.

"Toward the bathrooms."

Oh, right, that's where I was planning on going too. Earlier, before I forgot because, fuck me, he was cupping my junk again.

I loved that he'd let go of all the careful crap. No more tentative moves; he took me whenever he saw fit.

We stumbled to the bathrooms, and I groaned, both at Henry's kiss to my neck and the sight of the line. The alcove was full of people, but then I noticed not all of them were waiting to go to the bathroom. On the women's side of the line, I saw a studio-like setup with a long makeup counter. Makeup from ShadowLight littered the shiny surface, and a huge hashtag stretched across the mirror on the wall. #GiveYourShadowLight was being tagged from left to right by the women losing their shit over all the makeup.

The cacophony rang louder when Brooklyn and Sophie joined the others, and they had a photographer with them.

"You should try it," Henry murmured in my ear.

"What?" I chuckled.

"For me." He gripped my hips, pulling me back on his erection.

"You want me to wear makeup?" I glanced up at him in disbelief, turning in his arms. To each their own, but I had zero interest in painting my face. "Have you lost your mind?"

He shook his head slowly, gaze predatory. "Submission. I'd rather show you. Come here." He grabbed my hand and ushered me between the ladies and to the makeup counter. "Pick a lipstick."

Now I knew he'd lost his mind—or had too much to drink. Thankfully, nobody paid us any attention. Tucked away by the edge of the counter, not even the spotlights surrounding the mirror cared about two men eyeing the ShadowLight brand.

The tingling sensation in my stomach triggered me to obey so I could find out. So far, everything he'd introduced me to, I'd loved.

I knew fuck all about colors and whatnot, so I picked one randomly, and Henry took it from me. He discarded the plastic seal from around the black stick and removed the cap, revealing a dark purple.

"Put it on for me." He extended the lipstick.

Put it on for me. For me.

I swallowed, the fluttering getting worse. Then I faced the mirror nervously and inspected the object. Would it feel soft on my lips? Sticky? I remembered hating the lip gloss Meghan wore. It was like kissing glue. My eyes flashed to the mirror, and I leaned forward before I could overanalyze and ruin it for Henry.

He stepped closer, one hand stroking my back, the other on my hip. He was still hard.

I shivered and brushed the dark, plum-colored lipstick across my bottom lip. I didn't know if the fact that there were people everywhere turned me on or terrified me. Maybe a combination of both. Another couple swipes, and my bottom lip looked okay. *I think.* Then my upper lip, where I had to be more careful. The slight bow in the middle was more difficult to fill in.

How the fuck did women do this every day?

Henry pushed me farther. The counter dug into my thighs, and my left hand landed on the surface for support. When I was done, I lowered the lipstick. Both hands planted on the counter, Henry pressing against me. I looked at my reflection and was awash with humiliation and arousal. The latter won while the former somehow clung to my mind-set. Dragging me down.

He loves it. Leaning over me to kiss my shoulder, he showed me just how much he enjoyed the moment.

I couldn't make sense of my expression. My eyes were hooded, flashing with desire, intoxication, and...something else. Apprehension. How could I look both scared and dangerous? My lips looked like they belonged to someone else. They were dark, almost pouty but not quite, and felt soft. Pliable. I resisted licking my bottom lip, instead sinking my teeth into the flesh.

Henry groaned under his breath and yanked me up. He turned me around and cupped my jaw.

The shudder that tore through me traveled from the base of my neck and down to my knees. Knees that got weaker.

Take me.

At that moment, I wanted him to take me like a fucking savage.

The shock was next, shock as he drew his thumb over my lips, completely smearing the color.

"That'll do." His voice was a low rumble, a mix between a whisper and a growl.

It took everything in me not to whimper.

He didn't say anything else. Keeping me close, he guided me out of the alcove and through the club. The lights flashed, the dance crowd jumped. It was dizzying, and without Henry holding me up, I would've been lost.

He led me down a familiar maze of dark halls before he deemed the sounds from clubgoers were distant enough.

"If we're going back to the private room, I gotta take a leak first," I said.

Henry pushed me up against a wall and caged me, his mouth a millimeter from mine. I swore my heart fucking stopped. The excitement flooded me completely.

"Get down on your knees for me."

For me, for me.

I sank to the floor, instinctively going for his zipper. He undid his belt. My fingers shook. With his hard cock in my hand, I finally licked my lips. And I sucked him into my mouth until I gagged.

"That's my boy," he whispered raggedly.

I moaned, my lips stretching around his dick. In the dark,

his features were almost intimidating. The shadows devoured every trace of kindness, leaving me this commanding, dominant god. All I could do was submit. Fuck, it was all I wanted to do too.

He caressed my cheek and smeared the lipstick further as I swirled my tongue around him, sucked him greedily, and fondled his tight sac. With my free hand, I unzipped my jeans and stuck a hand down my underwear to jack my cock.

Henry sucked in a breath. "You're a dream come true." Fisting my hair, he pushed his cock along my tongue. "You want more?"

I nodded quickly and suckled at the slit, my cheeks hollowing. "Please," I managed to gasp. The lust spiked and sent me on a crazy trip. The urgency took me aback. I sucked him harder and jerked my cock faster.

He scratched my scalp lovingly and started fucking me in slow thrusts. "I want to empty myself down your throat." He brought a hand to my neck and stroked me gently. "When I get deep enough, I'll feel my cock right here."

There was no stopping the whimper this time. Breathing deeply through my nose, I warred against my instincts and took him deeper. The desire overrode the itch to choke, except for a few times, but I was determined. And hornier than ever.

I sucked Henry off in a dark hallway with lipstick staining my mouth and jaw until his cock throbbed and released in hot spurts down my throat. The whole moment was so surreal that I had to repeat it in my head over and over. It wasn't just LA that was the drug. It was Henry too.

Never in my twenty-seven years would I have thought of this. Was my brain capable of even conjuring a fantasy that was remotely close to Henry's wickedness? I doubted it.

"Ready to go home, baby?"

I nodded sleepily, burrowing closer into Henry's arms. If I didn't get home soon, I'd turn this couch into a bed, and Henry would be my pillow.

We were back in the private room, and once Sophie and Brooklyn had left with their husbands, I'd relaxed a little. I didn't have to worry about saying the wrong things anymore. Noah and Julian were lit, especially Noah, and they were more casual in a way. Less intimidating and Hollywoodsy.

"Where's Martin?" I slurred.

I could only count six people in here. Henry, me, Noah, Julian, a bartender slash waiter slash actor, and fucking Joseph. Every now and then, he slid his smirk my way.

"His ex picked him up an hour ago." Henry wasn't happy about that.

"You guys ready to head out too?" Noah stretched his arms over his head, then scrubbed a hand down his face. He was trying to sober up, but Julian distracted him. Before anyone could answer, Noah was groping his husband.

I snickered. They were sweet together.

"Bloody hell, love." There was a hint of a British accent in Julian's voice that I hadn't paid attention to before. "Let's get an Uber."

"Where do you live?" I asked, stifling a yawn.

"I think we'll stay at the beach house tonight," Julian sighed. "I'm not lugging him all the way up to Pacific Palisades."

I didn't know where it was, though I'd learned enough to assume Malibu was always farther away. "He's lugging me to Malibu."

"You can crash with me if you want," Joseph offered.

I looked to him warily, afraid it was Henry he'd wear down. Definitely not me.

"That's a firm no, but thank you for the kind offer," Henry replied wryly.

Fist-pump.

"All right, I'm ready to crash." Noah grunted and hauled himself off the couch. "Come on, hubby. I wanna molest you in the car so I don't have to think about the fact that we have work tomorrow."

Noah was a hugger, I learned. At least, when he was buzzed. He hugged both Henry and me, saying it was great to meet us, before bidding the others goodbye and dragging Julian out of the room. Julian and I just barely managed to promise each other to keep in touch and make plans to meet up.

The rest of us piled out at after, and I leaned on Henry, having had a couple drinks too many.

"Are you sure you don't want to have fun with Henry and me, sweetie?"

I jerked away from Joseph. "*Sweetie*, the only one who's having fun with Henry is me."

Henry squeezed my hand. "Not another word, Joseph."

"Lord, you two." Joseph rolled his eyes and walked a little faster. "All right, go be boring."

I breathed out in relief as he disappeared from sight. "Sorry if I crossed a line—"

"You have absolutely nothing to apologize for." Henry kissed my temple and put his hand around my waist. "He can be pushy."

Lovely.

CHAPTER 14

SUGAR AND SPICE AND...THAT'S A DILDO

On Friday afternoon, I braved the heat to pace a hole in the floor on the porch. Henry was on the phone with his parents, and he'd requested privacy for it. I didn't mind. I was just nosy and ready for Ty to get help.

We hadn't been able to get in contact with Henry's parents sooner, though it didn't matter anymore. They were back home in Camassia, and it was time to steal their grandson away from them.

"What's going on?" Martin came out from his shop.

"Henry's talking to his parents," I replied. "You would've known that if you two exchanged words instead of bitch glares."

Martin was unaffected. "This is how we function. It passes after a week or so."

I shook my head.

"So what's the plan?" he asked.

I told him about the contract Henry'd had his lawyer draw up, a contract stating that Henry's parents would get full custody if Ty would come down here and visit for one week. Henry didn't want to risk anything by asking for the remainder of the summer; he feared his parents would worry that Henry would get through to Ty. But a week was doable, and the elder Benningtons were arrogant.

"Henry's the one who's arrogant if he believes he needs only a week," Martin said.

"He's bluffing," I answered. "They won't actually sign anything beforehand, but he thinks seeing the contract will give his parents reassurance that it's happening. Ty's staying longer than that, and we need the bigoted 'rents to make sure he gets on the plane."

Additionally, Henry had the upper hand legally. His parents couldn't keep their son from seeing Ty, or even from moving him out of state.

"Well, I hope it works," Martin offered.

"Yeah, me too." I blew out a breath, feeling hot. "So, how're things with your ex? We've barely seen you since Wednesday."

"I'm very happy," he said. He didn't look it, though. Not that he looked unhappy either. His expression was just...plain. "We're together again, and it's different this time."

"Okay. Cool." What else could I say? He probably wouldn't like it if I said I hoped his boyfriend didn't steal another car from him. "Henry found a house, by the way. Like five minutes away from here."

It was up in the mountains, and I'd only seen pictures of it so far. I didn't wanna know the rent. Three bedrooms on the second floor, each one with its own bathroom, then a guest room downstairs, a den, laundry or whatever, and a big kitchen that opened up to the terrace. Of course, there was a big-ass pool too.

"How will it be to play happy family for you, honey?" Martin didn't say it with an ounce of malice. If anything, he looked concerned. "You and Henry seem...close."

I hesitated, then went with the truth. "Would it be naïve to hope for more with him?" It was something I worried about—often. Especially the part about being naïve.

Martin shook his head no. "No. I can tell he's in too deep already, as well. He just won't believe you're all in until you hit him over the head with it. Multiple times."

That, I could understand. While Henry had stopped being careful with the physical stuff, I knew I'd be the one taking initiative if—fingers crossed for when—we took the next step.

"You need to consider the facts too, Zach," Martin continued. "He's twenty years older than you. Maybe he's not too set in his ways, but he'll have your young age at the forefront of his mind. He'll assume you want anything but commitment. He might even believe he knows better and give you more than one out."

I grimaced. I wanted the opposite; I wanted him to claim me and be borderline possessive in that hot way, but I understood where Martin—and Henry—was coming from.

"I appreciate your advice." I nodded. "He's different from my previous partners." Not because he was a man either. "It's intense and confusing and scary."

Martin glowed warmly. "That makes me happy. He deserves a good guy. You just might be perfect for him, and I don't throw around those words casually. Henry has a lot of living left to do, but he deflates when he can't share it with someone. He becomes a homebody."

I chuckled and lifted a shoulder. "I've been kind of a homebody too. Spending time in LA has changed everything."

He grinned, eyes flashing with delight. "Darling, in LA, you decide who you are. Every neighborhood has its own culture and population. Once you find the right one for you, you're home. Los Angeles is a way of life."

Longing filled me as quickly as a generous dose of worry

did. Because I wasn't sure I could ever leave Camassia permanently. I loved my hometown.

Martin had given me a lot of reassurance, though. No one knew Henry as well as Martin did, and if he believed I stood a chance, I was going to trust that.

"You two need to bury the hatchet," I told him. "I think he misses bickering with you."

He laughed softly. "Well, our friends don't call us Felix and Oscar for nothing." At my confused expression, he added, "*The Odd Couple?*" I had no clue what he was talking about, and Martin sighed dramatically. "Lord in heaven, today's youth has forgotten Broadway. The play's even been adapted numerous times *and* been a TV show! You've never heard of it?"

"Uh, sorry." I felt properly chastised, though I was amused too. I'd grown to adore Martin. "I'll look it up, okay?"

"You do that." He gave me a look of mild disdain, then waved a hand at his shop. "Come on. I need you to try my new creation. You could use some sugar."

I could totally use some sugar. He snuck little treats to me almost every day, and he hadn't failed yet. My favorite was a cannoli of his, filled with some cream containing orange and dark chocolate.

I was licking frosting off my upper lip when Henry walked into the pastry shop with a tired smile.

"Hey, babe." I was testing out terms of endearment. Not sure that was a winner. I liked it when he called me baby and darling boy; he was harder to pin down. No pun intended. "Maybe I should just call you Sex God?"

He chuckled quietly and pressed a kiss to my cheek.

"So, it worked," he announced. "Tyler hates me and

wouldn't even talk to me, but my mother and father are taking him to the airport on Sunday." He walked behind the counter before I could hug his sexy self, and he stole a cupcake from the tray Martin was working on. "When you have a moment, call your brother, Zachary. I'll book him a ticket and make sure he gets seated next to Ty." He took a bite of the chocolaty goodness. "My God. If only your taste in men was like your baking."

"Can you not call it baking?" Martin asked irritably, and he literally slapped the cupcake out of Henry's hands. It landed on the floor with a splat, leaving Henry and me surprised. "I make artisanal pastry creations. I don't...*bake*." He sneered at the word.

Henry pointed at the floor. "You wasted your artisanal pastry creation."

I shoved half my cupcake into my mouth so I wouldn't guffaw.

A smile tugged at the corners of Martin's mouth, but he wasn't gonna admit defeat in their little feud. I could just tell a smile would imply immediate surrender.

"Get out of here," he said instead, waving us away. "I'm sure you have details to discuss. You're moving this weekend, for goodness' sake."

"We might wanna bring body armor," I joked. "I have no idea how Ty's gonna react when he sees me here."

On the other hand, I wasn't sure Mattie could keep that to himself—that I was already here.

Humor glinted in Henry's eyes, and I was glad he wasn't focusing on Ty's "hatred." Instead, he was determined to undo what his parents had done.

"How long have you rented the house for?" Martin asked.

"Mid-September," Henry replied. "Tyler starts school again at the beginning of September, but I booked a couple extra weeks in case we haven't made any progress and I'm not ready to let him go home yet."

That was smart, I figured. Hostile takeover, here we come.

Henry got the keys the following day, and I tried to keep my reaction to the house to myself. Wait, did I say house? I meant to say, fucking mansion. The architecture was Spanish, all hacienda-like, with rustic colors meeting bright ones. The turquoise shutters stood out against the terra-cotta of the stucco building.

When Henry had told me the kitchen was open, he hadn't been kidding. The French doors were pushed aside, opening up to the big terrace where a rectangular pool took up most of the space. The grill by the barbecue area was made of stone, and the cushions covering the chairs matched the shutters. They had to be the most comfortable-looking dinner chairs I'd ever seen. The loungers by the pool matched too.

Back home, we had two lawn chairs on our balcony. I'd found them at separate yard sales.

Hearing Henry approaching behind me, I said, "Having the AC running with the doors wide open can't be cheap." The indoors was a cool and breezy seventy degrees, while the outside was a hellish ninety.

He hummed and dropped a kiss to my shoulder, his hands finding my hips and then my stomach, under my tee. "Did you see the hot tub on the balcony upstairs? All I can think of is taking you there."

I shuddered, and heat rose. "That, um... That would be a first."

Perhaps I was getting desperate, but I wanted him to fuck

me. I'd legit begged him last night, before he'd distracted me with his mouth.

"Losing your patience, baby boy?" The fucker trapped my earlobe between his teeth and flicked it with the tip of his tongue. We'd discovered my ears were sensitive. Fuck if I'd known that before.

"Yeah." I swallowed dryly and blew out a breath. Someone was getting hard behind me. Good, that made two of us. If I hadn't affected him the way he did me, I would've thrown a fit. "By the way, when Mattie and Ty get here, are we gonna be discreet or something?"

That ended the buildup of sexual tension, and Henry gave my neck a soft kiss, then turned me around and cupped my cheeks. He pressed another kiss to my lips, lingering.

If I didn't know better, I'd say he wasn't sure of the answer to that himself.

"I can't," he finally admitted. "I promised myself a long time ago that I was done hiding. For the same reason, I can't do that to you—unless it's what you want." He paused, and I searched his eyes. Maybe I was falling in love. "You're..." His mouth tugged up in a soft grin. "You're something else, Zachary. I don't think I *can* be discreet with you."

"Good." I had to swallow again, this time 'cause it felt heavy. "I don't think I can do that either." Holy fuck, was I falling in love with him? Was that possible? It'd only been a week and a half.

In order to protect myself, at least a little, I decided that, no, it wasn't possible. Not yet. I wouldn't hold back or anything, but I had to consider the circumstances. He'd swept me off my fucking feet on the vacation of my life.

I reached up and kissed him. "I guess I have to think of a way to come out to Mattie."

He nodded and touched my cheek. "I'll be here for whatever you need." Amusement crept in. "May I ask what you're coming out as? We haven't really discussed your love life beyond the fact that you've had a few girlfriends."

I shrugged. "I don't think a label is necessary. I'll tell him I've been…I don't know, confused. That I've suspected I'm into men too—or primarily. Whatever."

Truth be told, I wasn't very worried about coming out to my brother and grandmother. The only thing that made me uneasy or nervous was being *out* back home. I wasn't so self-assured as to think strangers couldn't ruffle my feathers, and Camassia wasn't Los Angeles. At its core, despite getting better as younger generations took over, Camassia was a sleepy lumberjack town.

Many places in America were that way. Unlike here, where it felt like I lived in a safe party bubble of acceptance and good times.

"Anyway." I pushed that away for now. "Let's claim the biggest bedroom and unpack."

The front of the house faced the hillside leading toward the ocean, so the view from our bedroom had more yellow, shrubby mountains and valleys to showcase. Also, yeah, the hot tub on the terrace that stretched across the entire back of the house. I wanted to try it soon.

"Too bad we can't use it once Mattie and Ty get here," I said. 'Cause they'd have the same access from their rooms, and as open as I wanted to be with Henry, I had limits.

"We have twenty-four hours until then." Henry was putting away our clothes in the closet. There wasn't much else in the room. Huge bed, walk-in closet, a big flat screen mounted on the wall in front of the bed, and nightstands. There was a chair between the doors leading to the closet and bathroom, but I didn't count it as furniture. It looked more like what someone would call "art." It was just silvery wiring and weird loops.

Whereas the rest of the house was decorated to be homey and colorful, the bedrooms were stark white and clean. The bed stood at the center of the room—and at the center of my attention. We'd had a busy morning of going to the grocery store and running some other errands, so I wouldn't turn down a nap. Maybe it would lead to sex.

Henry rejoined me, and he had a book in one hand, a toiletry case in the other. It was my book; he must've found it in my truck, thinking I was reading it. He put it in the drawer of my nightstand along with my lotion. I'd actually gotten into the habit of putting it on after my shower every night, and fuck if it didn't make my skin soft. I guess some beauty products weren't awful.

Next, Henry moved to his own nightstand.

"Mattie gave me that book," I said. "Said I'd like it."

"Oh, yeah? What's it about?"

I had no idea. "It's possible I forgot it existed."

He chuckled, giving me the side-eye, then opened his case. "Not much of a reader?"

Whoa. I forgot the topic and stared. "Um." Lube. He stocked his drawer with lube, tissues, unnecessary condoms, but holy mother of sex toys, that was a dildo. "What, uh, what'cha got there, Henry?"

"My ex-lover." He smirked and shut the drawer. The black silicone cock was now hidden, except for the very goddamn vivid memory I had of it. "Consider that the only dick I'm willing to share you with."

I was willing to discuss this at length. And girth. It'd looked almost as impressive as Henry's cock, and I wasn't sure how I felt about it. It was exciting. A lot intimidating. Would he fuck me with it? And watch?

"Were you together for a long time?" I asked curiously.

"Far too long." He rounded the bed and tugged me toward the door. "He's a bit...anal."

I blinked, then started laughing, and Henry grinned. He was pleased to make me laugh.

On the way down the stairs, I couldn't help myself. "I bet he's seen some dark places."

Henry tried to hold it in—tried and failed. The rumbling laugh broke free. "Just one, but I suppose you're right."

I kissed his shoulder for no reason, and then we were back in the kitchen. Pizza was on the agenda, and I was in the mood for pepperoni.

While Henry ordered two pies, I decided to shower off the day so we could enjoy the sunset and pizza without smelling like I'd been lugging a hundred grocery bags up the driveway.

Forty minutes later, I got exactly what I wanted. Henry had showered too, which only soured my mood a little. I dug it when he showered with me, but I guessed this was more efficient. He was too good at distracting me by...you know, existing.

He was plating the pizza on the terrace, and the sun was almost touching the ocean. I grabbed a plate with two slices and picked the chair next to his.

My phone was digging into my leg, so I pulled it out of my sweats and placed it on the table. Mattie was in a texting mood tonight, and I'd received four of them while I was in the shower. All related to what he needed to pack.

He was excited about the trip. And, no, he didn't have to bring a jacket for "chilly evenings." Nan's suggestion, I'd learned.

I'd checked my weather app for tomorrow, and Malibu could expect triple digits.

Yay.

"Are you nervous about tomorrow?" I asked around a mouthful of pizza.

He nodded with a dip of his chin and handed me a napkin. "I am."

Might as well bring up something I'd been thinking about, then. "I'm ready to play bad cop, just so you know. Mattie says Ty's livid, so it's not a cheerful nephew you're picking up at the airport tomorrow." Before Henry could object, I added, "I'm fully aware you're prepared and ready to be a disciplinarian, but you haven't seen him in two years. A lot has happened, and I have some experience in handling him when he's in dick-mode."

I'd asked Ty to leave my home more than once, and I was no stranger to checking his privilege. There was no harm in making the transition easier before Henry took over.

"You'll get to see how I am when I'm more parent than big brother," I realized aloud. "I'm kind of different." Kind of, being a huge understatement. I was a working-class kid from my town's little ghetto, and I'd automatically cleaned up my act slightly when coming down here. "Shit." How had that even happened? Now I worried Henry wasn't getting the real me. I mean, at home, I dealt with bullshit every day. People came to the store asking for credit, which we didn't give. Teenagers shoplifted, and I booted them.

That was how I'd met Dominic, a fairly recent addition to my life. He lived in my neighborhood, and he'd been in the store with his daughter when two punks had come in to shoplift and be assholes. Between Dominic and me, we'd sent them running. Then he'd told me the punks were known down at the Quad, the youth center where he worked.

How would Henry react to a stroll through Camas? I wasn't stupid enough to think our town's poor district was as bad as one in, say, New York or Chicago. But you did need another mindset and attitude there, and I hadn't associated with that part of myself since I got to California. I'd relaxed and pushed all that aside in order to discover other shit.

At home, I didn't wear a T-shirt that said, "I Can't Think Straight," the last word streaked with the rainbow's colors. At home, I didn't go to clubs and get glitter on my cheek.

"Zachary...?"

I turned to Henry, realizing I was frowning.

He gathered my hands in his, kissing my knuckles. I didn't do *that* at home, either.

"Your mind is spinning." He brushed his thumbs over the tops of my hands. "I don't know what makes you look so frazzled, but if you're worried about your brother—or Tyler—remember that I'm here for you too." It wasn't that, though. "Of course, you've been different before. This is new to you—you're evolving."

Good word for it, I guessed. Evolving. Huh. So maybe I wasn't two different people. Maybe I was just one, and I was changing. *Evolving*. At the same time, could I imagine going home and wearing my new clothes? It was difficult to conceptualize.

"As for you playing the bad cop... How about we take turns?" Henry added another slice of pizza to my plate. "I trust you and give you free rein to speak to Tyler however you see fit. It will only do me well to observe and learn."

That was the problem. I was crasser at home. Sometimes, it was the only way for Ty to know I was fucking serious. He was shit at respect.

In the end, this was about him. If Ty wouldn't listen when I was polite, then I'd have to deal with the consequences of Henry's dismay when he heard me raise my voice at both teenagers. And then Henry's image of me would change too. Not that I was sure what this image looked like now. Who was I to him? I'd had my eyes open in wonder during my stay in LA. I'd been thirsty for new experiences and clueless to a lot.

I shook my head and looked down at my food. My stomach growled in both hunger and unease, a fucked-up combination. It wasn't worth overthinking right now. Ty and Mattie would be here in less than twenty-four hours.

My two worlds were about to collide.

Here we go.

CHAPTER 15

HAPPY, HAPPY FAMILY

"Tell him we'll see them," Henry assured as we entered the airport.

I nodded, plugging my free ear with a finger and clutching the phone a little tighter. "Yeah, just keep following the signs. Everyone's coming out from the same exit, and we're waiting for you there."

"Okay. Just got our bags." Mattie grunted, sounding like he'd picked up his duffel. "Wait, Ty's still waiting for two of his. The fucker checked four bags."

I chuckled wryly, glancing at Henry. "Ty's uncle has a matching set of Armani luggage. We better get used to it, Mattie."

"They were on sale, and they look nice," Henry defended.

I'd teased him about the bags since we got to the vacation house. Everything about Henry was so neat, books scattered all over notwithstanding. He even folded his boxer briefs, and there were little bags of good-smelly stuff in his underwear drawer.

"I'm ready to get away from Ty," Mattie grumbled. "I told him on the plane you're already here, and I swear he almost threw his soda at me."

"Well, Henry and I will take over in less than five," I told him. "I appreciate you coming with him."

"You kidding me? I'm here to learn how to surf."

I chuckled, and we disconnected the call.

Henry looked more nervous than ever, so I linked our hands together and squeezed his hand.

"It'll be okay."

He swallowed. "I hope so."

There wasn't much else to say. More arrivals poured out from the doors, and it didn't take long before I spotted Mattie's head. He always wore the same old ball cap, a rusty red one from a team no one had heard of. We had distant family in Bakersfield, and Mom had brought it home to me after she'd visited some aunt or cousin. Mattie stole it from me a few years ago and never returned it. Not that I cared. I wasn't a cap person.

"Lord, you could be twins," Henry muttered.

It wasn't the first time I'd heard that. Mattie's hair was a little darker than mine, that was it. Same six-foot height, same build, same blue-green eyes. Although, now as he got closer, I could see he was paler. Which meant I must've gotten some color.

"I hope you won't trade me in for a younger model." I thought that was funny. Henry didn't. *Oh, well.* I cupped my hands around my mouth. "Mattie!"

His head snapped up, and he grinned tiredly when spotting me. Then he nudged someone next to him—Ty, I assumed. He was a few inches shorter, and a guy who looked like he belonged in Texas with that cowboy hat was blocking my view. And when the dude sidestepped and I caught the first glance of Ty, I kinda wished I never did. Livid was correct. He wanted to be anywhere but here.

His bright hazel eyes fixed me with a death glare, and he didn't even look at Henry. Much like his uncle, Ty was a mix of warm colors—like his hair and eyes—and cutting features. He had the body of a runner; right now, a murderous one.

It pissed me off.

"Holy fuck," Mattie blurted out. "You changed, bro. Everything. I mean..."

I forced a smirk and ran a hand through my hair. It was what he was currently staring at with a strange expression.

"Hello, Tyler." Henry's voice snapped my attention back to where it was supposed to be, and I jerked my chin at my brother. We should give them at least a semblance of privacy.

We were surrounded but managed to get a few paces farther away, where Mattie immediately rattled off everything that was different about me. The haircut, I had a tan, new clothes, and "there's something else too..." His words.

I was busy watching the awkward reunion some feet away. I managed to catch a couple "whatevers" from Ty as Henry said he was happy Ty had come down. Next, Henry offered to help with the luggage, but Ty merely wrenched away and started pushing his luggage cart toward the exit.

I didn't think before acting. I let out a sharp whistle that got his attention—and possibly others' as well—and pointed toward another set of doors. "Wrong exit, and lose the fucking attitude."

Ty's jaw clenched, and he directed his glare at the floor instead.

"This is gonna be great," Mattie said.

I chanced a glance at Henry, only to avert my gaze. He was in for it now, and he already appeared surprised.

We shuffled toward Henry's car in uneasy silence that Mattie and I tried to break a few times without much success.

He stopped short when we were outside and the wall of heat hit us, and I said, "I know, right?"

Ty was out of the car the second we stopped, and while Mattie had eagerly taken in the sights on the way up to Malibu, Ty seemed unimpressed by the whole thing. I watched him stalk up the driveway, sans his luggage.

"Fancy digs, Mr. Bennington." Mattie looked at the house.

Henry paused, having just opened the trunk in the back. "I apologize, we didn't get a chance to say hello at the airport. Call me Henry, please."

Mattie nodded and shook his hand. "Matthew, but everyone calls me Mattie."

I joined Henry and hauled out my brother's duffel. "Don't get Ty's bags."

"Why?"

"Because he can get them himself." I shrugged and handed Mattie his bag. "If he wants to act like a kid, we should treat him like one."

"I missed you, Dad." Mattie flashed me a dopey grin.

I chuckled.

Henry thought about it, then nodded firmly. "You're right." He sent me a small smile. "I'm glad you're here."

The relief covered me like the softest, fuzziest blanket. I bet he could see it too. Rather than getting cutesy about it, I offered a quick wink and then followed my brother toward the house.

I told him the second bedroom upstairs was his. The third was Ty's, in case he got the stupid idea of leaving in the middle of the night. The floorboards creaking and the fact that he would have to pass Mattie's room as well as Henry's would hopefully be enough to change his mind.

"I get it." Mattie nodded. "What room is yours?"

Dammit. I didn't wanna lie to him, but we hadn't been here five minutes yet. I was planning on talking to him after dinner.

"There's a guest room downstairs," I said. Which wasn't a lie. There *was* a guest room on the first floor. "Anyway, dinner's in an hour. You can unpack and get a shower or whatever."

"Cool. I'm starving."

"Yeah, me too. Henry's ordering from some Italian place." I side-eyed him with a grin. "They don't cook at home much here. And I can't wait for you to meet Martin. He's hysterical."

"Who's that?"

"Henry's best friend." We reached the house, and I opened the door for him. Ty was already inside; I spotted him in the kitchen on the way to the terrace. "Ty," I called. "Third bedroom upstairs is yours, and when you want your stuff, it's waiting for you in the car."

"Whatever." He sat down by the pool with a soda and yanked off his hoodie. "I'm just gonna sit here for a week, and then I can go home again."

By now, I'd reached the kitchen, and I leaned against the open glass doors. "Okay. Watch out for the rattlesnakes."

"What the fuck?" Mattie exclaimed.

Ty had grown rigid in the lounger, and I smirked.

Henry had said he'd only seen the snakes a once or twice, though he heard them sometimes.

Speak of the devil… Henry appeared next to me with a menu. It was from the restaurant, so I quickly picked a dish that sounded good. Mattie took longer to decide.

Henry was watching his nephew, looking like he was trying to decide something too. There was an air of authority around him I couldn't see earlier today. The man had the ability to come off as a ruthless businessman even as he wore his cargo shorts and flip-flops, but Ty was his weak spot. They both needed to get to know each other again and see where they ended up.

"Tyler, come pick your meal, please." He waited for a reaction from Ty. So far, nothing. The kid had his back to us, and he was just looking out over the hillside.

Mattie silently returned the menu to me and pointed at the item he wanted. I nodded in acknowledgment.

"If you don't pick your dinner, you're not eating," Henry told Ty.

"Great, he's gonna starve me too," Ty muttered.

I opened my mouth to call him out for being fucking juvenile when Henry rested a hand on my arm, cautioning me.

"It's all right. Tyler isn't hungry. He can join us for breakfast in the morning if he wants to." With that said, Henry walked over to the fridge, and I followed so I could return the menu. I told him Mattie's order as he checked what condiments we had. Probably a double check to distract himself. We'd bought it all yesterday. The kitchen was full of pretty much everything.

Mattie ventured upstairs to explore and get settled in, and I figured a shower couldn't hurt.

I preferred dinner when Henry and Martin were glaring at one another. The awkward tension between the two Benningtons made for one stilted meal on the terrace.

Ty sat with us, though he had nothing to eat. Henry had caved momentarily and said the fridge was full, and still, Ty didn't move. He merely sat there with his empty soda can.

"Do you know why Henry wanted you to come down here?" I asked.

Ty lifted a shoulder and turned his head toward the ocean. "I guess he wants to play parent for a minute."

"Tyler—" Henry started.

"I tracked him down," I told Ty. "I wanted him to know what kind of man you're becoming. Wait, did I say man? I mean, what an absolute fuckwit."

Ty's head whipped back, and he glowered at me. Mattie's utensils clanked against the plate.

"You started this shit?" Ty seethed.

"Yeah, you're welcome," I replied. "You think I'm alone in thinking you're turning into an elitist bully?"

"I've told you this before, buddy," Mattie said quietly. "Our friends talk shit about you, and you're sort of giving them all the reasons to."

Ty swallowed hard and stared at his lap. His posture changed slightly, as if Mattie's words packed a punch. I hoped they did.

"Fuck them." Ty raised his chin, feigning indifference. "They don't matter, anyway. Just a bunch of losers."

"And me?" Mattie cocked a brow. "You said Aaron was too poor to chill with us. I work nights and weekends to afford car insurance and going to the movies. You dumped Jenny because her 'rusty pile of shit' broke down so she couldn't come over and blow you. *My* car is a rusty pile of shit, and my brother worked his ass off to give that to me for my birthday. You also told Gideon he should just give up on Micaela 'cause he wouldn't be able to afford to take her to nice restaurants. I couldn't take Andrea on dates all the time when we dated, so you tell me, Ty. Am I a loser too?"

I slumped back and rubbed a hand over my mouth, all but gutted by his words. More than that, I was torn. Proud as fuck because my brother was mature and damn wise. But...he'd been forced to grow up young, kinda like me. And I didn't like that. I would've wanted him to stay a kid for a while longer.

"Answer him, Tyler." Henry's command was low and

controlled, though I could sense the underlying anger. Knowing him, he was probably taking this as a personal defeat too. Another thing I didn't like.

"No," Ty gritted. "He's not a loser."

"Then why are the others?" I asked.

He refused to answer that.

"I'd like a moment in private with you," Henry told him and wiped his mouth with a napkin before standing up. "Follow me, please."

Well, shit.

Ty rolled his eyes but followed Henry into the house.

I chewed the inside of my cheek. How bad would it be to listen in?

"I'm proud of you, by the way." I faced Mattie and gave his shoulder a squeeze. "You know I always wanna be able to do more for you, right?"

"Shut up, Zach," he groused, shoveling food into his mouth. "He's the dipshit. I have no fucking complaints about what we have. You do tons already."

"I know, but—"

"I'll throat-punch you," he warned.

I frowned. "Why would you do that? You'd end up getting stitches like last time you tried to throw me down."

I hadn't seen how close he'd been to that table. Honest.

He snickered and touched the scar on his jaw absently, all while pushing more food into his mouth.

The next silence was at least comfortable, and I got to finish my dinner too.

Maybe you should tell him you like cock now.

I sat up straight and cursed at my own thought. Just like that, the discomfort returned. My stomach tightened, and I flicked a glance at my brother. He'd take it well, right? Nan and

I had raised him to be accepting and open-minded. Plus, he had friends who were gay.

"We gotta talk about something." I cleared my throat and pushed away my plate. Suddenly, the pasta and garlic sauce and all that damn cheese was forming a brick in my gut. "I, uh, I had another reason for coming to California."

"Oh?" He belched into his fist and grabbed an oregano roll from the container of side orders. "I hope you haven't checked out any colleges here. I know you want me to get my money's worth, but there's nothing wrong with the state college back home."

That was a whole other argument. And I did hope he would pick another school, one with a better engineering program.

"It's not that," I said. "It's about me. For the past couple of years, I've... I don't know how to put this, but I've had thoughts." I sucked at this.

"It's okay, big brother." He patted my arm. "It's called puberty. Happens to all of us."

"Fuck off," I chuckled. I shook my head. "Can you hear me out, goddammit?"

He made a go-ahead gesture and leaned back, a hand going to his stomach.

I sighed. It was time to blurt it out. "I wasn't sure I was straight."

Mattie lifted his brows and lolled his head along the back of the cushion until he met my gaze. "Uh, what?"

"You heard me." It would do me no good to get frustrated. "I didn't know, and I wasn't comfortable doing anything about it at home, so when..." I waved a hand at him. "You know, when you started bitching about Ty last winter and we talked about maybe getting in touch with his uncle, I thought...maybe I could explore. Or, I got that idea when you told me his uncle lived in

LA. And LA... I figured, it would be a good place to find out—Jesus, just say something."

"Um, sorry." He sat up straighter again, frowning. Then he scratched the spot below his ear, something he did when he was uncomfortable. Dammit. The only thing worse would be when he twisted his cap—yep, there he went. He turned his cap backward and readjusted it. Another tell of his. "I don't mean to be a dick, Zach, but..." He shifted in his seat, hesitant. "I kinda already assumed you were queer. Or gay, sorry."

My eyebrows shot up. "The fuck? Is there a sign on my forehead or something?"

"No, but there's gay porn on your computer at home," he replied frankly.

It was my turn to slump back, and I ran a hand through my hair. I couldn't fucking believe that gay porn I hadn't even particularly enjoyed had outed me.

"I wasn't banking on it," he amended. "I mean, I like Meghan and that other one—the redhead."

"Alice."

"That's the one." He bobbed his head. "But I don't know, you were checking out guys too." That was news to me. Not that I'd done it, but that he'd noticed. "And, uh, just so you know... the Peyton that Nan wanted to set you up with—her friend's grandkid or something? Yeah, Peyton's a dude."

"For chrissakes, Nan thinks I'm gay too?" I stared at him in disbelief.

He shrugged, then nodded once. "It ain't like we've discussed it at length."

"You only assumed—yeah, I got that," I muttered.

"But, so, now you're out, yeah?" He tested a smile.

"I guess so." I was still confused about the whole conversation. "We're cool, right?"

"Of course we are." He furrowed his brow. "Why wouldn't we be?"

I let out a tired chuckle, the relief hitting me hard, and his question was valid. He'd never indicated we'd be anything but cool, no matter what.

Maybe it was part of it—for many, anyway. There was always that risk, and losing my family which was already so small would slay me. I couldn't imagine what Henry had gone through. The phantom pain and emptiness I felt at the mere idea were enough to make me wanna run into his arms and hug him.

About that... I should tell Mattie it was Henry I'd sunk my claws into.

"One more thing." I shifted in my seat and blew out a breath. "I'm sorta dating Henry."

Finally, I had shocked my brother.

"What the—are you s-serious?" he stuttered. "Isn't he a little old for you, bro?"

"Hey," I warned halfheartedly with a lazy smirk. "His life experience is a big part of the draw. He's...fucking amazing." Not to mention I found the age difference a complete turn-on.

Mattie's discomfort was back now, though I could tell it was more related to not wanting to hear about his brother's love life than the fact that Henry was a man. "That's great. *Weird*...but great."

I reached over and flicked the brim of his cap in response.

CHAPTER 16

I THINK HOLY FUCK IS ACCURATE HERE

The next morning, I woke up to Henry's mouth leaving a soft trail of kisses along my shoulder blades. I smiled sleepily and stretched out, only for him to stop me. Or rather, he stopped me from pushing down my leg that was bent at the knee, conveniently giving him some extra access to my ass.

Good to know, lying on my stomach with one leg up would give him ideas.

The sound of a bottle opening sent a bolt of excitement through me, and I lazily pushed my ass out. *Give it to me.* Slipping a hand under myself, I grasped my cock and gave it a slow stroke.

Slick fingers parted my ass cheeks farther and rubbed me in sensual movements. He was taking his time this morning. And I didn't feel like breaking the silence, so I let my body language say all there was to say.

I exhaled heavily as he entered me with two fingers. His hard cock pressed against my thigh, and I shifted closer to him.

More, more, more. I felt his smile on my skin, more kisses following along my shoulder.

Three fingers. Long, teasing strokes, stretching me.

Then he slipped them out.

"Holy fuck," I breathed. "More."

"Shhh..." He grasped my chin gently and made me tilt my head back to him. "Do you want me to use protection?"

Holy fuck, I repeated to myself. Holy fuck, holy fuck, holy fuck. I shuddered, gulped, and shook my head quickly. At fucking last, he was gonna take me. And, no, I didn't want anything in the way. I wanted to feel every inch of his skin and then have him fill me.

Henry didn't say anything else. He caught my mouth in a kiss before he slicked up his cock. He was the only thing on my mind. I couldn't think of anyone or anything else even if I tried.

We stayed in that position, me mostly on my stomach, one leg pulled up, him halfway on top of me. He rubbed his cock between my ass cheeks for too goddamn long, and I turned my head again and groaned into the pillow.

By the time he began applying pressure to breach my opening, I couldn't even tense up. I wanted it too much. I was fucking ready.

The burn flared up, and I sucked in a breath. The moment meant something to me; it was two years of fantasies becoming reality, and with the perfect man. I screwed my eyes shut as the pain speared me, and I realized it wasn't the only thing fucking spearing me. I choked on a gasp. Henry was all in. Jesus, was he.

"I'm sorry, baby boy. I couldn't wait." He breathed shallowly against my shoulder and slid a hand down one cheek to squeeze it firmly. "I won't be able to stay away from you now." He pulled out slowly, then pushed in again, and the pleasure rippled through the pain. "I need this tight, fuckable little ass to be mine."

My eyes flashed open, and I mouthed a silent, "Oh my fucking God." The gasps followed, and I sank into him, wishing I could crawl under his goddamn skin.

"Say it," he whispered against my neck.

"Whenever," I groaned. "It's yours."

Henry shivered and withdrew from me. Then he turned me onto my back, wrapped my legs around his hips, and forced his way inside me again. I heard the muted slap as one of his hands grabbed the headboard. The other found my cheek, and I turned toward his touch.

I wanted mirrors on the ceiling. I wanted to see his muscles flexing as he thrust his cock into my ass.

"So beautiful." He pushed in once more and brushed his thumb over my bottom lip. "I'll want you in every position imaginable. Begging, sweating, gasping, shaking." He started moving faster and deeper, and he fisted my cock gently, as if I wasn't already losing my mind. "You'll spread your legs for me, won't you, Zachary?"

"Yes," I hissed. "Kiss me." I tangled my legs with his for leverage so I could meet his thrusts, and I tried to pull him down. "I want you, Henry." I didn't mean for that to come out as a damn whine.

"You have me." He lowered his head and captured my mouth with his in a wet, hungry, erotic kiss that left me breathless. "Tell me how it feels."

"I can't—" I couldn't fucking understand how he was still forming words. My mind was swimming, like I was drunk or high. "Oh God. Full—I feel full. Overwhelmed. Oh fuck, right there." I arched my back and dug my head into the pillow, and the euphoric sensations crashed over me. "It feels fucking amazing," I panted. "Fuck me harder."

He went harder and pressed a palm on my lower abdomen, right under my cock. I didn't know how, but it felt even greater.

"Get yourself off," he commanded quietly. "I want your gorgeous chest full of come so I can lick it up."

I whimpered and succumbed to the pleasure. My body took over. I stroked my cock quickly and bore down on him, the pain only fueling the intensity.

I heard us, the slick sounds of his cock sliding in and out of me, and I smelled us, the scent of sex and man making my mouth run dry. And I felt him...everywhere. I swallowed against the dryness and forced my eyes to stay open. Otherwise, I wouldn't be able to drink in the sight of him. Henry was immense in a way, especially when he was looming over me and playing my body like an instrument.

"I wanna come," I gritted. "Fuck." I slipped a hand farther down, cupping my balls and ghosting my fingers around my ass. That, when I felt him pushing in, was heady. I teased his skin and slid through the slickness, and almost got off at the sound of his sharp intake of air.

"Ahh—Zach... *Hell.*" He pounded into me and dropped his forehead to mine. My hand went back to my cock, and I chased my orgasm. "I'm there, darling."

With my thoughts racing ahead to his cock releasing his come deep inside me, I lost it all. I groaned as my climax surged through me, and then I stopped breathing. Rope after rope splattered up my chest. My taste buds reacted to the delicious scent, my mouth pooling with saliva.

Henry rocked deeper once, twice, and shuddered violently. I felt his cock throbbing as he emptied himself in my ass.

It was too much, lust overload, and I checked out. I had no choice. Every fiber of me was hypersensitive and rigid, and I rode out the orgasm until all I heard was the ringing in my ears.

I gasped for air, and Henry collapsed next to me. His cock disappearing from me caused me to wince in pain, yet it made me feel empty too.

I resurfaced from the haze to Henry leaving slow, open-mouthed kisses on my chest. I shivered like crazy and wanted him inside me again. The feeling of being fucked, taken...I'd never known it would be like this.

"Christ..." I exhaled and weaved my fingers into his hair. "I wanna be yours, Henry."

I tasted sex on his tongue as he gave me a toe-curling kiss, and I moaned breathlessly and wrapped my arms around him.

"I mean it," I mumbled into the kiss.

"I meant it when I said you're a dream come true." He smiled softly and teased my bottom lip with his teeth. "For the sake of my sanity, we're going to take this slowly. Lord knows I'm already yours, but you're so—"

"I remember my own age," I grated. Then I pinched his nipples. He hissed and smirked. I shook my head. "You're stubborn."

"I'm realistic," he corrected. The amusement in his eyes ensured the moment wasn't completely ruined. "The world is a big place. You have a lot to explore."

I nodded. "True. Before I can make my own decisions and know who I want to date, I have to fuck the entire gay population. Makes sense."

"Smartass." He left the bed and extended a hand. "Shower with me."

I guess I could do that.

My mood went to shit during breakfast when I learned how Henry's private conversation with Ty last night had gone. Apparently, Henry had apologized for not sticking around, stating he felt awful about it, which... Everybody knew that already. The man wore guilt like Kanye wore arrogance.

Ty had shrugged and said he'd just been relieved, 'cause he didn't want Henry around.

Having spent the last week and a half with Henry, I could picture the hurt slashing through his features upon hearing that.

He'd powered through, though. He'd told Ty that even though he had a lot to make up for, he was going to be strict. He wouldn't tolerate bullying and putting others down in any way. And the next time Ty acted like a douche, he would lose his phone. To be honest, I didn't understand why he still had it.

Mattie spent the morning in the pool and writing a list of things he wanted to see in LA. Because, I figured, taking him sightseeing would give Henry and Ty more alone time.

Around noon, I heard a car pulling up in the driveway, and Henry looked to me, confused.

"It's probably Martin," I said, losing my tee. Seeing Mattie in the pool made me wanna dive in too. "I texted him." I'd also found the balls to send Julian from the nightclub a message. "I told him I missed his baked goods, so he gave me a lecture on how they're called artisanal pastry creations or whatever."

Henry seemed surprised, in a good way. "You're very fond of him."

I smiled and lifted a shoulder. "How could I not be? He should be here too."

Henry didn't disagree with me, and in response, he leaned in and gave me a quick kiss.

"Holy fuck." Ty came out on the terrace, having spent some quality time brooding in his room. "You two? I mean—fuck, are you also a faggot, Zach?"

I was so stunned that I couldn't reply. I didn't know what to think.

"Tyler!" Henry was just as stunned—and horrified.

Faggot.

I'd never been called that before. I supposed I was in a good place mentally, because the word didn't hurt me. However, it filled me with anger.

Henry sighed. "I forgot to tell him about us."

Wh... What? No. No, that wasn't it. It was okay he hadn't told Ty, just like I'd forgotten to inform Henry that my brother knew. But what Ty had said was not fucking cool.

I pointed a finger at Ty. "Use that word again, and you and I are gonna have a serious motherfucking problem."

Ty flinched. He hadn't expected my reaction.

"Hey, what's going on?" Mattie jumped up from the pool, grabbed his towel from a nearby lounger, and walked over.

"He saw Henry kiss me." I didn't look away from Ty. "So he asked if I'm a faggot too."

Mattie groaned and looked exasperatedly at Ty. "*Dude.* What the fuck is *wrong* with you?"

Ty gnashed his teeth together and averted his stare to the ground.

"I think we need to step out for a while," Henry stated. To me, he lowered his voice a little. "We'll be back in a few hours. I want to take him to Second Family."

"Okay." I nodded and linked my fingers with his for a beat, then watched the two Benningtons disappear inside.

Other than knowing Second Family was a safe space for LGBTQ+ persons who didn't have a family to fall back on, I didn't have a sense of their activities. I'd have to google it later.

Or ask Martin, I thought, as he emerged in the wide doorway.

"I arrive, and Henry leaves with an angry little bee in tow." He sniffed and put a hand on his hip, and I couldn't help but grin.

"Aren't you a sight for sore eyes?" I hadn't realized I'd managed to miss Martin's presence in the forty-eight hours since we left their little corner of Malibu. "Martin, I want you to meet my kid brother. This is Mattie. Mattie, Martin—Henry's best friend."

"Thank you for not saying *oldest* friend, dear." Martin winked and extended a hand to Mattie. "My, my, are you legal?"

"Back off, cradle-robber. He's seventeen."

Mattie chuckled and shook Martin's hand. "Good to meet you."

"Likewise, honey." Martin eyed us. "You're certainly related."

"People keep telling us," my brother said. "I'm gonna jump in the pool again."

"Be right there." I nodded before facing Martin. "Want any help with that?" He was holding a paper bag with the cupcake sticker that was his logo.

He handed the bag over, then unbuttoned the top two buttons of his light blue shirt. "Remember to share."

"We'll see," I said. "Henry probably has a pair of trunks you can borrow upstairs."

"A day by the pool does sound lovely." He pursed his lips. "Okay. I'll go make a pitcher of margaritas." He turned on his heel without another word, and I grinned again. It was nice to have him around.

Tightening the drawstrings of my board shorts, I stepped closer to the pool where Mattie had gotten comfortable in an inflatable pool chair. It was bright pink and had a bunch of flamingoes on it.

"I know what you're gonna say," he told me. "Pink is totally my color."

I laughed and jumped in.

CHAPTER 17

IT'S STARTING TO LOOK A LOT LIKE I'M STARTING A LIFE HERE

Over the next four days, I didn't see Henry and Ty as much as I would've liked to. Every morning after breakfast, Henry took his nephew to a new place on the famous list, leaving me alone with my brother. Martin stopped by often too, and he spent the night twice.

He'd brought Eagle one day, and the cat wouldn't leave his carrier, so Martin had taken him home again.

One thing I could put behind me was the bitchy feud between Martin and Henry. They were on good terms again and found time to have a glass of wine and bicker about skipping brunch last Sunday; therefore, they needed a new spot for next week. Now that I was a "seasoned" Los Angelino, Martin had shifted his attention to my brother. It was he who now had to experience the best restaurants Malibu had to offer.

On Sunday, we were apparently going to a place in Venice. I let Henry and Martin deal with that.

I'd taken Mattie sightseeing a few times too. I'd gotten lost, effectively making me feel less seasoned, and shown him Sunset Boulevard, Venice Beach, downtown LA, and Beverly Hills. Today we were going to Santa Monica—for a couple reasons. Firstly, I wanted to show Mattie the pier. Secondly, we were having dinner with Julian.

Henry had been adorably miffed when he'd deduced I wouldn't be home when he got back with Ty.

"We won't be too late," I'd said, which had wiped away his frown. He'd kissed me soundly and repeated that he wanted me to have fun.

He and Ty were off to West Hollywood where they'd join some people from Second Family for lunch and a group session. I was still waiting for the details on that. In fact, I was waiting for a lot of details. At the end of each day, Henry was exhausted, and Ty was…I didn't even know how to describe it. He'd grown silent, almost depressed.

I guess I'd expected to be part of it more. On the other hand, it was probably best for Henry to establish this—whatever it was—with his nephew. For now, I settled for having my nights with Henry.

I was sore as fuck today.

"Are you ready?" I came down the stairs and checked the pockets of my new shorts. I'd followed in Henry's footsteps and bought a pair of army green cargo shorts and flip-flops. With them, I was wearing my white "Let Me Be Perfectly Queer" tee.

Mattie nodded, only to splutter a chuckle when he spotted the print across my back.

I smirked, pocketing my wallet.

On the way to the truck, he told me he'd talked to Nan, and she was sending us a "little vacation gift" so we could buy ourselves something.

"That never gets old," I chuckled. "Seeing my own

paycheck every month does nothing, but when she transfers twenty bucks for ice cream, I grin like a loon."

"I know, right?" Mattie snickered and rounded the truck.

I got in behind the wheel, *carefully*, then backed out until I could make a turn. "Did you think about Henry's offer yet?"

Last night after dinner, Henry had admitted he was trying to convince Ty to extend his stay, and he wanted Mattie to able to stay too. Ty was staying no matter what, but of course, everything would be easier if he stayed willingly. Anything to make progress—and postpone the inevitable fallout with Henry's parents.

"I don't mind sticking around." Mattie shrugged. "I'm getting a tan here. Girls love that."

I snorted.

As we reached the main road, he asked if I was staying too.

This was where shit got hard. "I've been away from work for too long." I talked to Pammie briefly yesterday, and she was good until next weekend. It helped that we only had the store open for evenings at the moment. She didn't have to run herself ragged. "If I leave next Thursday, I'll have been here three weeks."

Mattie nodded slowly. "Maybe it's best I stay another week or so. I wanna know what's going on with Ty. He wouldn't say a word to me last night."

Yeah, after today, I was done with the CliffsNotes. Henry only mentioned the basics during dinner. They went here, they went there, they volunteered, they bought supplies for minor charity events. He didn't say much about how Ty was taking it. Or if they talked.

I constantly went from wanting more info to wanting to give them privacy.

"Did they do something special yesterday that made him all...mopey?" Mattie asked. "Other than the phone thing."

I had no idea. "I mean, I can guess." We knew Henry had taken Tyler to Culver City where Second Family had a call center. Teenagers from all over the country could call operators there to talk. Often it was young people who were terrified to come out to their families. "I checked Second Family's website the other day," I mentioned, sliding on my shades. "They have a page for stats on kids who commit suicide and shit like that." I may have gotten choked up when seeing the numbers. "If Ty got a reality check, maybe that's what had him down."

I had my fingers crossed for it. It meant he could change.

"One can hope." Mattie took out his phone. "Second Family... So does Henry work there? Oh, there he is. Or, he's mentioned. He helped start it. That's cool."

"He helps out with finance shit," I said, side-eyeing the page. I hadn't read the history, which I should've. "I think he pays the rent for their headquarters when funding is low or something like that."

"Yeah, he's on the board with a fancy title," Mattie replied absently. "He helped start the nonprofit in 2013 with four others, two of them close friends."

Huh. "Is Martin mentioned?" Nah, I would've known if he was involved.

Mattie hummed. "Nope. An Elizabeth, a Bridget, a Marisol, and a Joseph."

"*Ugh.*" Why, oh, why? "Joseph Robertson?"

"Yeah, you know him?"

I shook my head and grumbled, "He's a friend of Henry's. They used to fuck."

Mattie barked out a laugh. "Are you *jealous*?"

"Shut up." I reached over and punched his arm.

"Just..." I sighed in defeat as Mattie closed his mouth around the bigger part of an ice cream cone. "Christ. Don't spoil your appetite."

"Mmm. I won't, Dad." He licked the strawberry soft serve off his lips and leaned against the railing. Thirty feet below, waves rolled in underneath the pier. The sun was blazing, and it felt like all of Santa Monica was here. "Hold up." He stuck a hand down into his pocket and fumbled to grab his phone. "Gotta take a photo of the Ferris wheel before we go."

"Send it to Nan," I said. Our grandmother loved those deathtraps.

"I will. Here—she'll ask why we're not in the picture." He stepped closer, and then we had the big wheel behind us as we smiled into the camera. "Great. Oh, are those churros?"

I pushed him toward the start of the pier. "You're not having another snack. We have dinner in less than an hour."

"Stop being so uptight!" he bitched.

"I'll show you uptight, you little shit." I slung an arm around his shoulders and hauled him close so I could lick his cheek.

He groaned and shoved me off of him while I laughed.

"People are gonna think it's me you're perfectly queer for now," he complained. "No offense, but my boyfriend would be hotter."

"Dumbass, you look like a younger version of me." I shook my head, grinning. It struck me how glad I was to have him here, so I could share this with him. It was nice to see him let go of all the responsibilities we had at home too.

Following the slow-moving herd of people, we made it off the pier and crossed the bridge that went over the highway between the beach and Ocean Avenue. On the way, I told him the little I knew about Julian, his husband, and their friends. Mattie made one comment as I mentioned Sophie Pierce and the other celebs, and it was, "Oh yeah, she's hot."

With tourists as well as locals crowding the streets this fine Friday afternoon, it took us almost half an hour to get to Fourth Street where the restaurant was. Henry had recommended it, and it was next door to the gay bar we'd gone to my first weekend in LA.

"I'm so full." Mattie puffed out his cheeks and sought out the shade on the sidewalk. Basically, it meant he plastered himself to the walls of the buildings. "You were right. I shouldn't have eaten so much. Now it's gonna take at *least* twenty minutes before I'm hungry again."

I rolled my eyes, then checked my watch. We were standing outside the restaurant, which had an interesting theme judging by the outdoor seating area. It was as if a steakhouse had undergone the same makeover I had to make it more stylish. It was minimalist. Wooden picnic tables and rustic mini crates for condiments were paired with linen napkins and plates that were square. A waiter walked by with a tray of drinks, each glass frosted.

"Aren't we having dinner kinda early?" Mattie asked.

"Julian has work at like four in the morning," I replied. "Something about post-production and being first in the studio." Other than that, it was good we ate early because Malibu wasn't around the corner. Depending on traffic, it was an easy forty-five minutes one way. A far cry from what we were used to back home.

Mattie scoffed. "If my boss ever tells me to work that early on a Saturday, I'm gonna quit."

My mouth twisted up. "That would be his husband." And as I said that, I spotted Julian walking toward us. His curly brown hair was a mess, like he'd had a taxing day. To my surprise, the aforementioned husband was with him too. Noah.

Julian smiled tentatively when seeing me, and I smiled back.

"I managed to drag Noah away from work early," he said. "Good to see you again, Zach."

"Yeah, you too." We exchanged a one-armed hug, and I said I was glad Noah could join us too. Then I placed a hand on Mattie's back. "This is my little brother, Mattie. Mattie, Julian and Noah."

"Nice to meet you, Mattie." Julian shook his hand. "Zach told me he was excited for you to join him in LA."

"That's because he can't live without me," Mattie answered with a smirk.

Noah laughed, and I shook my head in amusement.

"All right, let's get some grub." Noah led the way toward the hostess's desk near the front door, and he requested a table outside. Since we were early, we only had to wait ten minutes.

It didn't take longer than that for me to relax fully. We were a mismatched foursome, Noah probably in his early forties, then Julian and me in our twenties, and Mattie at seventeen. Different walks of life, different careers, different everything. But Noah seemed like a laid-back man, more so than Julian. In our few days of texting back and forth, I'd learned a bit more about him, and I was especially interested in how Noah was the one who'd gotten him into the film industry as a composer.

Most of all, it felt fucking amazing to make new friends.

"Ah, man, I almost forgot to tell you, Zach," Noah said, grabbing another rib off his plate. "Brook has a bone to pick with you."

"Oh, yeah." Julian's eyes lit up. "She can't stop thinking about you and your partner. Henry, yes? I'm sorry, I met so many people that night."

"Um. Who's Brook, and what did I do?" I took a sip of my beer.

"Brooklyn Wright," Noah explained, and I nodded. The woman who Joseph worked for at that makeup company. "Apparently, you and your man got hot and heavy by the mirror station at the club. You wore some makeup?"

Mattie dropped his fork and knife, and I felt my face turn redder than a fucking tomato. Oh my fucking God, this wasn't happening. I had no issues being open, but Christ, maybe Mattie didn't need to know the details.

"Er, yeah." I cleared my throat.

Mattie turned to stare at me like he didn't know who I was.

"Long story," I said.

"I have nothing but time, son," he replied.

I ignored him while my cheeks continued to burn, and I waited for Noah to elaborate.

He had an annoying little smirk going on, gaze darting between my brother and me. Then he chuckled quietly and went on. "Right, so she's in the middle of launching her new brand, but seeing you and Henry that night sparked some idea that would take her in another direction. Her words. Now she can't stop complaining when we see her. She keeps saying she can't feel it, can't get into it, 'cause this new idea is in the way."

I didn't know what to say, other than…I guess it was flattering Henry and I had inspired her? In fact, I sat a little taller, and I didn't care if Mattie knew.

"Henry made me try a lipstick," I told him. "It was bizarre and uncomfortable and sexy, and I rocked it." No need to get into how I'd sunk into this weird mind-set of wanting to put Henry on an altar and worship him.

Mattie shook his head in a daze, though he wasn't stunned enough to stop shoveling mac and cheese and brisket into his mouth. "I don't know who you are anymore." He wiped barbecue glaze off his mouth, and I snorted.

He said it in a way that I didn't have to worry about him thinking the changes in me were wrong, just different.

"I just came out to him," I clarified to Noah and Julian.

"Ohhh." Julian nodded in understanding. "Well, evidently you made an impression."

That was cool.

Before the evening was over, I'd gotten a new number to put in my phone. Noah and I exchanged digits, and it was implied we'd all meet up for a barbecue at their beach house sometime.

Mattie and I walked back to my truck, and I couldn't shake the anticipation. There was excitement building up, and it was because I was creating something new. This was for me—and Mattie, obviously, but...I really dug this. I was making friends and going out to dinner, for the first time allowing myself to have a social life.

Then I thought of Henry, and it was impossible to shake the smile. I was a dork. A dork who wanted to go home quickly and tell the boyfriend about this awesome dinner.

Unfortunately, when we got back to Malibu, we faced a shitstorm. From the driveway, we could hear Ty yelling at Henry.

"Oh, shit." Mattie slammed the door shut and jogged up to the house.

I was quick to follow. "Hold up, Mattie."

CHAPTER 18

OH, TY. OH, MARTIN. OH, FUCK

"Wait. Wait." I caught up to him and put a hand on his shoulder before he could open the door. "Don't go in."

"Why?" Mattie looked to me incredulously. "They're fighting—and Henry's been too polite."

"I know, but listen." I nodded at the door, waiting for him to understand. Because I could hear Henry; he was pushing Ty. After days of way too much silence, maybe it was this Henry had been waiting for.

"Just leave me the fuck alone!" we heard Ty shout. I automatically sought out the windows on the second floor, 'cause his voice came from up there. "What part of 'I don't wanna talk about it' don't you understand? Fuck!"

"Come back here *right now*, Tyler."

Mattie and I both took a step back at the force in Henry's voice. How he could command so much authority without yelling or cursing was a mystery.

"Damn," Mattie mumbled.

I murmured my agreement and sat down on the stoop, glad we were in the shade. It looked like we'd be here a while.

The next time Henry spoke, his tone was more patient, though it brooked no argument. He said he was done waiting to have this discussion, and I definitely didn't mind. Maybe I could finally figure out what they'd been up to.

"You had to excuse yourself when that boy was telling his story at the group session," Henry said. They had to be between the foyer and the living room for us to hear him so well. Only one window was open, and it was down here. "You may pull off the asshole act very well, but I don't believe it's genuine. Something he said upset you."

"Believe whatever you want," was Ty's reply.

"Come on, Ty," Mattie whispered, sitting down next to me.

"I have all the time in the world for you," Henry told him. "We're not done here until you've explained to me why you feel the need to push everyone away by behaving rudely."

I hummed, having not considered that. Was Ty purposely pushing people away?

I'd figured it was the influence of the elder Benningtons, who didn't seem to accept anyone who wasn't privileged. Though, privilege was the wrong word, because they didn't see their own. Basically, if you didn't live as well as they did, you were just a lazy fuck or making the wrong choices.

"You don't have all the time, though." Ty's words broke the silence. "Mom and Dad didn't."

"Shit." I brushed a hand over my mouth and tried to tap into his way of thinking. What he said raised a bunch of questions, mainly one. Had he been given enough time to grieve his parents?

"It's easier to leave before you get abandoned, right?" Ty went on, and my heart fucking broke for him. "You think I give two fucks about Grandma and Grandpa? You think I don't know how goddamn vile they are? But they're safe. My future is secure with them. As long as I do as they say, I know I'll be okay."

I was suddenly relieved I wasn't in there. I wasn't sure I could handle seeing Henry crestfallen, and I was fucking certain that's what he felt.

Waiting for Henry to respond, I imagined his brain going a mile a minute to piece together what was going on with Ty. And had been going on for years.

"Tyler... Christ. That's not the way to live your life."

I moved closer to the door as Henry's voice had lowered. Mattie followed.

"Did you know your father wanted to own a bookstore?" Henry changed the subject, although I suspected it was for a good reason. "When we grew up, he said he wanted a shop full of science fiction and fantasy books."

"Wasn't he a lawyer or something?" Mattie whispered.

I shrugged with one shoulder. I didn't think Thorne had actually been a lawyer; he'd been a business major, but it was something that'd put him in a suit each morning.

"Of course, our parents didn't approve," Henry went on. "Luckily for Thorne, one thing made him happier than any dream career—his family. You and your mother." *And you*, I wanted to add. "He lived a happy life, but he made a lot of compromises for our parents that he shouldn't have."

"I didn't know that," Ty said quietly. I almost missed it.

"I don't want you to have to make those compromises, Tyler," Henry murmured. "There will be countless occasions where you'll have to compromise, but not that. Not with your dreams." He paused. "You used to sketch. Every time you and your parents came down to visit, you'd draw me something."

"I was a kid."

"You're still a kid. You're a young man who has the time to

figure things out—if you want to. Whether you pursue your childhood dream of becoming an animator or you've thought of something else... But can you tell me you want to major in business at Columbia like your father and I did? Do you want to waste your creativity because my parents are a safe choice? You'll be suppressing who you are."

That struck a nerve even with me, and I was one of the lucky ones. Getting to know who I was becoming was vital to me. If I had to bury that now...

Henry had spent years hiding who he was.

I drew up my knees a bit so I could rest my elbows on them. Being *out* wasn't only reserved for sexual preference, was it? I mean, technically, it boiled down to being out as whoever you were. No hiding, no suppressing.

"Does it matter?" Ty responded eventually. "They'll never go for that."

"It does matter," Henry countered patiently. "I want nothing more than for you to choose to stay with me, but if you're not ready for that, I *will* be the prick who forces you to stay." Fuckin' A, he was going there. He was putting his foot down. "I have sole custody of you for another year, Ty. You're not going back to your grandparents."

"Wh-what?" Ty was... Shit, I didn't know. I couldn't tell. Was he angry? Shocked, in disbelief, numb?

"You do have one choice," Henry continued. "I would never tear you away from your life, so if you want to live in Camassia Cove, we will. But you will not live permanently with my parents because I can't sit by and watch them take over. Not when it's hurting you."

Mattie and I exchanged a look. Where would they end up? Hell, at this point, I had to be realistic and wonder where I would end up too. I'd gotten attached to Los Angeles, though I couldn't see myself leaving Camassia behind for good.

"And what if you die?" Oh, Ty was angry. Scratch that, he was back to livid. My phone vibrated in my pocket, and I ignored it quickly. This was more important. "Don't you fucking realize I wanted you gone 'cause you're so much like Dad?" Jesus Christ. That poor kid. "I told you once I wanted to get into animation, and what did you do? You bought me a digital sketchpad. Grandma called it silly nonsense for little children. When I told Dad I didn't wanna do Little League anymore, he said okay like it was nothing." Ty was getting himself worked up, his words coming out ragged. "Grandpa told me that boys who grew up to be good men had learned how to stand on their own on a football field first. With you—fuck! I can't do this. I c-can't get attached to another p-parent and then —" His voice was cut off by something, or someone. There were muffled sounds.

I blew out a breath and gave Mattie's leg a squeeze.

My phone buzzed again.

"I had no idea," Mattie said quietly.

"Me either." I ran a hand through my hair, hating feeling useless. I wanted to do something. Help out in any way. "This is good, though. If Henry was waiting for a breakthrough, he just found it."

Mattie nodded absently. "That's one messed-up coping mechanism. He's been pushing people away so he won't have to go through losing them."

"We don't know what happened right after his mom and dad died," I pointed out quietly. Mattie and I knew a thing about losing parents, but we'd somehow always had the support we needed to get past it. I hadn't had a choice after our dad left. Mom was ill, so I had to take care of Mattie. It was so long ago that the memories were getting fuzzy. Either way, we had Nan.

What we didn't have were two grandparents who drilled bigotry and ignorance into our heads.

"They all but drove Henry out of town," I said, "and I don't think they gave Ty much comfort."

"Mm..." Mattie nodded. "I hope it gets better now—"

"Jesus Christ, where's the fire?" I pulled out my phone as it buzzed again, and then I frowned. It was Martin who'd called twice and now sent a message.

Why is no one answering?! I just need to be picked up, for goodness' sake. I'm not asking for a kidney.

"What the..." I clicked on his number and put the phone to my ear.

"Finally!" he answered. "Where is Henry?"

"He's..." I wasn't gonna get into that. "He's busy—"

"*Good.* Anyone but him can pick me up. Joseph laughed in my face—figuratively, of course—so it will fall on you."

"Um, okay. Where are you?" I asked.

"Just—" He made a frustrated noise. "Just get on the road. I'm near Pepperdine. I should ask them to pray for me."

I didn't know what that meant, but the urgency in his voice was enough to get me moving. Pepperdine University wasn't far away, maybe ten minutes down the highway toward LA. I got Mattie to go with me too, because I figured Martin's car had broken down, and my little brother was better with cars than I was.

It was a frazzled and sufficiently ruffled Martin we picked up on the side of the road, and there was no Mercedes to fix. Mattie shuffled toward the middle of the seat, and Martin got in with a huff. When I asked him where his car was, he looked at me as if he was ready to tear me apart.

"Hey, I'm not the enemy here, princess." I turned the car around and headed back on the highway. "What happened?"

He got snippy. "It was stolen, okay?"

"How would—oh God." I pressed my lips together, only it didn't help. A loud laugh broke free, and I slapped the wheel. "Are you fucking kidding me? He stole it *again*?"

Perhaps this time, his ex would stay an ex.

No wonder Martin didn't want Henry to pick him up.

"I'd rather not discuss it." He turned to look out the window instead.

Whatever. It gave me time to explain the sordid tale of Martin's ex stealing his car once in the past, and this was round two. My brother laughed, as expected.

"But how could he steal it with you inside?" Mattie wondered, chuckling.

Good question.

"He feigned carsickness and said he needed to throw up." Martin folded his arms over his chest, the white fabric of his button-down yellowed in places by the road dust. "Being the good boyfriend I am, I stepped out to help him. That's when he took the wheel and drove off, calling me a cocksucker as he went."

I tilted my head. Something about this story triggered my suspicions.

"Martin," I said slowly, "why did he call you a cocksucker and take off with your car?"

He huffed again.

He wasn't gonna answer.

I had a feeling I knew where this was going, so I prodded some more. "Did he, by any chance, catch you giving head to someone else?"

Because who the fuck could forget that Martin had a thing for sucking twenty-five-year-old dicks?

My brother was following us like a tennis match.

"He didn't catch me." Martin waved a hand, dramatic. "I was trying to be a good partner by confessing and being honest."

"Well, that went *great*." I rolled my eyes and made a quick decision. Fuck taking him home. I was bringing him with us to the house.

Henry was gonna love this.

The house was quiet when we got back, aside from Martin's whining because we hadn't taken him home.

"You're being kind of a bitch, you know," Mattie said conversationally.

I stifled my grin, and Martin looked properly chastened and shut his mouth.

Mattie snickered and climbed the stairs, announcing he was sweaty and gross and needed a shower.

Trailing farther into the house, I found Henry on the terrace in one of the loungers with a bottle of beer. He had his eyes closed but probably knew I was here.

The sun had set, so I switched on one of the patio lights before stepping out further.

"Hey." I sat down on the edge, by his legs, and placed my hand on his thigh.

He opened his eyes slowly and offered a tired smile before closing them again. "Hello, beautiful. How was your day?" He brought the bottle to his mouth and took a swig.

"It was good. We had dinner with Julian and Noah." I stroked his leg, wondering what mood he was in. He seemed content. "We came home earlier, but we didn't wanna interrupt. You and Ty were talking."

He sighed, definitely content, and reached for my hand. "I thought I'd heard you."

"We totally listened in for a while."

He smiled sleepily and kissed my knuckles. "I don't mind. How much did you hear?"

"We left when Ty got upset." Leaning forward, I pressed a kiss to his lips, then stroked his jaw. "You okay?"

At that, he opened his eyes once more, and he inclined his head. "Very much so. The only thing that would make tonight better is a bubble bath with you and a bottle of red."

I chuckled and kissed him again. "I'll see your bubble bath and raise you one opportunity to gloat." I straightened in my seat and peered into the kitchen where Martin was lurking in the shadows. "Get out here, Mr. Can't-keep-it-in-his-pants."

"Oh goodness, now what?" Henry muttered and sat up straighter too.

Martin joined us with reluctance rolling off of him, and he sighed dramatically and made a get-on-with-it gesture.

"What happened?" Henry asked, standing up.

"When you were talking to Ty, Martin texted me," I explained. I ignored Martin's glare and rose to stand next to Henry. "He needed to be picked up on the side of the road because someone stole his car. Again."

"For crying out loud," Henry snapped. I snatched his beer from him because I knew they got loud and gestured a lot when arguing. "Martin! How many times do we need to have this conversation? Let me guess, you cheated again too?"

Oh, so this was a recurring thing. Fun.

"To be fair, I warned him," Martin argued. "I keep telling people I'm not good with monogamy!"

"Yet, you enter monogamous relationships!" Henry threw out his hands. "There are ethical ways to date several men, you know. I can't deal with you. Christ. This is why you can't have nice things!" He pinched the bridge of his nose, getting heated. In the meantime, I sat down and took a sip of the beer. I wanted to enjoy this show. "Okay, what next? I assume you need me to contact him so he can return your car."

That set Martin off, and he seethed. "Oh, get off your high horse, Henry. I do not *need* you to do anything for me. I am perfectly capable of—"

"Letting your dick think for you, yes, I'm aware."

My mouth formed a small "o." *Burn.*

"At least I have one that works," he scoffed.

I pointed the beer bottle in Henry's direction. "His works very well, honey."

I got the glower for that. Okay, so perhaps I should keep my mouth shut. Yeah, I'd do that. Martin was *mad.*

"I'm not getting into this," Martin said angrily. "Henry, consider our truce over. Zach, I'll be in the car. You're taking me *home.*" He pivoted and stormed inside, and shortly after, we heard the front door slam shut.

"Well, then." Henry turned to me, lips pursed in thought. "Bubble bath when you get back? I'd like to test the jets on all your lickable little places."

I nodded, my ass clenching. "Yeah, okay. I'm in."

"So will I be, my dear."

Oh, fuck.

CHAPTER 19

JUST CALL ME JET-SET BOY

"Henry!" I yelled. Rubbing the sleep from my eyes, I picked up Mattie's note from the kitchen island and reread it.

Henry trailed down the stairs shortly after, fully dressed and ready to face the day. See, I was one of those who ate breakfast in sweats. He wasn't, and I was going to have to change that. Clothes were evidently unnecessary today.

"The boys aren't up yet?"

I handed him the note. "They found bikes in the garage and went to the beach."

"'We'll be back for dinner,'" he finished, reading out loud. "Hm. Should we join them? After yesterday, I don't think Ty is a flight risk, but—"

"Mattie wouldn't let him leave," I reasoned and hooked two fingers into his belt. "Maybe we should let them spend the day together. They probably have a lot to talk about." My brother had mentioned Ty refusing to speak to Mattie the other day. "You and I could eat breakfast and do naked stuff." The hot tub on the upstairs terrace was calling my name, particularly after last night. Holy shit, the jets in the bathtub were out of this world. I could only imagine how forceful they'd be in the hot tub.

His mouth slanted up a fraction as I tugged him closer. "My sweet Zachary, are you hungry for even more cock? You slut."

I stuttered out something that sounded like, "Shhyeah."

"Hmm. I'll make it happen for you." He dipped down and gave me a slow kiss. "First, breakfast."

Right. We had to fill up on energy. Carbs were good for that, right? And sugar.

"I wanna know how it went between you and Ty after we left yesterday too." I adjusted my dick as Henry aimed for the fridge. "Did he agree to stay?"

Henry spoke from behind the open fridge door. "We didn't discuss it much, to be honest. He let me comfort him, though. He was so tired, the poor thing. He's been pretending to be someone he's not for a very long time." He closed the door, setting down eggs, English muffins, and fixings on the counter by the stove. "I don't believe he will put up much of a fight. He seems to know I'm serious about not letting him live with my parents anymore."

That was good. It was great to hear.

They'd have their rough patches, no doubt. Ty wouldn't break his habits in one day, and they were going to have to start over from the beginning. That's where they were now, at their beginning. It was a good one, I thought.

Henry agreed.

"Mattie would like to stay for a while," I added.

"I'm glad to hear that," he replied. "I'm impressed by how you've raised your brother, Zach. He's a wonderful young man. I can only admire you—and hope to be half as good with Tyler."

"That's so like you, selling yourself short." I joined him at his side so I could pinch his ass. "But, thank you. He's a good egg."

So were the English muffins Henry made us with eggs, sausage, and all the cheese in the world.

"Ohhh..." I groaned in contentment as I lowered myself into the tub. The water wasn't as hot as I thought it would be, and that was a damn good thing. Although we were protected underneath a sunroof with grape vines blocking the sun, it wasn't exactly a chilly day that called for a hot soak.

"Feel good?" Henry adjusted the jets after setting a bottle of something on the edge of the tub. I squinted at it to read the label. Water-resistant lube. Well, fuck me. He thought of everything.

"So good." I sighed and leaned back, my head landing on the edge. There were four indentions with foam lining the sides of the tub, providing cushions for lazy guys like me.

Henry pulled his tee over his head, then dropped his shorts. I stared 'cause I could and grinned a little when he winked. Then he got in and sat down next to me, a sighed "Oh, yes" slipping through his lips.

Wanting to feel him, I crawled onto his lap and nuzzled his cheek.

He smiled, and his hands were always quick to find my ass. "Perfect. I think you need to straddle me more often."

I smirked. "You just want easy access to my ass."

"That too, certainly." He captured my mouth with his and groped my ass cheeks, and he managed to make me yelp when he wriggled his pinkie finger inside.

"Jesus Christ, Henry. A little warning would be nice." I clenched down on him automatically, and it wasn't enough. A finger or two didn't cut it anymore. "I think you have an ass fetish."

"Oh, I don't think it. I know so." He swept the tip of his tongue into my mouth and replaced his pinkie with his middle finger. "Most people have fetishes, no?"

He couldn't possibly wanna carry on a conversation while he was fingering me.

"Sure. Maybe. I don't know." I shifted on top of him, wanting more. "I don't think I have any. I mean—other than loving when you fuck me. If that's a fetish, sign me up."

He chuckled huskily and used his index and ring finger to stroke my constricting opening. He liked to rub the skin there and tease me by dipping the pad inside, then circling some more.

"You're kinda kinky," I had to say. "Ass play, cock worship, lipstick domination."

His laugh was softer and muffled by a drawn-out kiss. "I believe we are both guilty of worship, darling boy."

"Mmm, true..." I kissed away the water droplets on his shoulder. "Fuck, that right there." When he scissored me open with two fingers—I fucking loved it. Oh God, I could feel the warm water just inside my hole, seeping in between his fingers. "I want your cock."

"Not yet," he whispered. "You may touch me, though. Both hands, please."

I moaned under my breath and found his erection, thick and hard. I used both hands and stroked him sensually. And scratch that. I was massaging him. In firm, unhurried strokes, I rubbed his cock, feeling all of him. As I gently grazed my fingernails up the base of him, I used my other hand to cup the head and twist it carefully.

"Incredible," he breathed into a kiss. "You obey perfectly. Did you know that?"

I shivered, and a breeze rolling through the balcony only made it more visible. "I like pleasing you," I admitted. "It turns me on, and it feels good." Like now, when he fingered me deeper and made me greedier. He always felt so *fucking* good. "Yeah, you're definitely kinky."

He flashed a wolfish little smirk. "Only for fun. I do have some fetishes, and being dominant is one of them." He elicited a long groan from me, because—fuck—those fingers of his. "At this speed, you'll wake up my bottom side soon." Since he had both his hands by my ass, he could use more fingers. Four of them, his middle fingers and index fingers formed an object big enough to fuck myself on. Even though he only allowed for slow movements. "Would it turn you on if I was the one begging to be fucked?"

"*Uungh*," I moaned. "You have no idea."

"Good. What about your fantasies, Zachary?"

"Why are we talking when you could be balls deep in my ass?" I pushed myself down on his fingers, wondering how the fuck he was angling them. He must've put them together, the sides with his nails facing each other.

"I asked you a question," he reminded.

I huffed, breathing heavily, and scowled. Okay, the bastard needed to be swayed. I'd all but forgotten my own seduction, so I redoubled my efforts with his cock and included his balls. They were firm, telling me how aroused he was.

I didn't know how to answer him, though. Only one thing came to mind as I thought back on the porn I'd watched. Funnily enough, it was from straight porn, and now I couldn't help but wonder if it'd been the role-play that'd turned me on more so than the gender.

I'd watched the video countless times, and it was part of why I had been so confused. Because of how turned on I'd been, supposedly because it had been a man fucking a woman. But now... Was it the kink?

"Sleep sex," I blurted, out of breath. I swallowed and exhaled heavily. "I saw it in porn. The man was fucking a woman who was pretending to be asleep or unconscious."

Henry's jaw tensed. "Somnophilia. That's what it's called."

"Okay." I couldn't gauge his mood, so I was quick to add, "Just as role-play. I don't actually wanna be passed out or—well, I mean, I don't think it's possible to sleep through a fuck for real, but the fantasy—"

"Quiet, boy." He kissed me and slipped his fingers out of me. Dammit. "It turns me on too. Count on me wanting to try it with you."

"Oh." Now I definitely needed him to fuck me. Hard. "Have you tried it before?"

He shook his head and reached for the lube. "No. I've only gotten off to porn with it." He pinched my ass. "Bend over the edge for me."

Finally.

I got off his lap and stood up. The water was just deep enough to keep most of my cock submerged. I gripped the edge and leaned forward, and that wasn't enough for him. He told me to rest my elbows on the top and stand on my toes.

It put my ass right at the level of his cock.

Henry rubbed himself behind me, the head of his cock bumping against my flesh. "We'll see how long I last after that filthy little confession of yours." He interrupted my gulp and my shudder by nudging his cock between my cheeks and shoving himself deep inside me. "*Fuck.*"

My lips parted in a silent scream before I lowered my head and bit into my forearm. *Holy mother of God.* The pain was the only thing that could stave off an instantaneous orgasm, so I was fucking glad it hurt as much as it did. I hadn't even touched my dick yet.

A muffled sob eventually broke free, along with a choked, "P-Please, *more.*"

Henry cursed viciously, then fucked me hard and fast for a few strokes before easing out. He gripped my hips and motioned me forward, until the rest of me was closer to the edge too. That was when I felt the jets hitting my balls, and I moaned embarrassingly loudly.

He fucked me more relentlessly than usual. Thanks to the water, he could slide his hands down my hips—his fingers tracing that sensitive crease where my thighs met my crotch—and support some of my weight. When he pushed his cock inside me on a particularly hard thrust, my toes left the bottom of the tub.

My eyes nearly rolled back. He hit so fucking deep, sometimes brushing against my prostate when the angle allowed it. To massage it, he could only use fingers. This way, he only managed to drive me goddamn crazy.

"Henry," I groaned. "I need you—"

"You brought this on yourself, Zachary." His voice was a low growl, his breath coming out harsh. "Tempting me with this beautiful ass, your fantasy—mother*fuck.* I can't get it out of my head." Slipping out slowly, he caught his breath and kneaded my ass roughly, and I bit back a whimper. "One day soon, I want you to pretend to be asleep so I can do all sorts of lewd things to your body."

Yeah, I fucking whimpered. Why even bother trying to hold that back? The man turned me into a flushed, desperate fucktoy.

He pushed in again, effectively stealing my breath. Next, he grabbed a fistful of my hair and brought me back to him. The sounds coming from my mouth—I didn't know what they were. Groans, sobs, pleas, choked gasps.

"You'll do it to me too," he whispered in my ear. Goose bumps rose all over. "Won't you, Zach? You'll be a good boy and take advantage of me in my sleep."

"Yes," I ground out. "*Fuck, please touch me.*" The words gusted out of me in a jumbled rush as I got increasingly close to bursting without a single stroke. My cock hurt, and the jets kept hitting me underwater. I wasn't merely teetering on the edge; he was fucking me on it.

"Perfect." He released my hair, letting me fall forward, and then he fucked us both toward climax. His hand fisted my cock and stroked me against the blasting water stream.

It didn't take many seconds before I was coming with a hoarse cry. The pleasure had me in a choke hold, flooding every part of me in sharp currents. My eyes burned with unshed tears, my ass ached hellishly, and my heart couldn't pound faster.

Henry sagged against me, his forehead landing on my shoulder. His shallow, rapid breaths hit my back, and I trembled in my efforts to stay upright. I swallowed a *hnngh* sound as I felt his cock jerking lazily inside me.

"Goddamn, baby," he whispered raggedly.

I nodded once and blew out a breath. I was done. So fucking done. My body was liquid.

Henry gathered me somehow, and I ended up seated in his lap. His softening cock was still buried inside my ass, and for some reason, that was exactly what I wanted. He'd positioned me sideways when sitting down, and this way, I could kiss him better. Kisses and touches came far easier than words. My heart wouldn't quit racing.

Cooking dinner together was one of the more coupley things Henry and I had done together. I enjoyed the fuck out of it. He had put on some music and was making a salad while I flipped steaks on the grill.

"How are the fries?" I hollered from the terrace.

"Not quite there yet," he responded. "Another few minutes."

I nodded and added the last of the steaks. The sun would set within the hour, so I hoped Mattie and Ty would be back soon.

Henry stepped outside a couple minutes later with a glass of wine for me. He and Martin had turned me on to the shit, possibly because the wine I'd had in the past wasn't always passable as wine.

"You've gotten some nice color today." He touched my cheek, to which I turned my head and gave his palm a quick peck. Then I took a sip of my wine and gestured at his neck. He'd been in the sun today too.

We'd been lazy all day. After the hot tub rendezvous, we had migrated to the main terrace and lounged around the pool and had way too much ice cream. Or I had, at least. Henry seemed to have better self-control.

"Oh, hell." Henry's tone shook the perfect atmosphere, and I followed his gaze toward the house. Past the kitchen, into the foyer. And *oh, hell* was right.

Mattie and Ty were home. They were stiff as sticks and carefully dumped their towels and a backpack on the floor.

"Sunscreen," I called. "It's a thing."

While they flipped me off, I sent them a thumbs-up.

"Christ, you two." Henry became all adorable. "Do you not realize how dangerous it is to be in the sun without protection?" He stalked through the kitchen and into the half-bath in the foyer, quickly emerging with after-sun lotion. "This has aloe in it. I'll get you some ice packs after dinner. Before we eat, though, you should take some ibuprofen. I'll go get it."

I smiled to myself and took a swig of my wine, then plated the last steaks.

I was dating a fretty fusser.

Mattie and Ty stepped out on the terrace with equally miserable expressions and aimed for the seating area. Still in their trunks, the reddening skin of their shoulders, torsos, faces, and even their legs was visible.

"Been in the water all day?" I guessed. My brother loved swimming in the ocean, and once he got in, it was difficult to get him out. It was the only way I knew they wouldn't feel the burn until it was too late.

"Maybe," Mattie mumbled.

Ty's complexion was originally even fairer than Mattie's, so he'd really unlocked the level of lobster. My brother wasn't far off either.

"I sneezed in the driveway and wanted to cry." Ty touched his burned nose gingerly.

I pinched my lips together to hide the amusement. Seeing the damage up close did have me worried too. But Christ, they were funny.

There was a big dose of relief related to Ty, as well. He seemed more at ease.

Henry returned with sodas and painkillers and a lecture on skin cancer.

The boys listened grudgingly while slathering themselves in after-sun lotion.

After a couple trips to the kitchen, I had set the table on the terrace and brought all food. "What have you eaten today?" I asked. They were eyeing the steaks as if they were starved.

"We bought hot dogs for lunch," Ty replied. He winced and hissed when lifting his arm to fill his plate.

"I'll do it." Henry couldn't relax. He remained in the fussing parent mode and served their dinner. "Did you take the pills?"

They nodded sullenly.

"Okay. Eat carefully, now." Henry sat down next to me, his forehead creased with concern. "You should take baths after dinner. I'll leave oatmeal and baking soda in your bathrooms. Don't towel off," he warned. "You don't want to upset your skin further. Then more lotion. I'll put it in the fridge while you take your baths."

Maybe it *was* possible to fall in love in a short period of time.

That was the thing with Henry. Being with him made me see possibilities everywhere. He was a genuinely good person, and I almost felt like I was a better version of myself when I was near him.

"Oatmeal?" Ty grimaced.

"It's gross, but it works," Mattie muttered. "Ain't my first sunburn."

"For the sake of my sanity, have you considered making it your last?" Henry asked.

I grinned, and I was pretty sure there was a faint blush underneath Mattie's burned cheeks. This was good for him too. To have an older male role model around who wasn't his brother.

I sighed contentedly, then dug into my food and enjoyed the moment.

CHAPTER 20

MURPHY'S LAW CAN SUCK MY DICK

We didn't have brunch with Martin on Sunday, which felt entirely wrong. He hadn't answered his phone when we called, so Henry and I left Malibu with two aging teenagers who could barely move.

In Venice, at a place called Casablanca, Henry introduced me to bottomless mimosas and my first—though, it had to be the best too—calamari steak ever. Henry was driving, so he stuck to one drink.

I was kinda tipsy by the time we got back in the car.

Tipsy meant courage, and that was the moment I had the balls to discuss the time Mattie and Ty would spend here while I was back home. It was a topic I'd quickly grown to hate. At the same time, I woke up this morning missing the sound of rain pelting the windows.

"Can you stop acting like I'm twelve?" Mattie groaned. "I'll fucking behave, Zach."

"Well, good." I faced forward and tapped my fingers along the armrest. "And don't take advantage of Henry's tendency to be whipped."

"Hey," Henry protested. "I'm not whipped."

"Of course not, sweetheart." I brought out my phone to write a list of expectations I had for the boys. They should help out and not get everything handed to them, they could ask Martin if he needed help in the shop, Ty could help Henry with inventory at the bookstore... It would do him good to see the place his uncle had started. Snacking—Mattie could get out of hand with snacks. Henry would have to keep an eye on my brother there, 'cause Mattie's favorite dinner was Cheetos, and then for dessert, he licked the dust off his fingers.

At the bottom of the list, I wrote, **Make a damn wish and hope you end up in the same place as Henry.**

"You're moping, honey." Martin hip-checked me to nudge me away from the counter where he was decorating mini cupcakes. They were for some celebrity's kid's birthday. Each little cupcake had vanilla frosting, edible glitter, and a handmade crown of chocolate.

"Sorry." I stuck my hands in my pockets and searched for a random topic. "What made you give up law school for this?"

He waved a hand. "I like to work with my hands, and studying law put me to sleep most of the time. That's not what you want to talk about, though."

"Can't I come down here to say hi?" I scowled.

"Of course you can," he placated. "But it's not why you came here this time. Now, out with it. Trouble in paradise?"

"No..." Wasn't that the issue? There was no trouble at all. Everything was fucking perfect, and I wasn't happy about leaving soon. But it was time. I'd pretended Los Angeles was my reality for a few weeks now, and I had to get back to Nan and the store.

After brunch, running some errands, and chilling all Sunday, time had sped up for us. Monday and Tuesday disappeared in the blink of an eye between pool fun, sightseeing, and playing house. Well, technically, it was still Tuesday. I'd headed out for a little while to meet up with Julian, who'd been in the area. We'd bought too-expensive ice cream and more or less ended up talking about our significant others for two hours.

On the way home, I'd taken another turn and ended up at Martin's instead. He was going to pull an all-nighter to get everything ready for this princess's birthday party.

Who had a party on a Wednesday, anyway?

"I wanna go home but not alone," I admitted. It was dark out by now. Henry would probably text soon to check in. "I miss all the things that Los Angeles people shudder at."

"Such as?"

"The rain. The forest, the... Just being home. Less traffic."

Martin chuckled softly. "We do not love the traffic, dear. We endure it."

"You know what I mean."

"Indeed. Rain is hideous. Have you spoken to Henry about this, though? Do keep in mind he is from your hometown."

I scrubbed a hand over my mouth and sat down on the little bench by the window. "I guess I'm greedy. He's said we'll see each other again soon, and it's not enough for me. Ty's really come around these last couple of days—what if he wants to move here?"

For the most part, Ty was focusing on Henry, as he should.

Mattie was the constant; Ty took breathers with my brother, with whom his dynamic hadn't changed. Then Ty dove right back into spending time with his uncle to find their middle ground. In short, Ty and I didn't talk too much. And that was okay. I went from being his buddy's big brother to his uncle's boyfriend. It made sense that he didn't know where he had me yet. I barely knew either.

"You can't see yourself living here?" Martin wondered. "You seem to like LA."

"I do." I nodded. Shit, I liked it a fuckload here. "It's just not home. Something is missing."

Martin made a humming sound and planted his hands on the counter. "Perhaps you need some alone time to process everything. You've undergone quite the change in very little time. Once you're on solid ground at home, I think it'll be easier to see where you end up. For now, you have unfinished business in that little flannel town of yours."

Unfinished business… I guess, in a way, he was right. For lack of a better word, I wasn't *out* back home. If I kept prolonging my stay, I'd feel like I was hiding. I had to see Nan, get back to work, and see my friends, few as they were.

Movement between the two counters caught my eye, and I watched as Eagle sauntered into the shop from the back.

Last night, Henry had mumbled Eagle's name in his sleep, and I'd struggled not to laugh.

"He misses the bookstore." Martin picked up the chubby fur ball and returned him to the back office. "No, you stay here, feline." He closed the door, then put on a new pair of plastic gloves. "Bring some treats back to the house, Zach. You'll need the sugar to turn that frown upside down."

I mustered a small grin. "I'm gonna miss you."

"Oh goodness, no. Don't you do that to me." He gave me a hard stare, looking upset all of a sudden. "You're coming back, for chrissakes. Whether you like it or not, this is your home away from home, and I will see you promptly for brunch in mere weeks. Make it happen, do you understand?"

"I understand," I said quickly.

"Good. Get home to your man now. I'll stop by with dinner tomorrow."

The next day when I placed my duffel on the bed, Henry came up behind me and hugged me to him.

"I don't like this. Not one bit."

I melted into him and closed my eyes. "This is where you promise me everything we have is real."

"So very real, Zachary." He turned me in his arms and kissed me deeply. "When school starts, I'll see you then."

Oh? That was news to me. I inched back to look him in the eye. "How can you be sure?"

He touched my cheek. "I have to face my parents at some point. Wherever we end up, we'll have to pick up Tyler's belongings at their house too. We'll fly up no matter what."

I swallowed the lump that formed in my throat and nodded jerkily. It was something, at least. I'd see him in a few weeks.

I searched his eyes as my vision blurred around the edges, and I didn't say the words I had at the tip of my tongue. It was the wrong moment. I couldn't know for sure I loved him yet. I wouldn't know until I didn't have unfinished business. I had to return to my reality first.

"My beautiful man." He dipped down and kissed me once more, a slow, deep, passionate one.

I shivered and locked my arms around his neck, pressing up against him. "I need you."

"I'm all yours, baby." He cupped my cheek, our foreheads touching. "I never stood a chance."

"I didn't either." Even as I said it, I knew he wouldn't believe me. It was starting to sting, though I reminded myself he'd lived more than I had. His view was gonna be different. "Come on." I tugged him backward and blindly pushed away the duffel. "I want you inside me."

He only hesitated for a second before he stalked over to close the door. Then he was back, lowering me to the bed and covering my body with his.

In order to beat traffic, I wanted to get on the road early. The sun wasn't up yet when I forced down some scrambled eggs and bacon.

Henry worked silently in the kitchen, wiping down the counter after being the sweetheart he was. The man had packed me a lunch. Leftovers from the Greek place Martin had brought food from for dinner last night. And snacks and drinks.

I was kind of annoyed with Martin. He didn't do goodbyes, so he'd made a swift departure once dinner was over, and he'd been gone with a kiss on my cheek and, "Brunch. Don't forget."

The truck was packed, and I'd filled up on gas yesterday.

Mattie and Ty trailed down in sweats and sleep-tousled hair a little before seven.

"Daily texts," I reminded my brother.

He nodded and slumped down on a stool next to me. "I remember."

"Can I get you some coffee, boys?" Henry offered.

Mattie replied with a, "God yes, please," and Ty nodded and yawned.

"Right, and no taking advantage of Henry," I added, half

irritated. "I don't wanna call in three days and find out he's your maid."

"Believe it or not, but I can take care of myself." Henry winked at me, then poured three mugs of coffee, one for himself. "I can balance the doting with structure."

Fine. It was a possibility I was overreacting. Whatever.

"So how long have you guys been married?" Ty asked.

Mattie bumped his fist, and Henry chuckled.

I didn't really react, other than enjoying that Ty was cracking jokes again. Or maybe there was a trickle of pleasure at the marriage part. For as much as I went nuts over my favorite drinks and having a great time in a club, the domestic lifestyle was where I got real comfortable. Being able to sit down and have dinner with my family, dividing chores...that was where I felt most at home.

"All right, I'm gonna leave you with the two comedians." I finished my juice and brought my plate to the sink. I linked a finger with Henry's. "I want frequent reports from you too."

He lowered his head and pressed a lingering kiss to my jaw. "No texts. I'll call so we can get off together."

I was on board with that.

Mattie was ready to drink his coffee and read the paper by the pool like some old man, so I gave him a hug and kissed the side of his head.

"Drive safe, love you." He waved lazily on his way out to the terrace and yawned.

I could tell Ty didn't know what to do, and fuck that hesitation. I hauled him in for a hug too, which didn't seem too unwelcome.

Then Henry followed me out to my truck.

"It's not too late to fly, you know."

Nah, this was cheaper, and I wanted to get my truck home.

I leaned against the door on my side and pulled him close.

"When I told Martin I was gonna miss him, he got huffy with me."

The corners of Henry's eyes crinkled with his smile. "Well, I will certainly miss you."

"I'll miss you too." Pulling him in for a kiss, I wrapped my arms around him and soaked up the last of the physical touch I was gonna get for several weeks. "Thank you for everything, Henry. Seriously. What you and Martin have given me..." I had no words for it.

"You've given us more than you realize too," he murmured. "I want you back in my arms as soon as possible."

I nodded and kissed him again.

"One thing." He cleared his throat and gathered my hands in his. He kept his gaze there too. "You asked me yesterday to tell you this is real, and it is. Hell—" He shook his head, smiling wistfully. "It's unlike anything I've ever felt in my life." That declaration made my breath stutter. "And because I want you to keep coming back to me, I want you to know I won't hold it against you if you meet—"

I quickly untangled my hands from his, ice and hurt tearing through me.

"Zachary, please listen to me. You haven't explored much yet, and... I apologize. I only want you to get everything you desire."

For a second, I fucking died. I grew distant and cold, and I nudged him aside to open the door. How could he *do* this? Right now? Motherfucker. I blinked and swallowed, wanting to get on the road before the emotions surged up.

"I can't fucking believe you went there." I got in the truck and slammed the door shut just as he said my name again, this time more urgently. I couldn't. Key in the ignition, I started the engine and backed out of the driveway.

Holy fuck, this hurt. He wanted me so badly he wasn't gonna hold it against me if I fucked someone else?

Mother*fucker*.

I rolled down the winding path toward the main road, and I slammed my hands on the wheel. Anger flared up and up and up until I was goddamn furious. Fuck him. Fuck him so fucking hard.

In a split-second decision, I took the wrong turn and headed straight for Martin's shop.

I'd fucking told him. I'd *told* Henry all I wanted was to be his. Why couldn't he make *that* happen? No, instead he gave me the green light to fuck around. Way to make me feel like I belonged to him.

My truck upset the dust as I tore into Martin and Henry's parking lot, and I was out of the truck before I could turn off the engine. It didn't matter. I wasn't staying long.

Bakers, or artisanal pastry makers, were up way before the sun, and the door to his shop was open.

"Is that you, Mariella?" he hollered from the back.

I rounded the counter to join him, and I was happy to see Eagle first thing. Martin's back office was his packing station. White boxes were stacked in piles everywhere, even on the workbench where I assumed he and his niece did the packing.

Martin spun on me, clearly surprised. "What're you doing here, hon?"

I pointed to Eagle, the fur ball that was conveniently resting in his carrier. At least one thing was working in my favor this morning. I went over to Eagle's corner and quickly closed the carrier door before he could claw his way out. He hissed at me, and I hunted down his litter box in the nearest bathroom.

"Should I ask what you're doing, Zach?" There was a note of worry in Martin's voice.

"Henry just hurt me," I said, carrying out the litter box.

"More like stomped on my fucking heart. So I'm gonna hurt him too. Where's Eagle's food?"

Martin was useless. He wanted to discuss what'd gone wrong, and I wanted to get the hell away from here. Without help, I located all the cat shit I needed, and I had it packed in my truck in two trips. I'd saved Eagle for last.

"Okay, gotta go." I walked out of the shop and secured his carrier in the passenger's seat. "Don't look at me like I'm crazy. I don't know what I'm doing."

Martin jogged out right before I got in behind the wheel. "Zach, what did he do? And Eagle is too pretty for the pound!"

I made a face and shook my head. If he thought I was taking the cat to give him up, I was fucking insulted. So I ignored it all and left Malibu with a cat that I sort of just kidnapped.

"Oh God, I'm like Martin's ex." I wanted to get in a hole and die. How goddamn embarrassing.

Nothing would clear your head like two hours of silence in an old truck that was warring against the sun. It was shaping up to be a record-hot day in southern California, and I'd passed countless trucks that had overheated already.

"Martin warned me," I said to Eagle. "He warned me, dammit. Henry doesn't know what a catch he is."

"It's unlike anything I've ever felt in my life. And because I want you to keep coming back to me, I want you to know I won't hold it against you if you meet—"

I flinched, replaying his words. They physically hurt my chest. It seized up tightly and made my breathing ragged.

It was going to be a while before I could forgive and forget, but I admitted I'd acted like a lunatic. Jesus, I'd actually stolen his cat.

Somewhere along the road, shortly after catching Malibu in the rearview, I'd turned off my phone. Now I was slightly afraid what I would face when I turned it on again.

"Ugh, this day can't get any worse."

I spoke too soon. The day could get worse. Instead of beating traffic everywhere, I was stuck in Bakersfield because my truck was acting up. I'd pulled over once, and I hadn't turned on the AC at all, yet it was still showing me it was overheating.

"You want the good news first or the bad?" the man asked. It said Landon on his coveralls that were splattered with oil spill and grime.

"Good, please." I stood just inside the garage bay of the auto shop, and my truck was occupying one of the four spots.

"It's only a malfunctioning thermostat and overheating," he told me. "Won't take long, and it ain't gonna set you back much. Bad news is we gotta wait until the engine's cooled down, and she's not in the best shape. How long you have her for?"

"It was my grandfather's," I sighed. "But, so, nothing's wrong with the radiator, right?" Because Mattie had looked it over before I drove down to California, and he'd said it was as good as it was gonna get.

"Nope, but it won't last forever," he replied, another man joining him. "Cam here's gonna take care of your truck. You can wait here, or there's a Taco Bell across the street."

"Taco Bell won't help me now. I need a fucking therapist," I muttered to myself. Of course, the men had heard me, and I flushed in embarrassment. "It's just not my day, sorry. I may have kidnapped my boyfriend's cat."

Landon's brows rose. "Well, okay, then."

The other guy, Cam, chuckled under his breath and walked over to my truck.

Not wanting to make a bigger ass of myself, I thanked Landon and said I'd be across the street. Shit, I was mortified. I couldn't make a very good escape either, because I couldn't bring Eagle into the Taco Bell. I had to go over there, buy a soda and some snacks, then go back to the garage, get Eagle's carrier, and return to the other side of the road. There were benches in the shade, meaning they couldn't chase me away because I was traveling with a stolen pet.

I wasn't even hungry.

Sitting there feeling sorry for myself, I tried to summon my logic. It was hidden in my brain somewhere. Cars came and went, pausing in the intersection, then vanished. Bakersfield wasn't very big. Supposedly, I had distant family here, though Mom had never brought me along as a kid. Maybe it was for the best; it was hotter than the surface of the sun.

"I'm sorry you had to suffer during my stint of utter insanity," I told Eagle, sucking some soda from the straw. "I guess your daddy's got my brain on a spin. I hear that happens when you fall in love. You do some stupid shit that you can't explain."

He wasn't angry or hissing anymore. That was something, right? He seemed quite comfortable in the carrier.

I watched as a nice car pulled up outside the garage. A man stepped out, holding a paper bag, reminding me of the lunch Henry had packed me. And I had forgotten it. Dammit, it must still be on the kitchen counter.

There was a girl too, who stayed by the car but waved happily to Landon and Cam. To my surprise, the newcomer kissed Cam as he extended what I assumed was his lunch. Next, Cam followed him back to the car, where he got another kiss, then one from the girl too. She had to be their daughter.

Well, the emotions I was waiting for boiled over right then

and there. I blinked back tears and cleared my throat repeatedly. How could I already miss him? I did, though. I missed Henry so fucking much, and I wanted that. What those two men and their daughter had—I wanted it. Henry and I would ace the family life, and I wanted it more than I could ever want club nights and purple drinks.

I blew out a breath.

The next few weeks were gonna suck.

CHAPTER 21

HOME, SWEET WHAT THE FUCK EVER

The dense forests of Oregon blurred as I drove past truck stop after truck stop. I told myself, the next exit I was gonna get some rest. Then I didn't. I kept driving. I'd spent the night in northern California in a shitty motel where I'd paced a hole in the floor before chickening out and leaving my phone off.

I'd turned it on again this morning, and the messages had poured in, both texts and voice.

I'm sorry, Zachary. Please call me. I don't want us to fight.

Get back to me as soon as you read this. Please, baby. I'm very sorry.

Bro, did you and Henry fight? He's mopey as fuck.

Martin called, darling. Did you really take Eagle? Can you come back? We have to solve this.

Holy shit, you kidnapped Henry's cat, bro! Have

you lost your mind?

"This is Martin, honey. I know how this is going to go. Henry's gonna overindulge in chocolate and let himself go completely, and next time I visit him, I'll have to wade through bottles of wine and CDs of sad music. Yes, the man still listens to CDs. For all our sakes, call him!"

There were several other messages from Henry, most filled with apologies, and I'd had a rock the size of Mount Rainier in my stomach. The guilt had flooded every part of me—until I read the message that came in this morning right before I got on the road.

I stand by what I said. I can't even describe what I feel for you. Can't you see I'm doing this because of that? I want you to be able to have both worlds.

Except, whatever worlds I ended up in, I wanted him and only him by my side. The hurt hadn't eased one fucking bit. I wanted it to be him and me, only us. Wherever we were.

I'd never liked the term unconditional love. For children, sure. I sure as shit loved Mattie unconditionally, but I didn't want that with Henry. I believed relationships needed boundaries and rules. I wanted to deserve him, not be given him freely. I wanted goddamn conditions.

If this was love for Henry, how would we work together?

"Does this mean we're friends?" I kept one hand on the wheel and used the other to pat Eagle's head carefully. I'd let him out of the carrier when we got on the road this morning, *after* I'd checked the laws on it. No, it wasn't okay to let a cat roam free, but dammit, he'd been in pet prison for too long.

The lazy thing spent most of the time sleeping in his carrier anyway, and he rejected three out of four stops on the road. Now, though...I mean, this was progress in our relationship. He was resting his head on my leg.

"If this is an apology for tracking litter all over the floorboards, I'll take it." I gave him another careful pat, then returned my hand to the wheel.

Washington was getting closer, and my truck was getting older. It probably wouldn't survive another road trip like this.

An accident was causing a traffic jam outside of Portland in the late afternoon, and I used the time to catch up with my brother. I'd sent a message this morning, and then they'd been out all day.

We had the best pizza for lunch. The house is different, and all Henry did today was drink scotch and listen to Adele. Surfing tomorrow. Are you home yet?

My anger hadn't faded enough for me to feel bad for Henry.

Stuck in traffic near Portland. Will be home around seven or eight, I think. Tell Henry that his cat is mine now. He doesn't deserve Eagle.

A minute later, Henry called.

"Great." I rolled my eyes, even as my stomach fluttered. Christ, I was lost over this man. As pissed as I was, I only wanted him more with each hour that went by. I caved and put the call on speaker. "I'm driving, so I can't handle an argument."

He sighed. "It's good to hear your voice."

I swallowed hard. It was good to hear his too. "What do you want, Henry?" I asked tiredly.

"I want to make this right, of course."

"I've already told you what I want," I said. "I'm not being unreasonable here. I don't look for promises or fairy-tale endings. I just want you to expect more from me. It fucking hurts when you think I'm gonna go out and fuck some random stranger."

"It wouldn't have to be a stranger—"

"Seriously, Henry!" I raised my voice as my fury simmered in warning. "It's real simple. Commit to me when you trust me to commit to you. Not a minute sooner. Doesn't matter how deep our relationship runs; if we date, we do it exclusively or not at all."

I was met with silence, which meant only one thing. He didn't trust me.

"Say something," I gritted, getting upset again. I couldn't wrap my head around it. If the timing was wrong, if he thought it was too soon to speak of commitment, then why could he tie himself to me but not the other way around? It'd be another issue if he wasn't ready for either of us to commit.

"I want to believe, Zach."

"But you don't."

"No." His tone was low, almost a whisper, yet it cut through me like a blade and echoed in my head as if he'd yelled it. "You'll wake up one day and realize there's so much more than—"

I hung up the phone before I could tell him where to go.

Home, sweet...home? I guess. I stepped out of my truck and inhaled deeply. It was crisper up here, even in the summer. Regardless of where you were in Camassia, you smelled the forest and the ocean in the air.

The apartment I shared with my brother was on the second floor of a brick building that looked like it'd seen better days. One window on the fourth and top floor was sealed shut with boards and a garbage bag. It'd been like that for a year.

I got Eagle settled in first, making room for his litter box in the bathroom. We only had one, and it was across the hall from the two bedrooms. By the time I came back from the truck with the rest of my shit, the cat was still in the carrier, though he had inched out a little.

I found myself standing in the living room, taking in the familiarity that somehow felt strange and out of place now. It *shouldn't*. Despite our half-shitty situation, we'd made this a home. We'd moved in a couple years after Mom died, needing a fresh start, and this was closer to the store on Olympia Square.

The couch was ratty and old but comfortable and covered in blankets Nan had knitted. A couple patchwork quilts too. Back from when she could still operate a sewing machine. There were pictures on the walls. It was something I'd been adamant about. They included drawings we'd made as kids. One bookshelf with games and DVDs. The flat screen Nan gave us last Christmas. Two comfy chairs, one of which Mattie had declared his. It had a footrest.

The heavy oak coffee table was the only piece of furniture we had left from the old place. From the days Mom was alive.

Checking the time on my phone, I decided it was too late to check in with Nan to say I was home. I wasn't hungry or particularly sleepy. Tired as hell, but not sleepy. To be honest, I wanted to shower, drink myself into a stupor, and cry over Henry.

Perhaps that was why I stupidly went on Instagram to check out my photos. I'd been good about uploading something every day. And there we all were. Henry, Mattie, Ty, Martin, and me. Standing right there in the middle of my living room, I zoomed in on Henry's ruggedly handsome face. He was smiling faintly, eyes hidden behind shades. I'd taken it of him outside the bookstore as he was locking up. Kind of random. I only remembered thinking he was too hot for words, so I'd wanted a picture.

I had a few photos of the two of us that were more couple-like. I hadn't uploaded them yet.

I rubbed at my chest and the stinging pain that fluttered through. His reactions to everything made me doubt myself. Had I overreacted? Did I demand too much? Then I circled back to the fact that he had no issues committing to *me*. And I trusted him, dammit. Why couldn't he trust me?

Eagle interrupted my depressing thoughts when he brushed up against my leg.

"Can I take you to dinner?" I offered.

Saturday was my last day off work, and I planned on spending it with Nan. I picked up pastries on the way to the home, which, of fucking course, made me think of Martin.

Her old folks' home was down in the Valley, and it was perfect for her. The others she'd looked at in the area were either too expensive or too boring. "I don't understand why they treat these places like they're just a place to wait for death. I still have living to do, you know," she'd told me once. Then we'd found this facility, new at the time. It'd once been a factory, and now it was trendy little apartments with a park in the back. They promoted physical activities and had their own workshop and hall where they offered classes. Sometimes it was a cooking class, sometimes academic classes. No matter what, there was always something to do.

The building next door belonged to an ad agency called Three Dots, and it was where Meghan worked these days. It'd been a while since we met up.

I entered the lobby of Nan's building and greeted the receptionist.

"Zach!" She smiled. "Your grandmother told us you were

visiting today. You've been on vacation?"

"Yup, saw a little of Los Angeles." I returned the smile, then continued toward the elevators. There was no hospital smell here. Or pale-yellow walls. It was brick; there were big canvas paintings, dimmed spotlights, and colorful couches.

Nan had her apartment on the top floor, so I clicked on three and checked to make sure I had everything. Pastries, a couple souvenirs, a magazine, and Sophie Pierce's autograph on a napkin.

Each floor had its own common room, and it was always a safe bet to start searching for Nan there. More often than not, she was playing canasta with her girlfriends or robbing the older gentlemen of money in poker.

It was canasta today. I found her in the corner with four ladies, and she smiled widely when she spotted me.

Home.

Seeing her was like coming home. It chipped away a bit of my cautiously placed armor that I'd put on this morning. Today wasn't about Henry. I'd cried enough last night.

"If you'll excuse me, girls, my grandson is here." She rose carefully and reached for her walker before I could reach her.

"I can help you, you know," I pointed out. I kissed her cheek, then nodded at the other women. "Hello, ladies. New glasses, Margaret? I dig."

The delicate little lady blushed and adjusted her glasses. "Oh, thank you, Zach. That's sweet of you to say."

"It's been a while, Zach," one tutted, while another complimented my hair.

I grinned.

"Let's go before they talk your ear off, sugar." Nan nodded toward the hallway, and I grasped her elbow. The walker wouldn't be enough for much longer. "Rose is right, by the way. I do like your new hair. Very stylish."

"Thanks." I made a mental note to start looking for a wheelchair. My grandmother was a cool little lady who was too young to be old. She always wore dresses, her silver hair always impeccable in a braided bun. One of her friends helped her with nail polish every four weeks, and she hated it when there was something she couldn't do on her own. So for us to get her even to use a chair on a daily basis would require some creativity. It couldn't be a chair they provided for outings.

The woman didn't even have hard candy in her apartment because it was such an "old people" thing.

Once inside her studio, I helped her over to the table by the window. She liked to look out over the district we called Little Seattle. The Valley was all cobblestone streets, factories-turned-lofts, townhouses, vegan sandwich shops, and local businesses. It was the home of the town's college too, and it was the district I used to think about settling down in. A faraway goal because it was expensive unless you wanted roommates.

"I want to hear *everything* about your trip. Mattie has told me a little."

"Oh, really?" I chuckled wryly and walked over to her kitchenette. "What did he say?" I plated the pastries and waited for her tea.

"That you met someone," she admitted.

"Jesus Christ." I looked up at the ceiling and sighed.

"I don't think you'll find Jesus up there, sugar."

"Can I come out to *anyone*, or am I gonna be the last to know I'm gay?"

Nan raised a brow over her glasses. The neck strap's rhinestones glinted in the morning sun shining in. "Your brother didn't say it was a man, actually."

"Oh." Shit.

"I'm joking," she laughed softly. "He absolutely told me."

For fuck's sake! "Tell me about him, Zach. Is he good to you—oh, drop the scowl. A grandmother knows."

"*How?*" I was getting fucking frustrated.

Okay, after the three weeks I'd spent in LA, there was no question. But before then...?

"I can't put my finger on it." She pursed her lips and tilted her head. "I think it's your reaction when you meet certain gentlemen. Do you remember Xander?"

I cleared my throat. "Uh, yeah." He was Margaret's youngest son.

"*That.* That right there." She smiled. "You get this adorable expression. I'm not sure you realize it."

I didn't.

Xander wasn't extremely attractive, though he wasn't bad to look at either. And he had a pinch of that authority that Henry possessed.

"All right..." I poured her tea and grabbed a soda for myself. Then I sat down across from her at the table and spun the plate of pastries so she could reach her favorite cream-filled madeleines. "Did Mattie also gossip about *who* I was dating?"

She narrowed her eyes. "He did, and you said that in past tense."

Yeah, well. I opened my soda and pushed down the hurt. "We broke up, I guess."

"Why?" she demanded.

"Because he has major trust issues, evidently." Okay, I was bitter about it, and I ended up spilling my guts to my grandmother. The only shit I withheld from her was either related to sex or makeup. I admitted everything else, from the first night we went to a gay bar to how we'd basically played house in Malibu.

She interjected with a question here and there, otherwise staying quiet and listening to every word I said.

"Has he been cheated on, perhaps? That leaves scars."

"Not that I know of," I answered, only to dive into the next story. About his parents and how they'd treated him. Because I wasn't completely clueless. He'd been betrayed in other ways. Left behind, rejected.

I hesitated when thinking of Joseph and Henry and how they'd, um, shared partners. Henry had mentioned his partners had rarely turned down Joseph, though I got the impression it'd been mutual. Joseph's partners had been fond of Henry too. In the end, I spilled the beans about that too, keeping it as PG-13 as possible. Not that I was too worried. This was a woman who loved Urban Dictionary and googled curses like cuntbagger and twatstain.

"Oh, my." She smirked a bit, as uncomfortable as she was intrigued. "I clearly missed out in my day."

"Nan…"

"Pish!" She waved a hand. "The choice is simple. One way or another, he's been hurt and grown cynical. It could be a combination of his dicksquat parents—" She sighed at my spluttered laugh. "Will you let me speak?"

"By all means." I pressed my lips together.

"—and old relationships that have changed his outlook on things," she continued. "It's not fair to you, Zach. It's quite the prick move of him to, whether he intends to or not, give you guilt by committing to you, then rejecting your promise to be true. I might even call him a right asshole for underestimating you."

I smiled. "But?"

"But you are not on equal ground in life, sugar." Her expression grew gentler. "If you want him to see you for who you are, then you have to accept him for who he is too, and life has knocked him around for quite a few years more than you're used to."

My shoulders slumped. I hadn't been fair to Henry.

"I wish he wouldn't underestimate you," she added disapprovingly. "You're one of the most loyal souls I know, and when you make a decision, you make it because you're certain. But perhaps three weeks isn't enough for him to see that."

"It mainly hurts 'cause it was okay for him to make those promises, but not me." I didn't want anyone to think I'd stormed out because we hadn't promised each other forevers. I only wanted to be given the same chance, and for however long we dated, we did so just the two of us. Instead, what he'd done, how he'd acted before I left it gutted me. It made me fear he wasn't as serious about us as I was.

"I understand." She nodded and sipped her tea. "Unfortunately, you two are a generation apart. Almost twenty years is nothing to scoff at, and everything you take on together will be viewed from two very different perspectives. Give each other time to adjust and synchronize."

Well, fuck. The embarrassment burned inside me, and I felt stupid. I'd acted like a child.

"Can I blame him for acting irrationally?" I asked, hopeful.

She snickered softly and picked up a pastry. "Can he blame you for his fears?"

Wait, what? "Why would he be afraid?"

"Oh, Zach, you sweet fool." She shook her head, her eyes alight with amusement. "Of course he's afraid. He's afraid of losing you. He thinks giving you the option of seeing others means the honesty isn't going to kick him in the family jewels. Poor boy is fooling himself something fierce."

I sat back, my mind spinning. Fears sucked balls. I didn't want Henry to be afraid. I wanted him to have me. Fuck, he already did, probably since the day I stepped foot in his bookstore.

CHAPTER 22

MEN SUCK!

"No, of course you can stay." I adjusted the phone, trapping it between my cheek and shoulder, and continued restocking the soda fridges in the back of the store. "As long as it's all right with Henry."

"He said I could fly up with him and Ty before school starts," Mattie replied.

I wasn't too surprised to hear this. Mattie had gone from staying an extra week to, well, this. He was on his third week, one week since I left.

Ty's grandparents were furious. Since they didn't know exactly where Ty was staying, they couldn't do much about it; though, according to Mattie, they sure tried. They called Henry and Ty every day with empty threats.

"Has he decided where he wants to go to school?" I asked.

Finished with Coke products, I continued with unpacking Pepsi.

"Um. I don't know." Mattie was withholding something. He sucked at it. "Why won't you and Henry talk?"

"Because we fucked up," I replied flatly. "Whenever we try, we end up fighting."

I'd called Henry after the Saturday I saw Nan. I'd apologized for acting like a kid, and I reluctantly offered to get Eagle back to LA somehow. We'd been civil, and he had politely told me I could keep Eagle for a little while if I wanted to. I did. Other than that...not much. Not even when I explained everything the way my grandmother had put it; he wouldn't budge an inch. He claimed it wasn't trust issues as much as it was his being older. He'd legit told me I had to trust his life experience on this one.

Just sayin', he was acing the mansplaining.

He knew me better than I did, in his opinion.

Idiot. Thinking about it got me pissy.

"I gotta get back to work," I said, irritated. It wasn't Mattie's fault, and I didn't wanna drag him into it. "Text Nan. She misses you."

"Okay..." There was something else he wanted to say, but I couldn't be assed to push him. I was tired. "Yeah, okay. Talk soon."

The following weekend, I needed to get out of town for a bit. I managed to get Meghan and Dominic to tag along, which made everything easier. I couldn't stand being alone lately. It left me with my thoughts, and that tended to go straight to hell.

Meghan had brought a friend from Seattle too. David.

"Adrian told me I needed to make more friends." Dominic spoke of his man as he gazed up at the hiking trail we were gonna take. Standing in a nearly empty parking lot at the edge of town made the mountain look bigger. "I kinda wanna sack his sorry ass right now."

I grinned, attaching the chest strap of my backpack. It was rough terrain all the way up to Coho Pass and would probably take us a few hours.

"He could've tagged along," I said.

"Like I'd let our girl wander in this wilderness." He scoffed and uncapped his water bottle. "You know how many mountains we got back in Philly and New York? *None.*"

"You sound like my father." Meghan chuckled as she pulled her dark hair into a ponytail. "You're what, twenty-five? Stop acting like a senior citizen."

Dominic grimaced and eyed the mountain again. "Aight, let's go."

I took the lead because I knew this trail like the back of my hand. It didn't take more than ten minutes before we might as well have been the last four people on earth. We lost cell service, the sounds of society were gone, and the forest was the only thing speaking. It'd rained last night, so the drippity-drop was constant and soothing.

That didn't mean my thoughts didn't stray to Henry and Malibu too fucking often.

Missing him was the worst.

Missing Martin hurt a lot too. We texted plenty, and rarely about Henry. Thankfully, they were slowly getting over the grand theft auto debacle, but there was nothing Martin could do about our situation. He kept saying he was trying, and it was Henry who wouldn't listen.

Goddammit, quit thinking about them.

I blew out a breath and listened in on the others.

David, like all of us, could hear Dominic was a New Yorker

by his accent, so David struck up a conversation with him about East Coast teams. Dominic didn't sound particularly interested, though he pretended fairly well. That meant it was Meghan's boots that were squishing through the mud to catch up.

"Hi, there." She sent me a cheeky smirk when I side-eyed her. "So when were you gonna tell me you're gay?"

"You saw my Instagram," I guessed. Last night, I'd been feeling extra sorry for myself because Mattie had posted beach pics that made me wanna be back in LA. To make myself feel better, I'd uploaded a new avatar, and I'd deliberately chosen my "Straight Outta The Closet" tee. "That was how," I went on. "It backfired when I came out to my family. They knew before me, so I figured why not just post a photo. Saves me the countless other coming-out convos ending with 'Oh, I already assumed.'" I rolled my eyes.

Meghan gigglesnorted and patted my arm. "Countless. Hon, you don't know that many people."

"Wow. Someone had an extra serving of scrambled bitch this morning." I hid my wry smirk and nudged my elbow to her arm.

"Hey, I was allowed one dig," she replied with a sniff. "You were my first boyfriend. You have to realize I went through the mandatory 'Holy shit, did I make him gay?' moment when I saw your photo."

Oh Christ. I couldn't *not* chuckle. She was too funny.

I draped an arm around her shoulders and kissed her temple. "I adored you, Meg. You know that, right? And trust me, I wasn't thinking about anyone else when we slept together."

She blushed, only to jab me in the gut. "Good. So...does this make you bi?"

I shrugged. "Maybe? I think I'm more drawn to men. I was just confused as fuck for a long time. Before then, plain oblivious."

That seemed to amuse her. "Well, now that you're not oblivious anymore, mind helping me out with David?"

I furrowed my brow and held a branch out of her way. "Watch your step. Help with what?"

She ducked her head and sidestepped a wet, mossy rock. "I can't figure out if he's gay or not. He seems interested in me, but he hasn't made a move, and his favorite bar in Seattle is popular among gay guys."

"Jesus," I muttered. "Have you considered asking him out?"

"Don't be ridiculous," she cackled.

Yeah, straight-up saying what you wanted didn't seem to be in fashion.

Around noon, the sun made an appearance, and sweat was trickling down my back. As we paused to chug water and catch our breaths, I yanked off my hoodie and tied it around my hips.

Dominic was holding up his phone, checking for service. He'd done well, though. I guessed his boyfriend had made sure he wore good shoes, and he hadn't complained about the trek once.

"There should be service when we reach the top," I told him. "There's an inn and some tourist stuff for hikers and campers."

"Cool." He nodded and wiped his forehead. "I have to go to a restaurant before the month is over. Youse interested in grabbing a burger after this?"

"Count me in," Meghan said.

"Me too." David drained his water bottle and stuffed it in his backpack.

"Sounds great." Anything to keep me from coming home to an empty apartment. "Why do you have to go to a restaurant?"

Dominic rolled his eyes. "Apparently, I think about money too much, so Adrian and I made a deal. I have to go out once a month, and he won't fret about me working security at a club in the Valley. He's a worrier."

I smiled. "That's sweet." I missed my fretter. In a half-assed attempt to help Meghan with David, I suggested one of the few gay-friendly places in town. "I hear they do great burgers at Eleven on Hemlock."

It was settled, and Meghan mouthed a subtle thank-you to me.

Crazy girl.

I could understand her confusion; David was definitely flirting with her, though he seemed kinda flirty with Dominic too. The latter was oblivious. I knew what that was like. Anyway, all the more reason for Meghan to simply ask the dude.

Dominic's loud "There's a fucking tramway?" when we reached Coho Pass kinda made it clear that we were taking the tramway back down. Meghan and I, who'd known each other the longest, took a few silly selfies at the highest point, and then Dominic could breathe out in relief. 'Cause we bought tickets to go down the easy way. I didn't think any of us minded. We'd hiked for hours, and we were ready to switch granola bars for burgers and onion rings.

Dominic was the first to enter the big car, and he walked to the back and widened his arms. "I fucking love this town." He probably wasn't talking about the spectacular view of our town, the forest, and the ocean. "I love tramways too." You could see all the way to the Chinook Islands now that the weather had cleared. "I can't believe I hiked all the way up here. Jesus fucking Christ."

I chuckled and set down my backpack on the floor, then leaned back against the railing that went around the whole thing. There were no places to sit, because the ride only took like fifteen minutes, give or take.

"I shoulda taken one'a those selfies." Dominic frowned. "I'm not sure Adrian will believe me."

I laughed. "Don't worry, we can vouch for you."

While he still had a signal, he called his boyfriend and told him to get his "sexy ass" to the restaurant and to bring Thea.

"Your daughter?" Meghan wondered.

Dominic nodded. "She's already declared she's gonna marry Zach."

That made me laugh again. His three-year-old—or maybe four, I wasn't sure—was a cute ballbuster. She didn't speak; she was autistic and nonverbal, I'd learned, but she signed fluently and communicated on a tablet. She'd taught me my first and only term so far in sign language, which was ice cream.

"She has good taste, then," David said with a smile.

Was that…? I mean. He could've just been polite. But yeah, definitely understood Meghan's confusion. Maybe he played for more than one team.

Meghan and I exchanged a look that basically said we had no clue.

On the way down the mountain, I chose four photos to upload to Instagram. Two of the scenery, one of Meghan and me where she was kissing my cheek, and one of just me making a funny face.

They were superbly edited by the time I had service again and I could upload them. At the same time, I received two messages, the first from Julian.

Hi, Zach. How is it being home again? Hope

you'll visit soon. Brooklyn asked if I can forward her your number. Talk later.

I replied right away.

Forward away, buddy. I hope her ill-timed inspiration won't get me into trouble. Everything is good here, but I look forward to when I can come back.

The other text was from Henry, and my stomach flipped automatically.

I miss you.

I swallowed and clutched my phone a little harder.

I miss you too.

Adrian was a lovely guy. Quite a bit older than Dominic, well-spoken and polite, yet he was casual and wore as many tattoos as a gangster. He taught history at Camas High, and Dominic called him Teach. Most of all, they were fucking adorable with their little girl. Thea bounced from one daddy's lap to the other's.

I'd officially become one of those people who couldn't look away from happy couples, even as it made me sick to my stomach. I wanted what they had so much. It was the Bakersfield moment all over again.

How would it look if Henry and I had a daughter?

How would it look if you two got your shit together, might be a better question.

I made a face to myself and took a long swig of my beer. For the record, I thought we'd look cute as hell with two girls. Maybe twins.

"You gonna finish that?" Dominic licked barbecue glaze off his thumb and jerked his chin at Adrian's leftover fries.

He was amused, Adrian, all while never losing the affection in his eyes. "Have at it." Next, Thea jumped over to him again. "Oh, you want to sit with me now, princess?"

She nodded and poked his bearded cheek.

Ugh. It wasn't getting any easier, dammit. Maybe I *had* fallen for Henry, 'cause if this wasn't what a broken heart felt like, I didn't wanna know.

The Saturday crowd was growing. It'd been pretty full already when we managed to claim two bar tables to push together. We were in a corner and the stools were comfy, so I had no complaints. Except for one thing. One might think a bar with a big pride flag hanging above the shelved bottles would know what a goddamn Purple Haze was.

Sensing that everyone was occupied with finishing their dinner and chatting, I brought out my phone again and sent Henry another text.

Is my age the only reason you won't trust me or even give me a chance to earn it?

There was nothing I could do about the former if he wouldn't accept the latter.

He responded, asking if he could call, so I excused myself and headed outside.

The town was in full preparations for the annual festival that was at the end of August. Back in the day, it'd been a harvest celebration. Now, the cobblestone streets were lined with booths for street vendors and marked-off lots for food trucks and beer tents. Local breweries and the apple contest dominated the festival, which lasted a whole week.

Ducking in between two buildings, I dialed Henry's cell and waited.

He picked up on the first ring. "Zachary?"

Fuck.

The sound of his rich voice was all this fucking day needed.

Emotions flared up, and I looked up at the sky and exhaled. Two strings of Edison lights were drawn between the buildings.

"Hey." I sniffled.

For a few seconds, all I heard was his steady breathing. He cleared his throat twice. "I...I don't quite know how to explain this. I trust that you believe it when you say you know what you want. This is just experience speaking, dear." Not this again. I couldn't fucking handle it. "What I don't understand is why this is a problem for us. I'm not telling you to find another partner. I'm merely pointing out that it's okay if you do."

"Is it?"

"Pardon?"

"Is it okay," I repeated, "if I find someone else while I'm with you? Because if that's the case, there's nothing to fight for. I'm not one of those polyamorous people you claim Martin is. I'm asking if it's personally all right with you."

That gave him pause, though I didn't know why. It was a yes or no answer.

When he finally spoke up, his voice was quiet and held traces of pain. "No...it would be excruciating, but if it meant I could keep you in my life long term—"

My groan cut him off, and I pinched the bridge of my nose. "Baby, don't you see how fucking crazy that is? *Please* look at this from my perspective. You're giving me an out—you're giving me permission to *hurt* you. And if you think it's okay for a partner to betray you, you probably can't think less of yourself."

"It wouldn't be a betrayal," he insisted.

"Fuck your fucking semantics!" I shouted.

I stiffened, my voice echoing between the buildings, and a handful of passersby peered into the alley. I cursed and slumped back against the brick wall.

I wanted to shake him.

How much more of this could I deal with? Nothing good

came from our conversations, and I didn't think we'd reach an understanding until we were face-to-face.

"I gotta get back to my friends," I muttered. "I need a drink. Or seven."

"Where are you?" he asked, guarded.

I narrowed my eyes at the ground. "I'm at a bar with some friends. We went hiking earlier."

"I see. I want you to enjoy yourself."

"Yeah, I got that. It's a gay-friendly place, so maybe I'll find someone to blow me. Have a good weekend, Henry." I disconnected the call and went back inside, feeling worse than ever.

It wasn't healthy. I could envision future "Where did you go?" and "Who were you with?" just pushing me down further. He made me feel like shit. And fuck it, the screen on my phone lit up one more time, and I sent him a message while I stumbled through the crowd.

__Just so you know, that makes me feel really awful. I'm not doing anything wrong, but every time you will ask me who I'm with and what I'm doing, I'll feel like a cheater when I'm anything but. You will always be suspicious.__

"You okay?" Meghan asked as I reached the table.

Had they raised the volume? The music seemed louder. It made sense that Dominic and Adrian were getting ready to leave. It was no longer a place for a kid.

I nodded absently in response to Meghan, scanning Henry's text.

__You're right. I'm very sorry for that, Zach. Please forgive me. I didn't consider that. In the future, I will give you space and not ask those questions.__

He didn't get it. I grinned, because if I didn't, I'd break

down in the middle of a bar. "I'm fine," I lied—splendidly. My throat felt thick, and my eyes watered. God, that bastard. One last message, and then I was done. No, really, I was turning off my phone.

You figured it out, Henry. Exactly what I want. Space. Well done.

CHAPTER 23

LET'S THROW SOMF PUNCHES

"Nan, you don't have to do that. I can do my own dishes."

"Why would you deprive me of feeling useful? Do you want to break my heart?"

"Wow," I mouthed, picking up Eagle. "One might think she's Catholic." Entering the bathroom, I stepped onto the scale with the kitty in my arms. "Let's see..."

Fuck yes, exercise worked. Who'da thunk it? Even the guy at the pet store was skeptical, stating very few cats would allow themselves to be leashed. Well, the haters could suck it. I'd been taking Eagle for a round of play in the park every morning for almost two weeks, and he'd lost a pound so far. All I had to do was find a somewhat dry spot—Eagle was *not* a fan of wet things—and then throw him a fake little mouse to wrestle.

"If you wanna make it to the first apple round, we should leave now," I told Nan, returning to the kitchen. Eagle headed straight for the little corner bed I'd made for him, and he lay down next to it.

Can't win 'em all.

"Almost ready." She finished the last plate, her hand trembling slightly when she put it in the rack. "Can you check my purse for the voting card, please? We got them with the paper. It's so we can pick our favorites and vote for those who participate. Between you and me, the Nolan family should win. I just adore Chloe's pies."

Her purse was in the hallway, and the mentioned voting card was sticking out. I folded it so it wouldn't fall out. "Yup, it's right here."

I returned to see her dry her hands and fix her hair.

"Excellent. Must we take the chair, though?"

"We must." I nodded. She didn't need one—yet—at the home or when she went on supershort trips to the store. For a walk on the opening day of the festival, though? Ohfuckingyes.

It waited for us in the hallway, and she made a show of how much she detested it. To be honest, I wouldn't mind trying it for a day. The festival brought in people from all over, and they tended to make room for the elderly.

We took the elevator down, and I helped her into the truck. Checking the time, I saw we had to hurry. Finding parking this week wouldn't be easy.

"Are you excited to see Mattie tomorrow?" Nan asked as she was rummaging through her purse. "I *know* I put my voting card in here. Did you see it, sugar? They're new for this year. They sent them with the paper the other week, this little ballot where we can vote for the contestants."

My head snapped sideways, and I frowned at her. "It's..." Holy shit. "Yeah, it's right there." I dug a hand into the purse and pulled out the folded card.

As I backed out and began driving toward the Valley, I pushed down the sinking feeling and made a mental note to mention this to the nurses. She hadn't had any troubles with her memory before.

It made me queasy.

I couldn't bring myself to say anything to Nan, though. She wore a smile all the way to the Cedar Valley, and she was excited about our outing.

"New color lipstick?" I asked.

If there was one thing I'd learned from the ladies at the home, it was that they loved to be noticed. Not all of them had kids and grandkids who visited.

"I've worn it once or twice." She nodded and checked her pocket mirror. "It's quite lovely. Beth's granddaughter sells them."

"Cool."

Perk when driving Nan was I could park in a handicapped spot, meaning it didn't take us too long to find parking.

"Don't think I didn't notice you dodging my question about Mattie, sugar."

And then sometimes, she was sharp as a tack. I huffed, opening the tailgate to get her chair. Okay, I could be honest about my brother; his travel companions, not so much.

"It'll be good having him home." I rolled the chair to her side and helped her into it.

"Henry and Tyler are flying up too, yes?"

I sighed. "That's what I hear. You know I haven't talked to him since the bar."

He'd sent a handful of texts. I hadn't responded, and it wasn't to be a dick or anything, but every fucking call ended in disaster. What was the point?

"I do look forward to meeting him." She sniffed and clutched her purse in her lap.

"Oh God, why would you meet him?" I was half horrified at the thought.

Between the backstreet where we'd parked and Hemlock Avenue where the celebrations started, the atmosphere went from quiet and nice to hectic and crowded. The festival took up several streets, two squares, and part of a park, and it was a great place to see if a relationship could last. Children screamed, siblings argued, parents cursed broken condoms, teenagers tested their fake IDs.

The noise was background music to Nan's explaining on why she simply had to meet the man I'd supposedly lost my heart to. I probably had.

I got a message as we got to the street where they had all the tables with people joining the apple contest. It wasn't from a number in my contact list, so I checked it out.

Hello, Zach. This is David, Meghan's friend. I was wondering if you would mind if I asked her out? She's been talking so much about you, and I know you have history. I don't want to step on any toes.

That one drew a genuine grin from me. There were good guys left out there. Completely unnecessary to reach out, but appreciated. I told him to go for it and that I was happy for them. Thinking back, that probably gave Meghan away, but whatever.

"There's Chloe's table, sugar. Oh good, they're doing both pies and cider."

All right, time to test all things apple. Pies, preserves, cake, freaking *chutney*... The man who did the chutney was hot, though. I forced a smile, tasting the weird creation that many others seemed to love. Nan blushed when he winked at her. Adam was his name, co-owner of a steakhouse in the area, according to the business cards they were giving out.

"You certainly deserve the runner-up, dear," Nan decided.

"Second place?" Ruggedly hot Adam placed a hand on his heart and pretended to be wounded. Rugged...almost like Henry.

"I simply cannot get enough of Chloe Nolan's apple pie," she admitted.

Adam flashed a grin. "Then I won't hold it against you. It's her cider I'm using in my recipe."

Okay, enough with the chitchat. The sun was beating down pretty hard for Washington, even in August, and every hot guy only made me think of Henry.

"You ready to cast your votes, Nan?" I asked.

"I believe I am," she said with a firm nod.

Awesome.

If one could be hungover on festival food, that was me the morning after.

I skipped breakfast and headed to work, where I had the first shift. Pammie would be here when it was time for me to pick up my brother.

He'd told me not to go all the way to Seattle since they were renting a car. I knew that meant I would be forced to face Henry today, and every time I thought about it, my gut did a somersault. I was *nervous*, and it bothered me. It was supposed to be a sweet-then-sexy reunion. Instead, we were seeing each other as...exes?

Walking over to the magazines, I grabbed an issue of *Northern Living* to waste a couple hours. During the festival, my little corner store was quiet. And no one was happier about it than me.

Around noon, two men entered the store, and I nodded politely, then went back to an article on hiking in the peninsula. I'd gone a few times. They had some good climbing near Hoodsport.

The guys were only here for a couple sodas, and I rang up their purchase and—

"You one of those fags?"

I shot my stare at them, specifically the bald dude who was nodding at my T-shirt. "Wanna See My Rainbow?" was printed across my chest, silver on black, and it was the first and only item of clothing I'd bought since I got home.

I raised my gaze again. I had two choices. Brush it off and hope for the best, or give him the retort my anger demanded and...hope for the best.

"Are you one of those dim-witted morons?" I asked slowly. My fists clenched and unclenched.

Give me a reason.

Back down, the voice of reason told me. There were two of them; I was alone. They were bigger too. Not taller, just bulkier. I also had more to lose.

My pulse skyrocketed as Baldy glared. "The fuck did you call me?"

"I didn't. I asked a fucking question." My jaw tensed. *Back the fuck down, idiot. They can ruin the store. They can break your face.* Except, I *couldn't* back down. "Do you want me to repeat it slower so you understand?" What was *wrong* with me?

Now they both wore matching death stares.

"Disgusting little cocksucker," he spat out and reached over the counter to fist my shirt. I flew forward faster than I could react, fear immobilizing me. Then pain exploded across the left side of my face as his fist connected with my cheek.

I was catapulted backward just as quickly, and my brain

slowed down further. I couldn't think past the pain. Everything hurt, and I waited. I fucking waited, and then, finally, the rage unfurled in me. My eyes shot open right before I jumped over the counter and rammed into the bald bitch. I kneed him in the gut and clocked him hard in the jaw.

"Fucker!" he yelled. "Get him off me!"

"What, you don't wanna dance with me, you ugly piece of shit?" I growled. I got in another punch that split his eyebrow.

My fun ended by being yanked back and pushed to the floor. The stand closest to the register fell over me, covering me in clearance items. Fruit, candy bars, snack packs. I groaned at the pain in my spine, then more pain. *Oh God.* It blinded me. The other guy kicked me in the stomach and hurled unoriginal insults about taking it up the ass. I couldn't focus on the actual words.

"Leave him before someone shows up," Baldy grunted. "He ain't worth it."

I coughed, receiving a final blow.

A croaked moan escaped me, and I tasted blood on my tongue.

The sound of the doorbell let me know I was alone.

"Fuck," I coughed.

I didn't know how many minutes passed while I lay there trying to regain my breathing. Eventually, I crawled over to lock the door, and I collapsed right there. Tears sprung to my eyes, though it wasn't because of the pain. Maybe it was shock, or that I was processing. With a grunt, I hauled myself up to sit, and that was a bad idea. My ribs shot a fireball of agony through me, sharp as hell.

"Assholes," I whispered raggedly. I hoped they'd smiled for the cameras. Was there a single store in this country that didn't have surveillance?

"Some good news, Mr. Coleman. No fractures," Doc announced, entering my room with a chart. He faltered upon seeing the cop next to me. "Apologies, Officer." He didn't leave, though. He continued to my bed, studying my chart.

But yeah, good news. Broken bones would've been worse.

Pammie was on the other side of the bed, looking increasingly annoyed with the police officer.

"He's answered all your questions," she said. "If you'll let me take you to the store, I can hand over the footage."

It hurt to talk at the moment, so I patted her hand. The woman could've been my mother, and sometimes she acted like it. But I didn't want her to get too stressed out over this. She already had four kids who drove her bonkers.

"I'll be fine," I mumbled and touched my lip. It was swollen but not split. The only spot that needed stitches was my left eyebrow. It looked worse than it was, with the dried blood. I'd also bit my tongue, which irritated me.

"It's okay, we're done here," the cop said. "You shouldn't have riled them up, kiddo."

"Do you tell that to girls with short skirts too?" I shot back. "Huh? Are they asking for it?" I spoke through the dull pain in my mouth. "Trust me, I know it would've been smarter to keep my mouth shut, but *damn* if I'm gonna stand by and not defend myself while others can do whatever the fuck they want."

The cop gave me a look of warning, and I got it. Not my wisest move to get cocky with a police officer. However, he hopefully acknowledged I was right, 'cause he kept his trap closed, other than wishing me a speedy recovery.

After he left, I released a heavy breath and let Pammie adjust the pillow behind my back.

"Are you sure you'll be okay?" she asked.

I nodded. "Go with him, hon. Then go home." We were keeping the store closed until tomorrow. "Mattie will see my message soon."

"Boy, you..." She sighed. "I damn near had a heart attack when I found you."

"I'm sorry," I offered.

She looked like she wanted to smack me for that one.

She was next to leave, after a whole lot more fussing and promises to check in. I'd have to thank her for giving a crap later. Right now, I was only interested in painkillers and going home.

Doc smiled patiently "How are you feeling?"

"Like two bigots used me as a punching bag. Can I have all the drugs in the world for my headache?" It was getting so bad that I had to squint. The light was too harsh, and there was throbbing at the back of my skull.

"Very soon, I assure you." He tapped the clipboard. "Like I said, no fractures—this is good news. You do have a concussion, however." He joined me at my side, and then I had one of those tiny flashlights pointed in my eyes. "You said there was no nausea? No vomiting or numbness?"

"None." I'd been through this already. "Massive headache, soreness, and I guess light sensitivity. Is that a thing? It hurts to look at the lamp."

He nodded. "That's normal. You need to rest plenty, and I advise you to leave the TV and phone alone. It lets you recover easier." He paused, carefully touching the back of my head. He hummed to himself. "Little to no swelling. I want you to monitor your situation carefully. If you do feel worse—nausea, slurred speech, difficulty focusing—I want you to come back in for an MRI."

Yeah, costly stuff. No thanks.

In the end, I was given mild pain relief for my headache and ribs. Instructions to rest for a few days, and a bill that would give me another headache when I could be bothered to care.

He was reluctant to let me go home alone, but I promised I wasn't driving. I lived two blocks away, so I'd be in bed within ten minutes. Plus another five if I had the energy to shower.

I told him I wouldn't be alone for long; my brother was almost home, and yada yada, then I was on my way. Ribs aching and bandaged, eyebrow stitched up, mouth banged up a bit, and this motherfucker of all headaches.

"Quit it," I grumbled, half asleep. I assumed it was Mattie who was wiping a wet towel gently over my face. It rasped over my five-o'clock shadow.

His quiet voice confirmed it two seconds before I smelled his body spray. What was it with teenagers and Axe?

"Dude, you're freaking me out. I talked to Pammie. She told me everything. I'm sorry I didn't get your message—"

"Shhh, *please*." I kept my breathing steady for fear any fast movement would set off my headache again. "I'm okay," I whispered. "Tired. Glad to have you home. Lemme sleep."

"Okay." His voice came out thicker, and it was an automatic reaction to open my eyes and make sure he was all right. Seeing his wobbly little smile and glassy eyes was its own gut punch.

"I'm really okay." I grabbed his hand and squeezed it a bit. "Good to see you." I managed a weak smile.

"You too." He'd gotten more color. His hair was a shade lighter from the sun. He looked great. "I'm sorry this happened to you."

Yeah. I guess it was a rite of passage I hadn't experienced yet. The hatred...all because of who I was... I racked my wounded brain, searching for the hurt. Maybe it was there somewhere, buried under the shit pile of anger.

"Um." Mattie looked over his shoulder, toward my door. "You have visitors, but I can tell them to wait if you want."

Ty and Henry. Hell, they were here? In our apartment? I was suddenly glad I hadn't crashed on the couch earlier. I'd certainly considered it. My bedroom felt safer; I was away from the "This is how they live?"

I winced internally. Ty had been here countless times, and Henry wasn't one to judge. Now wasn't the time to get insecure.

Henry's out there.

"Can you send in Henry and some water?"

He nodded quickly and stood up. "Be right back."

I released a shaky breath and stared up at the dark ceiling. Only the lamp on my nightstand was lit, casting a low glow and shadows everywhere.

At the sound of the door opening once more, my gaze fell, and so the gut punches kept coming. Seeing Henry for the first time in weeks all but tore me apart. Had I ever seen something so beautiful? It was almost haunting. Despite the dress pants and button-down that fit him perfectly, everything was wrong, yet so right. He'd lost a couple pounds. He was unhappier than I'd ever seen, and his scruff had reached beard status.

He walked in, steps measured and almost cautious.

I blinked as he became blurry for me, and I could sense it was only the beginning. My throat closed up, and my eyes burned.

Henry set the glass on my nightstand, then sat down on the edge of my bed. There were no words. Not a single one. Maybe neither of us knew what to say. Although, he knew what to do—thank fuck. He came closer and closer until his forehead carefully touched mine, his warm fingers gingerly brushing my unharmed cheek.

It broke the levees for me. I blinked, this time causing tears to fall down.

He sucked in a quiet breath and shook his head minutely. I curled my fingers into his shirt, and my breathing became ragged. I sniffled and hurt and trembled. I'd missed him. His nose grazed my cheek, his lips ghosting closer to where I needed them. Every touch was so careful yet laced with an urgency that mirrored what I felt.

He kissed me tenderly, avoiding the corner that hurt the most. I defied my pain and applied pressure; I just needed a taste. Just a little. I cupped the back of his neck and teased his parted lips with my tongue, and he let out a soft groan. It resembled the one he'd made the first time we kissed. The defeat—I'd never forget it.

"I was so worried." His whisper broke at the end. "God—" He shuddered and dared one kiss that gave me all the comfort and passion and love. It wasn't in my head. It couldn't be. "We only had Mattie's text message to go on," he murmured in between featherlight kisses. "'Call me,' it said. 'Call me ASAP. At the hospital.' And then you wouldn't fucking answer the phone." When his gaze met mine, I brushed a thumb under his eye. "I think I broke every law to get up here while your brother got in touch with your grandmother."

I hadn't even thought of her. I didn't wanna worry her since I would be fine.

"I'll be okay in a few days." I wiped my cheek. "Concussion and some bruises."

"Darling..." He sighed quietly and closed his eyes, our foreheads touching again. The contact was good—I craved it. "I fear I won't be able to let you out of my sight for a while."

I'd smile if it didn't hurt too much. "I can live with that."

"That's good, because I know I don't deserve it." With a final kiss, he straightened, robbing me of his warmth, and held the glass of water out to me. "Tyler gave me the business yesterday, and—" He shook his head quickly. "We can talk later. You need to rest. Do you have any medication I can give you? Have you eaten?"

My fretter was here.

CHAPTER 24

WE ARE SO FUCKING ADORABLE

Come morning, I'd gotten another seven hours of sleep, and I felt marginally better. The pain around my mouth had lessened significantly, and my ribs ached dully, which was far better than the sharp bolts whenever I moved.

"Hey." Mattie came into my room with breakfast. "Henry went out and bought some stuff."

"Thanks." I winced and sat up against the headboard. I was glad I didn't know what I looked like. The idea of taking a shower after the hospital had proved to be way too optimistic, so that was on the list for today. I needed to take a leak too.

Mattie set the bag on the nightstand before digging up breakfast sandwiches, containers of yogurt, tea, and thin pancakes. I loved those. Henry knew it too. He also knew I liked my OJ.

"No juice?"

"Um." He looked into the bag, then shook his head as if he remembered something. "He said something about—like, if you had cuts around your mouth? It could sting or whatever. I told him you drink tea sometimes, so he got that."

Tea was for when I was sick. Did this count? Either way, Henry still managed to make me all sappy when he was so considerate. Who the hell would think of that juice thing otherwise?

"This is great." I yawned and checked the time on my alarm clock. "I think I wanna shower first."

"All right. Need any help standing up?"

I shook my head. "Get Henry for me?"

He'd insisted on staying the night on the couch while Ty had driven over to the inn where they'd booked a room. I bet Henry regretted staying now. The couch was fucking awesome, but it wasn't big.

"Oh. He's running errands, but he told me to say he'd be back before lunch."

Ah. Well, all right, then. I wasn't gonna pout.

"Zach?"

I made a sleepy noise and moved closer to the hand that was playing in my hair. *Henry.* He'd replaced my pillow with his chest, and I drew my fingers through his sparse chest hair.

"If this is a dream, I don't wanna wake up," I mumbled.

I felt his chuckle rather than heard it.

It wasn't a laughing matter, dammit. In my dreams, we were together, said I love you every day, demanded good grades of the teenagers, and had two girls. I was leaning toward twins more and more, to be honest.

Reality looked a lot different.

Stretching out carefully, I yawned and looked up at Henry.

"I didn't mean to fall asleep again. Thanks for bringing breakfast."

He touched my cheek gently, concern etched across his features. "You can sleep again. I only thought you might like some pain relief and something to eat."

I *was* awfully sore. I pushed myself up to sit and grunted under my breath. Realizing how hungry I was made me look at the time, and I was surprised I'd slept so long. It was already three in the afternoon.

Henry got out of bed and pulled on a T-shirt. He was back to casual clothes—shit, it was the first time I'd seen him in jeans.

"Did you nap with me?" I cocked my head.

"I may have." He grew a little guarded, ready to be defensive. "I needed to be near you."

My mouth twisted up. "And you didn't take advantage?"

That loosened him up, and he smiled ruefully. "Don't think it didn't enter my mind, but no. I've behaved like a complete tool. I felt that sharing your bed was pushing it enough."

I was interested in hearing more about how he'd behaved like a tool—after I'd gone to the bathroom and taken painkillers.

"I'll be back soon." Henry leaned over the bed and kissed my forehead. "Does soup from Panera sound good?"

Oh God, yes. Perfect comfort food when I was all pitiful and hurt. "Broccoli cheddar, please. Um, in one of those bread bowls?"

"Naturally." He quirked a grin and said he'd bring back some other treats too.

While he was gone, I took another shower, a cold one. I was flushed with the wrong kind of heat and figured it was my body working to recover. The cut across my eyebrow looked cleaner, and the swelling around my mouth was gone. Ribs and head continued to hurt, and I knew that could take a few days.

After my shower, I stepped out and wrapped a towel around

my hips. I inspected my face in the mirror as I shaved, and though there wasn't any swelling, I had blotchy little bruises here and there. Under my eye and at the corner of my mouth, there were two angry marks that had darkened overnight.

Mattie had to be home. There was music coming from his room, so I hollered out for him as I returned to my own room.

He poked his head out. "Something wrong?"

I paused in my doorway. "Can you fill me in on what I've missed?"

"Yeah, sure." He shut off the music and followed me. "Nan wants to see you as soon as you're up for it. I told her you were feeling better."

"I appreciate it." I stepped into a pair of sweatpants and thought fuck it to the rest. I wanted to stay in bed. That's where I ended up after I'd dropped the towel in the laundry basket. "Any news about the Bennington drama? Have they gone to see the 'rents yet?"

He shook his head and sat down on the foot of the bed. "They don't even know Ty's back in town. Henry wanted to wait until you got better. Plus, they've been doing other stuff. They went to Ty's parents' grave yesterday."

There was a pinch of relief there. It could've been one of those things Ty needed. If his grandparents hadn't given him enough time to heal after Thorne and Shelly had died, maybe he had to go through a new grieving process.

"That's good." I nodded, reaching for the painkillers on the nightstand. "How's he doing otherwise?"

"Better." Mattie smiled. His own relief was clear as day. "He slips a lot—he gets defensive and hostile, but he catches himself. Henry's helping him change the coping mechanism or whatever he called it."

"I'm glad to hear it."

"Oh, and Pammie gave the security footage to the police."

"Okay, good." I would have to call her later.

I didn't think much would come of it. The case was no doubt low priority, even if not a whole lot happened in this town. Now I knew I'd done what I could, though.

Mattie was hesitating about something. Without his cap on to twist back and forth, he scratched the spot below his ear and chewed on his lip.

"Spit it out," I chuckled.

He huffed, frustrated. "Did you have to wear that shirt? I know how it sounds, and I don't want you to adjust to make others comfortable, but I don't wanna find you beaten up somewhere either."

I should've anticipated this. It was something I had to think about. Part of me felt like I had to shout louder only because I now happened to belong to a...what, minority? Christ, I was a white man. I belonged to the most privileged group that existed, and nothing short of a neon sign—or graphic tee—would change that to the outside world.

The other part of me wanted to live my life in peace. Standing out had never been my thing. Then, after learning more and more how people were affected... Henry had been ostracized by his own family. Joseph had been beaten half to death by his father. The stories of abuse and suicide I'd read from Second Family's website were what nightmares were made of.

"That's a no," Mattie sighed heavily.

"I'll be smarter next time," I conceded. "My temper got the best of me yesterday."

"But you'll wear those tees," he grumbled.

Yes, I would. Maybe they were silly; for me, they were fun. But when push came to shove... "I'll take a hundred beatings if just one kid passes me on the street, sees the shirt I'm wearing, and finds comfort in the fact that he's not alone."

He nodded jerkily and swallowed hard. "I get it, bro. You know I do." I did. He was worried, and that was okay. "Can I get one that says 'I'm not gay, but my brother is'?"

I snorted a laugh and kicked his knee with my foot. "Only if it's pink and there's a unicorn on it."

He smirked.

There was a quiet knock-knock on the doorframe that let us know Henry was back. Judging by his compassionate expression, he'd heard plenty too.

"Soup for the wounded." He walked in and held up two bags. "One burger and fries for the brother of the wounded too."

"Aw, yeah. You're awesome." Mattie jumped up and accepted the bag from Jack in the Box.

I lifted a brow. My brother was obsessed with Jack in the Box burgers. Henry had taken the time to get to know him, hadn't he?

Mattie said he was gonna eat in his room, and I reminded him to take out the trash before he disappeared. Then I accepted a huge bread bowl filled with broccoli cheddar soup, the heavenly smell making my stomach growl.

Henry had picked a salad for himself. Fucking *salad*.

"You're one of the most extraordinary young souls I've met, Zachary."

The spoon with dribbling soup got stuck midair, and I looked over at Henry in confusion.

He smiled faintly and mixed his salad absently with his fork. "I'm not sure how to explain myself. It's a feeling. It's your energy. You're the small-town, everyday hero who inspires and protects. You make people smile all around you. It's…"

"Are you okay?" I reached over and felt his forehead.

"Smartass," he sighed, then chuckled once and shook his head again.

Humor had been the easiest way to respond. I didn't have

anything else for this moment. What he said made me nervous, because I didn't know where he was heading, and because I didn't see myself that way. It seemed like big shoes to fill.

"You make me want to be a better person." He gave my knee a squeeze.

I felt the same about him. More than that, he made me see possibilities. I had hopes and dreams that hadn't existed before him. Before my time in LA.

"If you don't give us an honest shot, I don't know what I'll do, Henry."

Couldn't he fucking see how good we were together?

He swallowed and nodded once, giving up the notion of food. He set the container on the other bedside table. "I owe you so many apologies I've lost count," he murmured. "What Martin's been trying to tell me for weeks was more or less slapped in my face by Tyler the other day. He was quite the asshole about it."

"Good. What did he say?" Did I dare hope?

"He may have called me a blind bastard and pointed out I was pushing you away the exact way he pushed me away." He shifted, visibly uncomfortable, and cleared his throat. "I was taking the safe option."

Well, look at that. I'd have to buy Ty flowers. Or a video game with bloodshed and gore.

"I'm a hypocrite," he admitted bluntly. "I was telling him how that wasn't a way to live his life, protecting himself for an end goal that was only okay at best, and there I was, doing the very same thing."

"Don't you just hate it when kids get smart?" I asked around a mouthful of soup.

The situation was serious, but I was too giddy to put my severe face on. He finally *got* it. And Ty had put it into words not even I had considered.

Henry ignored my remark, eyes flashing with apprehension. "Will you give me a chance to earn your forgiveness?"

I couldn't stick to the funny anymore. Not when he looked at me that way. Setting down my delicious soup, I winced at the pain in my ribs and scooted closer to Henry.

"Will you give me the chance to earn your trust?" Ending up on my knees, I bent over a bit and brushed our noses together. "You'll want me for yourself?"

"Yes," he whispered. "I've only ever wanted you for myself, Zachary."

"But now, we'll make those boundaries." I kissed him lightly. "Yeah? You and me, no one else."

He closed his eyes and inhaled deeply through his nose. "You'll be all mine."

"Ditto." My smile broke free, and I kissed him harder.

"Jesus, baby." He met the kiss with passion and stroked the back of my neck. "It's a good thing I'm sitting down. This level of hope can bowl a man over."

"I want you to be hopeful," I murmured. "I'm hopeful as fuck. For one, your cat is kinda ours now." I grinned at his cute huff. "Secondly, now I won't feel as alone in my dreams for the future."

His expression softened, and he took himself another kiss. "Our future."

"Ours." My ass landed on the mattress again, and I pressed my lips to his shoulder before reclaiming my soup.

"Speaking of Eagle, has he lost weight?" Henry asked. "He deemed me worthy of a cuddle earlier, and he feels lighter."

"*Yes.* You're welcome. Being kidnapped suits him."

He laughed softly and moved to sit closer. "I almost didn't believe Martin when he told me you'd barged in and taken him."

"I was so mad." I shook my head, remembering. "I hit my

lowest point when the truck overheated outside Bakersfield and I had to call a mechanic. So I sat there outside a garage with a stolen cat and two crappy tacos, feeling sorry for myself while the man working on my truck was visited by his husband and daughter who were bringing him lunch. I even may have cried. Partly because I forgot the lunch you'd packed for me, partly because we would've looked damn good with a family."

Henry's gaze quickly met mine, and he searched my eyes, and I hid nothing. I did find myself holding my breath, though.

Give him more. Make it real for him.

"This isn't about exploring for me anymore. I'm not sure it ever was with you." I bumped his shoulder with my own. "I keep seeing these girls everywhere—first, the dudes in Bakersfield with their daughter, most recently, a buddy of mine. Dominic. He's thinking about proposing to his boyfriend, and they have a girl together. And that's the shit flying through my head, Henry. It's not about discovering a new club or no strings attached. Whatever I explore, I wanna do it with you by my side."

Henry dropped his forehead to my temple, and he cupped my jaw, tilting my head toward his. "Girls," he echoed with a small smile.

"Maybe twins."

His smile softened. "You don't think I'm too old to change diapers?"

"No." I gave his bottom lip a little bite. "And no one's said they have to be infants. Isn't there a catalogue in the baby store where you pick out your kids?"

He chuckled at my joke and stroked my cheek, then kissed me.

Spending the rest of the afternoon making out with Henry was totally worth a ruined bread bowl that got too soggy by the time I came up for air.

CHAPTER 25

MY ASS ISN'T HURTING

The headache faded after another two days, and that was when Henry decided we should all go to dinner together. As a family. I'd told him he didn't have to prove anything to me, but he was adamant, and we were going to a place that made these really awesome seafood platters, so I couldn't refuse.

"I'm a little wounded that Martin hasn't checked in on me," I admitted and buckled up. Mattie and Ty got in the back, and Henry took the wheel of his SUV rental. "The photo I posted today of Eagle and me even shows my bruises, and Martin liked the pic. He's *seen* my severe condition, and not a word."

"Uh." Oh, goodie, Ty was gonna make a smartass remark. "Isn't it funny how everything was fine when it wasn't, and now that he's almost healed, he's dying?"

Yeah, he'd grown a funny bone lately. Truth be told, it was awesome to see him being more of a regular teenager. He'd let go of a huge weight that'd kept him depressed and angry.

I could tell he was still testing the waters. Sometimes, he

looked to Henry and Mattie for their reactions, and he had slipped once or twice since they flew up here. Yesterday, he said something crass about girls, so Henry had cleared his throat and cocked a brow, to which Ty had cursed. The flash of contrition had followed, as had Henry's reminder that it was going to take time.

It was a piece of advice I planned on using against Henry if he found himself struggling too. Because I wasn't expecting our issues to go away overnight. It would take time before he could relax fully and allow himself to believe I was all in.

Leaning back in my seat, I caught a glimpse of my brother in the side-view mirror. I cocked my head. Didn't he look weirdly nervous? If anyone had a reason to be nervous, it was me. I'd postponed seeing Nan until my bruises were fading, and she was getting snippy with me on the phone. It was a whole lot of "Zachary" and no "sugar."

"What's up with you, Mattie?" I asked.

He searched me out, eventually seeing where I'd spotted him.

"Maybe I don't feel like smiling all the time," he defended.

My brows went up. "All right. And maybe you're full of it."

"He and Tyler have news to share when we get to the restaurant." Henry patted my leg and hit the interstate that went between Camas and Downtown. "It's nothing bad, I promise."

Then why did it look that way on my brother's face?

We drove through the forest in silence, except for Henry who was humming along to the song on the radio.

Martin would've liked Downtown. It was the face of Camassia, with all its Victorian homes in pastel colors, the marina, boardwalk, and *artisanal* shops. Those who lived here wanted to preserve the town's idyllic feel and protested whenever a larger corporation checked out property. But maybe I was wrong. At some point, I'd thought Martin had liked *me*.

It was possible I was a bit disgruntled.

Henry found parking in the marina as the sun was starting to set, and the four of us aimed for the fish camp near the start of the boardwalk. I'd taken Mattie here a few times when we had something to celebrate and we could afford it. The place wasn't particularly fancy, but the seafood platters weren't free. I liked it here, and the guy who owned it was cool.

"Do you want to sit inside or out?" Henry asked. "It might be too chilly out here."

Three guys from northern Washington gave him matching stares.

"You've been in LA too long," Ty chuckled.

"Well, then." Henry smiled ruefully and turned to the hostess. "Table for four, please. Outside."

Most of us were in jeans and tees. Not Henry, though. The jeans were there; so was the knitted, formfitting pullover.

Luckily for Henry, we were seated near a heater, and I grinned as he snagged the chair that was closest. But not before he'd pulled out a chair for me, ever the gentleman.

Orders were placed, mindless chitchat was covered, and our drinks arrived before I'd had it. Yes, yes, it was great that Henry was enjoying being back in his childhood town—we could talk about that later.

"Tell me the news," I said.

Mattie and Ty exchanged a glance, and Henry cleared his throat and straightened in his seat.

"I suppose I should start," he said. The others didn't argue. "Tyler has chosen to do his senior year here in Camassia. Mattie too, of course. So I got in touch with a Realtor the day after we arrived. We're officially looking for a house in Westslope." As he'd once dreamed of as a kid. I was sure the forest district with all its hermits and woodsy people had a ranch or something in his price range.

"Isn't this fucking awesome?" I asked. Happiness flared up within, though it battled with the suspicion of something else going on.

"I hope you think so." He grabbed my hand under the table and wove our fingers together. "Boys, you're up."

Ty was less concerned. If anything, he looked excited. "I'm going to college in LA."

"Yeah, me too." Mattie was waiting for my reaction. "I guess I changed my mind."

"No shit?" I smiled, confused. Still waiting for the bad news. "Okay...that's great. You have good grades, and we have your college fund if you don't get a full ride."

Henry gave that last part a dismissive wave. I knew what *that* implied, and we'd probably have a solid fight about it in the future. Followed by awesome sex. The latter was something I missed a fuckload, pun intended. Then I met a kinky bastard who became Virgin Mary while my ribs hurt.

"We're hoping that you will move with us." Henry tightened his hold on my hand. "They may very well change their minds, but as it is now, they don't want to stay here after graduation."

Uh. I furrowed my brow at Mattie. "You wanna leave permanently?"

He shifted uncomfortably in his seat. "I'd come up and visit Nan a lot."

A lot. Was he made of money all of a sudden?

"Um, okay." My mind spun, and I guess I didn't see the rush. In four college years, a whole lot could happen. "Why is this a discussion now?"

"Because it's a factor when we start looking for a new house in LA," Henry reasoned patiently. "These past few days, I've realized how much I've missed living here. At the same time, I love my life back home."

"So, we're gonna do both," Ty finished and took a gulp of his soda.

I kept my gaze on Henry. Was that it? Were we somehow going to end up in both places?

"What do you think?" Henry wondered carefully. "Would you consider living here in, say, the summers, and spend the rest of the year in LA? Actually—"

"I kinda like the fall here," Mattie said. "When I'm out of school, anyway."

"I was just going to say." Henry nodded. "Summer and fall."

The fuckers had been conspiring against me! This wasn't a conversation you just thought of in ten minutes. While the three of them had spent time together in LA, they'd begun forming plans and shit.

"What if I don't want it?" I had to know.

"Well, we won't have to buy a house," Henry replied. "A condo would suffice if it's mainly the boys staying there."

Nan was my biggest concern. There was no way we could move her back and forth, and she had her life here.

"I gotta think about this." I ran a hand through my hair, struggling to get a grasp on everything. "Henry, you know I love LA. Staying in both places seems almost too good to be true, and I do wanna spend more time there. But—" This was a huge but. "And I'm not stupid," I interjected first. "I see where this is going. You can afford everything, and you'll wanna give me all this—on and on it goes. But I can't do that. I can be ridiculously hooked on you and want everything you've mentioned for our future, but you gotta let me catch up at least a little. I need to make something of myself."

"I understand, dear." He nodded slowly, processing.

"We have a whole year here right now," Mattie pointed out.

"My fuckawesome tan is gonna be a distant memory before I get to see LA again."

True. I could work with a year. It was a start, anyway.

"There's also Nan," I said. "For as long as she lives, I won't make another city my primary home. We can visit whenever Henry manages to convince me to pay for the tickets. Otherwise, this is home." As I looked at the guys, I suddenly felt bad. I didn't wanna be the buzzkill, especially when everything Henry was suggesting was things I longed for. "I'm sorry," I sighed. "I want it, I just… Fuck, I don't even know what I wanna do for work. I keep saying I want more, but I have no clue what."

Mattie was about to respond, only our food arrived before he could. It put the conversation on hold while our table filled with crab legs, shrimp, oysters, calamari, and sides that were all things fried.

"Good thing is we don't have to get rid of the store," he said as we dug in. "If you find something else, you can hire more people to take shifts with Pammie."

I nodded, squeezing some lemon over my shrimp. "Bottom line, I'm not gonna let my pride stand in the way, but I wanna level up a bit before we start talking houses in LA. Does that make sense?"

Ty and Mattie nodded.

Henry didn't. "One problem. I fully understand your side here. That said, one year to find the right house where we'll be interested in living is already putting us on a tight schedule."

"You're just no help at all," I muttered. To show I was kidding, I leaned over and smacked a kiss to his cheek. "Find the damn house. I'll suffer in silence and try to figure out what to do with my life."

"You know I want nothing more than to help you, right?" He was neatly picking apart the food with shells, making little piles on his plate. "They're always looking for people at Second

Family. Martin is expanding to a franchise—I'm sure he'd jump at the chance to include you. In a city like LA, you use your contacts."

I chewed on a fried pickle, wondering if I was being too negative. Look at Henry; he was born rich, though he'd still gone to college and worked hard. My brother was, in a year, gonna be the first in our family to go to college. Then there was me.

Mattie made a face. "I know what you're doing. You wanna be macho and say you gotta create your own success? I'm sorry to say, but you're a little lipstick too late for that."

I widened my eyes at him.

Henry let out a laugh that he quickly failed to hide behind a cough.

"*Kidding aside,*" Mattie went on, frustrated, "you've raised me practically on your own since you were eighteen. How about you cut yourself some fucking slack and accept what's offered?"

I couldn't do that.

"You're a smart young man, Mattie," Henry said.

I couldn't do that, I repeated to myself, but I did see his point. Could I borrow time? Maybe that would work. I was a man of my word. We could start living our life together, and I could catch up eventually. Somewhat, I added quickly. 'Cause I had to remind myself that I *was* younger. It was unreasonable to hold myself to Henry's standard when he'd lived nineteen years longer than I had.

I felt better now. I nodded, as if to seal the deal, and grabbed a crab leg. "We have a bigger problem," I stated. "Henry hasn't asked me to move in with him." To be fair, I didn't think either of us was ready for that step. For when we moved to LA, though... A guy wanted to be wooed, dammit.

"Who said I was planning to ask?" He lifted a brow. "I thought I would just kidnap you and chain you to our bed."

Ty groaned. "TMI."

I chuckled. "Good to know." I supposed I could woo him by taking him to an adult store.

As the issue was deemed resolved by Mattie and Ty, they chatted amongst themselves instead. I heard names mentioned, classmates. It suited me fine, because I had a question for Henry.

"How long have you been thinking about this?" I licked lemon and salt off my fingers.

He pecked my cheek. "You're not the only one who's dreamed about the future, darling. I was never going to give up, even when it looked hopeless."

I smiled.

There was no question anymore. I loved him.

"Hon, you missed the exit," I said.

"Hmm, don't think I did." Henry kept driving through the forest, passing Camas where my bed was calling my name, and continued toward the Valley.

Oh. It came to me, and I was the dumb one. Of course, he was heading there first. We had to drop Ty off at the inn.

It would be the last night before he and Henry moved in to a vacation home. They were having stuff shipped from LA too.

I bet the bookstore was doing *great*.

When we entered the Valley, Henry made another questionable turn. This time, I wasn't gonna mention it. For all I knew, he had access to some secret underground way to get to Cedar Inn. I shook my head to myself and watched the brownstones we drove past.

"You chillin' with Ty tonight, Mattie?" I asked. Because this guy wouldn't mind some privacy with Henry. One way or another, I was getting off. Fuck my fucking ribs.

"Yup," he said. "Henry gave us a hundred bucks to go nuts. I can take a hint."

"Oh God." I palmed my face and groaned through a laugh.

"We're not doing anything nefarious," Henry insisted, offended. "Zachary is still hurt."

My ass wasn't hurt. That was what I wanted to rectify.

Henry slowed down outside of another place, a picturesque little bed-and-breakfast. We'd ended up by the park near the town's only college, and I gave him a confused look.

"You're booked at Cedar. You know that, right?"

He smiled and pointed toward the B&B. "He's not."

I followed his gaze, only to see Martin there. The porch and the little front yard were lit up dimly, so I could see his wide smile.

I was out of the SUV before I knew it, and I stalked across the street. "You asshole. You don't call, you don't write?"

He laughed merrily, opening the picket fence gate. "That's the welcome I get for coming all the way up here?"

I grunted some nonsense, then hugged him as hard as my ribs could handle. It was so fucking good to see him again.

"I'm sorry, my dear." He patted me on the back. "I was at a spa and had all my calls directed to Mariella. I didn't know about your hospital stay until the day before yesterday. I just got here a couple hours ago. Let me look at that handsome face of yours."

I eased up, and he grasped my chin, inspecting the bruises with a shake of his head.

"No word from the police, I take it?" he guessed.

"Doubt that'll happen." My mouth twisted up as I regarded him. "It's good to see you."

"You too, honey." He winked and patted my cheek. "Since Henry's decided to become half a Washingtonian, we'll have to make use of our miles and visit each other for brunch. I'm thinking once a month, certainly nothing less."

I choked on a chuckle, finding him crazy. There was no way we could fly back and forth that often. For *brunch*.

There was also no way I'd be the one to relay that news.

Henry joined us on the sidewalk, his hand slipping into mine. "Thank you for coming up." They exchanged a cheek kiss. "How're meetings going?"

"That's why I went to a spa." Martin waved a hand, a gesture I'd missed. "Who knew starting a franchise was so stressful?"

"Hey, Martin," Mattie hollered from the rolled-down window.

"Darling boys." Martin waved to the guys, then faced us again. "How was dinner tonight?"

"Good." Henry squeezed my hand. "We somewhat successfully managed to convince Zach that we need two homes, and we've decided I'm taking on my parents this weekend."

Oh yeah, I wasn't looking forward to Saturday. Like a good boyfriend, I'd offered to come with him. He stated it was best he did this himself. He wasn't even going to bring Ty. Instead, he was gonna go over there, stand up to his folks, and pack some of Ty's stuff. Henry had also told me, half jokingly, half affectionately, that he preferred it when I got hotheaded only in bed. And I couldn't blame him. I knew I was likely to get us into trouble if the elder Benningtons got shitheady, which was sort of a given.

In the end, not a lot could go wrong. Henry had sole custody, and Ty no longer wanted to see his grandparents. There was nothing they could do but accept it.

"Well, the more time you spend in LA, the better." Martin spoke with finality. "Leaving Malibu makes sense, but for this?"

"Hey," I protested. "You haven't given it a chance."

"We went on a cruise a few years ago," Henry revealed. "I had to do the island excursions alone because Martin doesn't like bugs."

Martin shuddered.

I snorted. My phone interrupted me then, and I checked it to see who was calling me at almost ten in the evening. I didn't recognize the number and was fully prepared to block another telemarketer.

"Yeah, this is Zach," I answered.

"So we'll do brunch on Sunday before I go home, yes?" Martin looked to Henry.

Releasing Henry's hand, I stepped away from them to hear the woman on the line.

"—and I've been driving my husband up the wall with my second-guessing, but I just can't get you out of my head, Zach." The voice. I recognized it vaguely. "We finished the last shoot for our launch campaign this week, and here I am, ready to move on to the next project only because of you. I'd like to schedule a meeting with you."

Holy shit, it was that lady. Brooklyn, Joseph's boss.

"Um, meeting?" I must've sounded like an idiot, but she might as well have been speaking another language. "Can I ask for what?"

She spoke so fast it was hard to understand. "I have this diversity campaign in mind for the holidays. It's been done before, but I want to go bolder—darker. I need spokesmodels to stay with us, to be able to handle more daring shoots. I want it genuine, so real you can feel it in the photos—aw, hell, I'm sorry. I'm rambling. You have no idea how much I've struggled with this, and then Julian told me you were going out for dinner, and I just checked out. I have to meet with you."

I opened my mouth, and no sound came out. What the fuck

was going on? I turned to Henry and Martin and gave them a helpless stare, but they were useless. Bickering old women.

"I'm interested," I heard myself saying. I didn't know why or how I was interested, but the excitement called to me. They wanted to meet with me, for whatever reason. "I, uh, I'm not in LA at the moment."

"That's fine. I'll have my assistant call your people. Who reps you? I haven't seen you anywhere. Anyway, they'll set up a meeting as soon as possible, and we'll make sure you get all the details beforehand."

"Um, right, yeah, that's great," I stammered. I was in way over my head, yet I managed to prattle off a phone number like I was the most evil mastermind in the world. I just hoped they wouldn't call it right now, 'cause my brother would be answering.

"Perfect, Zach." Brooklyn sounded like everything was suddenly right in the world. "I look forward to seeing you."

We ended the call shortly after, and I gusted out a breath. Oh, so *now* I had Henry's and Martin's attention.

"I…" I gestured to the phone, at a loss. "I need people."

CHAPTER 26

I NEED HIS ROCK HARD...REASSURANCE

"Mattie's gonna want his phone back soon," I muttered, chewing on my thumbnail. I couldn't tear my eyes away from Martin, who was pacing in my little living room with my brother's phone stuck to his ear. "I'm nervous. That's not weird, is it?"

"Of course not." Henry hugged me from behind, helping me relax slightly. "And you're positive she said spokesmodels?"

"Yeah." I'd assured them both of that ten times already. Last night, there wasn't much to do. Martin had seemed frustrated I couldn't relay more details, and Henry had looked weirdly proud. For what, I didn't know. I hadn't done anything.

"Certainly, certainly," Martin was saying to...someone. Brooklyn Wright's people. She had people.

"So, it's like an audition for something?" I asked quietly. "I mean, that's what we're dealing with here. I might have an audition or interview with her makeup company."

What confused me the most was how Brooklyn thought I

was "repped" by someone. Hadn't Julian told her I was only a guest at that club? I'd texted him, and he hadn't responded yet.

"From what you told us..." Henry hummed and pressed a kiss to the back of my head. "I'm not sure, baby. It sounds like more than an interview."

"I'll have my PA send it to you," Martin said. And he was lying, right? He didn't have an assistant. "Yes, that's perfectly fine, and I will book his ticket this afternoon." That made my eyebrows fly up. "I'll forward it." He jotted something down on a notepad.

"Whatever it is, I think you're leaving soon," Henry murmured. "This is exciting, sweetheart. I hope you get the job."

"Doing *what*?" I whispered, frustrated.

Henry chuckled and kissed my neck this time—a slow, openmouthed one that sent a shudder down my spine. "Isn't that obvious? You'll be a model, of course."

"Model," I tested the word. Crazy. "That's crazy. Straight-up batshit."

"Nonsense. You're incredibly sexy. By far, the most beautiful man I've ever met."

I rolled my eyes, though my face felt hotter at the same time. "You say that 'cause you love my ass."

"I do, so much." Fuck, he needed to lay off those kisses if we were gonna stay dressed. "I miss having you."

I swallowed and looked up at him with a brief glare. "You have yourself to blame for that, buddy. Scratch what I said, you don't love my ass enough."

"Soon," he whispered and kissed me. "I don't want to worry about hurting you."

Fretting fucker.

Turning back to Martin as he wrapped up the call, I adjusted my dick and waited expectantly.

"*Well.*" He released a breath and put a hand on his hip. "You, my dear, have a meeting with Brooklyn Wright and her team on Monday."

"This Monday?" I asked incredulously. It was way too fast. I was supposed to have a year to figure out what I wanted to do, and now I had an interview with some makeup brand in LA for a *modeling* gig. On fucking *Monday*.

"Don't you worry," he told me. "As of ten minutes ago, I am your fabulous manager, and I will be there every step of the way. It's a pretty straightforward gig. If they like what they see at the meeting, they'll book you in for a couple weeks, and then you're done."

A couple of weeks. Shit, okay, I could do that. Besides, before the meeting, there were no guarantees. No matter the outcome, I'd be back in Camassia soon.

Pammie was just gonna love this. With Mattie starting school, he couldn't work that much. Maybe it was time to bring in a part-time employee.

"This is actually happening," I stated.

"Oh, it's absolutely happening." Martin was thrilled.

I wasn't. Was I? There was excitement buried somewhere; I could feel it, but there was more. I was nervous, uneasy, and in serious need of reassurance from Henry.

Was this okay with him? What was he thinking?

"Can I have a moment with Henry?" The unease kept growing, and I wasn't sure why.

"Of course, honey." Martin walked toward us and extended Mattie's phone. "I gave them my number instead."

"Okay, thanks." I pocketed the phone, then nodded when he said he'd go to the coffee shop on Olympia Square.

When it was only Henry and me left, my brain started spinning again. This wasn't how we'd planned it. We were gonna have a year of dating and hopefully soon exchange I-love-yous and grow together like a family. I was gonna get closer to Ty; Henry was gonna get to know Mattie better and meet our grandmother.

"It's going fast," I admitted. "My biggest plans this weekend involved asking you to dinner and giving you a blow job for comfort after you've seen your folks." I guess it was my turn to pace. "We've never really been on a date. An official one. I want that."

"Zach, we'll get it," he reasoned gently. "You'll be back before you know it. By then, I will hopefully have found a house."

"So you think this is a good idea?" I needed to know.

Part of me wanted him to say no. It was the part of me that was intimidated, I guessed.

He chose his words carefully, and I stopped him before he could even begin.

"I want your honesty here, Henry."

That gave him another pause. "You're right." He inclined his head and took a breath. "I am working through my insecurities, so I will have to ask for your patience. And permission to come visit you on the weekend if you do stay the whole two weeks. Possibly three, if you think about it. They probably won't get you started the minute the meeting is over." The irony wasn't lost on me, because as he got himself worked up, my comfort grew. I allowed myself to relax. "I suppose what I'm saying is, I will encourage every new challenge you face because I will make sure to be there with you as much as possible."

He said the exact words I had to hear. If we'd been together for months or years, the need to check in and constantly be close wouldn't have been healthy. But we'd just gotten back together and were ready to combat those worries. He wasn't the only one with insecurities if I got anxious this easily.

"Thank you." I exhaled in relief and returned to him,

wanting his arms around me. "I wanna focus on us, if that makes sense."

"Perfect sense." He lifted my chin and kissed me. "I do look forward to you asking me out."

I grinned into the kiss. "Henry, do you wanna go on a date with me when you visit me in LA?"

Because now that I'd gotten the reassurance from Henry, the excitement built up rapidly and spread like wildfire in my veins. Brooklyn saw something in me, and I was gonna ace that audition...or whatever it was.

"I'd like nothing more," he murmured.

"Good. You put out, right?"

He laughed, even as his eyes darkened with lust.

The next day, Henry, Martin, and Ty were arranging things in their temporary home, and it was a good time for me to drag Mattie to see Nan.

The bruises were thankfully starting to fade, and no one looked at me twice as we located Nan in the common room on her floor. Mattie and I did our part, asking the ladies about their lives and whatnot, and then we helped her into her apartment.

"I'm disappointed you didn't bring Henry, sugar," Nan told me. "I thought you two worked things out."

"They did." Mattie got crackin' with the tea and plating the pastries while I helped Nan into her chair by the window. "I swear, every time I turn around, they're all over each other."

Wow, he was exaggerating.

"*Good.*" Nan eyed me over the frames of her glasses. "That's how it's supposed to be. Where is he?"

"Getting settled in," I replied, sitting down across from her. "I'll bring him next time, I promise."

"Perfect." She was appeased. "Now, come closer so I can see your face, Zach."

I suppressed a sigh, and my forearms landed on the table. "I'm okay. No headache anymore. I'm just a bit sore when I twist my upper body."

She gripped my chin and tilted my head slightly, angling it. "It sickens me. Did you get in a few punches?"

I smirked.

She nodded. "I'm glad. Oh, if I could get my hands on those cowards."

Mattie brought over the beverages and pastries. "Zach, tell her about your trip."

"Dude, we just got here."

"What's my pumpkin talking about?" Nan looked between us. "Are you leaving again?"

"Yeah. It's a temporary work thing. And it's an interview—I don't know if I'll get it." After talking to Julian, though, I had high hopes. A misunderstanding had made Brooklyn believe I was a professional, but after Julian had corrected her, she was even more interested in meeting with me. "I'll be back in a few weeks."

"Well, what's it for? Don't hold out on me." She put a pastry on her plate and stirred her tea. "I don't suppose it's a conference for store owners."

Mattie laughed.

I chuckled and shook my head. "It's a modeling gig, I guess."

"And if he's hot enough for that, then I gotta be too," Mattie reasoned.

Nan looked intrigued. "This is certainly different, sugar. I want to know everything."

I realized how tense I was when Henry joined me in bed that night. He had been busy with Ty and the house search all day, plus getting some essentials for their temporary place. With Martin around, essentials were never enough.

"I missed you today." He hugged me close, and I let out a breath and tried to unclench. "Are you okay?"

I nodded, then hesitated. "I had a fight with Mattie, and it's possible I overreacted."

For never seeing Henry's age as something to worry about, I sure focused a lot on other people's ages. Namely, my brother's. He was seventeen, and I felt guilty for leaving him alone. He started school next week too, which made it worse. Like I was abandoning him, and yeah, I could hear how crazy I sounded. We'd been on our own from time to time since I was fourteen and could babysit him. So when Mattie called me out for being ridiculous and pointed out he'd been alone with Ty while I was in LA the first time, I may have resorted to yelling.

When I explained it all to Henry, I was glad he didn't laugh at me.

"For all intents and purposes, you're the boy's dad." He pressed a kiss to my jaw and stroked my back. "Of course, you worry. I'll be here, though. I would like for him to stay with us if it's all right with you. That way, we can have dinner together, and I can make sure they get to school on time."

"I'd like that." I burrowed closer, slipping a hand underneath his boxer briefs. "How did it go with the Realtor today?"

"Excellent, as a matter of fact." He smiled in the dark, the light on my bedside table almost not catching it. "There are some beautiful lodges and ranches in Westslope. We found one overlooking the river. Ty loved it."

That was good news. Henry had already promised to send me pictures of the places they looked at while I was gone. It helped to keep me relaxed if I had the future to focus on, and that was what every photo would represent. It was the home I'd one day share with Henry whenever we were in Camassia.

"Remember when I came to you in Malibu and explained everything about Ty and said Mattie saw him as a brother?"

Henry smiled and brushed our noses together. "You said you wanted to keep it that way."

Yeah. Now it was getting real in a way I sure as hell hadn't expected.

"Before you leave in two days, there's something I have to tell you." Henry shifted me onto my back and crawled over me, and I was the last person to complain. Fuck yes, I hoped this meant he was done fussing over my ribs. "I understand completely if you're not there yet, but waiting two weeks won't work for me. Hell, even one week is too much."

"Oh?" I wriggled beneath him and rubbed his chest. My mouth followed, leaving a trail of kisses along his sternum. "We need to fuck, baby."

He huffed. "Zachary, I'm trying to tell you I'm in love with you."

My gaze flashed to meet his, and I was momentarily dumbfounded. Then I replayed the words I obviously hadn't paid attention to, my lips slowly stretching into a grin.

He smiled carefully. "I can't get over how beautiful you are, inside and out."

"I'm in love with you too." I pulled him down on me, and Christ, it was so right. His weight on me could set me on fire.

His hazel eyes were nearly liquid with heat and affection, and his kiss promised all sorts of wicked and tender things. His hands on me were reverent while his cock pressed demandingly against my thigh.

He groaned and thrust his tongue against mine at the same time as I managed to work a hand between us to palm his cock.

"Do—" He shuddered. "Do you feel better?"

"Yeah." It would've been my response even if I hadn't. "We need this."

He nodded and broke the kiss.

"Nightstand drawer." I explored his chest and neck with my fingers, pushing my cock alongside his hip, and he reached for the table.

"When did you buy this?" He kneeled between my legs and got rid of his underwear before slathering his big cock in lube.

"The other week." I eye-fucked him while I shed my own boxers. How could he be so damn sexy? His erection jutted out, thick, long, intimidating, and glistening. The ridge of his vein glinted in the low light. "Since I didn't have you, I had to use my fingers."

He caught me watching him and slowed down his stroking. He showed me how he got himself off, the unhurried edging, the twist, the pressure at the base, his other hand cupping his balls.

"Ugh, so much better than porn." I bit my lip.

"We'll get you a vibrator for when you're gone," he murmured huskily. He kept stroking himself slowly but used his other hand to prepare me. I shivered as he spread my cheeks and slipped the tip of his pinkie inside me. "I love feeling you like this."

"I know." I grinned and pulled up my knees so my feet were planted on the mattress. "You do that little wiggle thing."

He did it and smirked.

"I want to do it in public." Easing two fingers inside, he elicited a moan from me. "When you're not prepared. Grocery shopping or at the movies. Just slip my pinkie inside and feel you."

"Dirty," I chuckled, breathing heavier. "Speaking of toys... I may have checked out a site where I can get a kit for making my own dildo shaped after your cock."

He rumbled a low curse and stretched me, doing that scissoring thing that got me so hot. "I'll get you one. Then I want you on all fours with a webcam that will show me everything. Every clenched little millimeter of you."

"Jesus," I breathed. I closed my eyes briefly, picturing the vulnerability. He'd sit on the other side of the screen and watch me while I fucked myself. He'd stroke himself and give me commands. "We haven't tried the sleep thing yet."

"We will." He wiped his hands on the sheet, then lowered himself over me. "We'll try everything, my love." He kissed me unhurriedly and rubbed the blunt head of his cock against my asshole. "I have so many things I want to do to you. I want to mark you. With my hands..." His rough hand landed on my throat, shocking me with the bolt of arousal. "With my teeth," he whispered and nipped at my bottom lip. "With my come." In a swift push, he buried himself.

The hand on my throat stopped my cry, instead, drawing a choked gasp from me. The explosion of pleasure turned into an implosion instead, and it sent me spiraling too quickly. I begged and clung to him like a whore. When I pushed too much, the pain in my side was easy to ignore. Henry was fucking me deeply, perfectly, effectively stealing all my focus.

He massaged my throat while whispering filthy things in my ear. "I'll never let you forget you're mine, boy." Pushing in deep, he ground his hips and angled himself to get me *right there*. I cried out hoarsely, and it earned me a hand over my mouth. "Shhh, darling. You don't want to wake up your brother, do you? It's probably best only I know what a perfect ass-slut you are for me."

I gnashed my teeth together so hard I thought I'd crush my molars. "H-Harder." And faster. I couldn't deal. I needed him to fucking rail me.

"I'll take you however I wish, won't I?" He smiled into a brushing kiss. "I love how your body responds to me—how you clench down, just like that. Fuck. How you arch your back, and how your cock leaks with come all over your belly. Do you feel it trickling down? Do you smell it?"

"*Hnngghh.*" I dug my head into the pillow, meeting the next thrust. It shot fire through me. "Oh, fuck. I love you. Shit. Oh, *fuck.*"

He nuzzled my jaw, then sucked on my earlobe. "You make my fucking mouth water."

"*Henry,*" I whimpered. "Fucking—I need it. All of it."

"Okay, baby. Promise to be quiet." He pulled out of me, and I nodded quickly. Then he smacked my thigh and told me to get on all fours for him. "Let me see that tight little hole stretch around my cock."

I flushed all over and got into position, ready to back into him when his hand made impact on my ass. I sucked in a breath through gritted teeth as the sting flared. My cock betrayed me by throbbing and growing painfully hard.

I got what I wanted after that. He fucked me ruthlessly from behind and ordered me to cover a hand over my mouth. Because his "baby boy wouldn't *shut the fuck up.*"

The fucker owned me. He made me stutter and hiss, choke and grunt.

"Unbelievable," he breathed. He brought me backward and wrapped his fingers around my cock, smearing the fluids, and nipped at my ear. That erogenous zone did things to me. Full-body shudders and goose bumps. "I love you, Zach."

"I love you," I groaned breathlessly. "*Ungh*...love you..." My head lolled back to his shoulder, and I simply took what he gave me. With one hand on my hip and the other working my cock, he fucked me on him, in charge of every motion. I just obeyed.

"Almost there."

Me too. I couldn't verbalize it. I tensed up as a ball of heat dropped to my stomach, and the tingles began creeping down my spine. His tightening grip of my cock pushed me to the edge, and I pushed myself down hard on him. The sensations engulfed me, and then I was flying.

The dirty bastard held my cock close to my stomach so the come splattered my skin. I was too gone to do anything about it, though I wasn't sure I'd change anything. He was corrupting me. The dirtier and messier, the hotter.

Henry went rigid next and rocked deeper. I felt the pulsing of his cock as it released each shot of his orgasm. His fingers dug into my hip.

I gasped for air and collapsed against him, a sweaty, fucked mess.

I couldn't form words for several minutes, and exhaustion was taking hold of me. It seemed Henry couldn't speak either, because he spent the next few moments cuddling the hell out of me. My mouth stretched into an involuntary grin as he cleaned me off where it tickled, but it was totally cool when his kisses took over.

Each brush of his lips across my chest made me feel adored.

"I would never jeopardize this," I whispered. "I just want you to know."

He sighed contentedly and gathered me close, kissing me on the forehead. "I don't want to picture my life without you."

"You don't have to." I smiled and popped a kiss to his nose. It earned me a cute grin from him. "Whatever happens in LA... I'm ready for the crazy, as long as I have you with me."

"Oh, there will be crazy." He chuckled quietly, stroking my cheek. "This is only the beginning."

"For us."

He nodded. "For us."

I was ready for it.

EPILOGUE

LET'S MAKE LOVE TO THE CAMERA

"Someone's in a better mood today," Brooklyn sang.

"Maybe?" I couldn't wipe the grin off my face though, so no use in playing coy. It'd been nine days and four hours since I saw Henry. Nine hectic, mind-blowing days where I'd hit the bed face first every night and spent the days being bossed around and poked at. In front of a camera.

I was *not* a model.

Why Brooklyn had hired me almost on the spot was beyond me. She said she liked my face, and once I'd embraced her pro tip on modeling, I did do a bit better. *"We want humble models who look superior and like they don't give a fuck."* I was a dude, so mostly I just had to look cocky and broody. But yeah, that I-don't-give-a-fuck attitude worked.

She was so invested in this project that she was doing the makeup herself. It was how she'd started, doing makeup on the set of a daytime soap opera. Now she ran this successful company and was weeks away from launching the ShadowLight makeup brand.

The makeup room was next to the studio, and I sat down in front of a wall-sized mirror so she could do her thing. Joseph came in shortly after to do another model's makeup. There were fourteen in total, but three were going to have more exposure.

I was one of them—as the gay guy. I'd grown closest to Akira, a Japanese male-to-female transgender model who told the dirtiest fucking jokes at the least opportune moments imaginable. She cracked me up. Lastly, there was Maliah. She was Brooklyn's daughter, and I would've hoped we'd be closer, if it weren't for her overprotective father who felt the need to personally guard every shoot she was in.

"When does your man get in?" Brooklyn started by pushing back my hair, fastening it with a clip.

To my annoyance, it was Joseph who answered. "He lands at five thirty."

I ignored it. He was an outrageous flirt, and I'd lost count of the times he'd tried to hit on me. Which, technically, worked against him. 'Cause it wasn't really me he was interested in. Not beyond a fuck or two, anyway. It was Henry; I was fucking sure of it now. And Henry wasn't happy about his advances.

Another makeup artist entered the room, followed by Akira, and that filled the three spots. She waved sleepily at me, and I said good morning with a little smirk. She was hungover.

"I guess that means you're not coming for dinner tonight?" Brooklyn winked at my reflection, getting ready with some wipe thing.

"No, I'm gonna get fucked six ways to Sunday." It was the truth. "According to Henry, anyway."

Brooklyn and Akira guffawed.

My grin was still there when it was time for the foundation, so I closed my eyes and relaxed. This was the type of makeup that made regular people insecure about their complexion. I wasn't supposed to look like I wore anything.

Brooklyn was demanding yet easy to work for. If she had a vision, she possessed the skills to explain it so no one wandered around completely clueless on set. Since I was new, she'd sort of taken me under her wing, something I appreciated a ton. She invited me over for dinner every night with her family, and I accepted for the most part. When I was surrounded by so much wild shit, it was nice to have a place to unwind.

Akira was way wilder than I could ever be. Or want to be. She could party all night and kill it for the photographers. I'd gone out with her and some of the others twice, and dancing and sipping Violet Hazes was fucking awesome, but a dude needed his sleep too.

"Breakfast orders, people." An assistant poked her head in, and everyone prattled off something.

"OJ and a plain bagel, thanks," I said.

"I miss carbs," Akira yawned.

"Don't we all, hon," Joseph agreed.

I shrugged to myself. I wasn't quitting carbs for a job. Modeling was...an experience, just not one I'd devote my life to. Brooklyn had hinted at wanting to book me for something else later on, and I'd let Martin deal with it. I was gonna go along with it while it was fun and it didn't get in the way of something more important.

I was also the dork who'd made a fool of himself when I'd seen what I was getting paid. I'd legit called Brooklyn and said there was something wrong—a misprint. She'd laughed at me.

Then, so had Martin and Joseph.

In my defense, I wasn't used to being paid this much.

"All set, gorgeous," Brooklyn declared. "You can eat after the first setup."

I nodded, and then I was shuffled along to the huge studio

that was set up to look like a depressing diner from the fifties. The saddest Christmas decorations sat on the diner's counter, which the photographer directed me to stand behind.

They used elaborate sets, and Phil had photographed us in everything from a train to a church. Some of them were, uh, what did they call it...on-set shooting? Maybe. Shit, I didn't know. No, on location. Something like that. We weren't always in a studio.

"We want you bored, Zach—bored and yearning."

Uh-huh, so I was gonna do brooding and fuck all. Got it.

Unlike the sets, the wardrobe couldn't be simpler. We were all in black jeans and wife-beaters. Martin *loved* that.

One thing I'd learned about modeling was that it took forever. They had to direct me, check the lights, take test photos, and change things up. However, once we got started, I wasn't going anywhere.

I leaned over the counter, elbows on the top, and looked out as if there was a window. Phil seemed to approve. I'd fucked up on my first day, overthinking all the instructions: "Show us some biceps," "Remember to look resigned," "Relax," "More attitude." And who could blame me? It'd been too much to remember, so I'd grown frustrated and wary. Now I kept that in mind; it was more important I stuck to the key instructions. Brooklyn's vision, what she wanted to portray, was my focus.

"Frown at the counter, give me the frustration because there's something you want but can't have."

I suppressed a sigh and rephrased it to myself. *Imagine not being able to see Henry tonight.*

My jaw ticked, and I absently pressed the palm of my hand against my other hand's knuckles, cracking them. There were no words to describe how much I missed him, and the best part was that our reunion would be better this time. We were on the same page and talked every day; we put us first. If he wasn't feeling a hundred percent, I didn't get off the phone until he was better. If I was too overwhelmed by this lifestyle, for lack of a better word, he was with me until I could breathe out. Yeah, not seeing him tonight would mess me up.

"That's great, Zach. Let's take ten so you can eat your breakfast."

"*Calm* yourself, hon," Brooklyn berated with a laugh.

"I'm sorry." I grew sheepish and refocused. One hour to go, then he'd be here. Henry had landed. Now he was facing traffic at rush hour. Distance didn't matter whatsoever. It could be around the corner from the airport, and he'd still be a while.

"I want your A game," she said, holding up a lipstick. "This next one is what started it all. The look you gave the mirror in that club—I want you to give that to the camera now."

I nodded once, then stayed still as she applied the lipstick. It resembled the one Henry made me wear, dark plum, only this one had no shine or gloss to it.

Each ad in this campaign, I'd learned, would have a strip of three photos. They all had depressing backgrounds with some type of half-assed, cheap holiday decorations. In the first shot, we got the longing, brooding, and defeat. In the second one, we were staring at whatever makeup product Brooklyn chose. So far, I'd gotten lipstick and an eye pen. The item of makeup would be at the center of our attention, as well as the photos'. Then the third photo was where we wore the product. And we got bold.

When Brooklyn said she was going for bold, she wasn't messing around.

The second shot had taken me the longest today. Then after lunch, I'd been whisked to an outdoor set where Maliah had been doing her shoot. My part had been to push her up against a streetlamp and brush my thumb over her shimmering cheekbone.

Asher, Brooklyn's husband, wasn't happy with me at the moment.

I'd reminded him I had a boyfriend.

"Akira to set!" someone hollered.

I refrained from touching my lips. It was possible I'd done that once or twice before.

"Perfect." Brooklyn stepped back and followed me back to my spot behind the diner's counter. On the way, I rolled my shoulders and stretched my legs. "Akira, I want you behind Zach."

Akira was by no means short, but she wasn't taller than me.

In heels, she reached high enough to sink her teeth into my shoulder, which Brooklyn told her to do.

"Lord, woman." I winced. She had sharp teeth.

"Shush. I know you like it rough," she giggled.

I laughed and didn't deny it. When I was tipsy, I shared stories about Henry and me.

Brooklyn placed one of Akira's hands under my beater to rest along my abs. "Okay, careful now." She guided Akira's other hand to— "No, wait. Too much." Brooklyn studied us for a beat and tapped her chin. "Skip the abs. Rest it on his hip instead. I want focus on his mouth." She carefully drew Akira's hand to my jaw so her fingers landed over my mouth. "Stay still." Next, she dragged the fingers downward, and I killed my smirk. She really had Henry's actions in her thoughts. The dark lipstick smeared with Akira's fingers, down my jaw. "There, keep your fingers there." She smeared the lipstick a bit more before backing off. "Give me bold, darlings! Zach, I want the same fuck-me eyes you gave your man in the mirror. Can you do that for me?"

Oh, I could do that. All I had to do was think of him.

Feet aligned with my shoulders, I lifted my chin and pretended Phil's camera was Henry. It was his teeth sinking into my flesh, his fingers making a mess on my jaw. My LA nights flooded my thoughts, and I put all the attitude I could into it. The determination to face anyone who wanted to walk all over me, the take-me-for-who-I-am pride because it was okay to stand out, the sheer desire to please my boyfriend, and the...challenge, the *dare*, to find yourself in a club bathroom with glitter on your face.

Brooklyn's squeal offered the biggest relief. It made me hope my eyes had flashed with at least a fraction of the heat the experiences had given me since I'd met Henry Bennington.

He and Martin had insisted I mingle on my own that first night at a gay bar in Santa Monica. Because of it, I'd embarked on a journey that was gonna take me places. I could do both. And that was the thing. Henry remained insistent I try new things, and I was eager to jump in now, 'cause I had him. Whether he was right by my side or waiting by the bar, he was there. He would be the last person to hold me back, but when I needed my safe place to land, he caught me.

I wanted to try it all. Be it modeling, getting involved with Henry's organization, or helping Martin decorate freaking cupcakes, I was gonna do it.

"Joseph!" Brooklyn shouted. "Get out here!"

I took a calming breath. It was hard to push down the motherfucking joy that surged through me.

"Grip his hip tighter, Akira," Phil said.

"Same with his jaw, hon," Brooklyn added with a nod. "Make it look like you're digging your fingers into him."

Akira complied and snickered softly at my wince. I was gonna give it to her later. Fuck her if she made me laugh.

Joseph came out from the makeup room just as I spotted a

shadow in the corner of my eye. *It's him.* It had to be. Gray slacks, black shirt, a roll-aboard carry-on. It meant Mattie and Ty were having dinner with Nan tonight and taking care of the store tomorrow. It meant I had the whole weekend with Henry.

"Look at him," Brooklyn said, beaming. "*Look* at him. He's my new face."

I groaned through a chuckle and gave up. "How the fuck am I supposed to give the camera bedroom eyes *now*?" The woman was making me self-conscious. More than that, my entire being was buzzing. I wanted to run over to Henry.

Brooklyn noticed Henry then, and she tinkered a laugh and waved a hand. "Okay, let's take a break."

Fuck, yes. I legit jumped over the counter, taking a quick detour to the box of tissues Brooklyn held up, and then I was stalking closer to the exit while wiping the lipstick off. *My man.* Holy shit, I'd missed him. Had it really only been nine days?

He gave me the warmest grin, and I didn't stop until I had my arms around his neck and was yanking him in for a hard kiss.

"I love you." I hugged him harder to me, enjoying catching him off guard for once, and spoke in between kisses. "I love you, I love you, I love you."

He let out a surprised noise and smiled. "Hello to you too, my love." He touched my cheek and took over, controlling this kiss and the next.

I was gonna be in charge soon, though. We'd have a quick dinner, probably with Martin, who was bitching about his struggles with the franchise startup, and then I'd get Henry back to my hotel room and take all the advantage.

The best suites in the world were the ones your employer paid for as a "job perk." I may have prepared it for Henry's arrival, including snacks for energy, all the lube we could need, and the dildo he'd made me use for him.

"When do you get off?" he asked, dragging my bottom lip

between his teeth. "I still have to punish you for sending me cock shots at three in the morning."

I laughed. Violet Haze was a wild drink. It wasn't my fault. Couldn't forget the captions either. On each picture, I'd typed, "We love you hard."

"I get off when you're inside me," I grunted. "But if you're asking when my day here is over, it's seven."

He hummed and took himself another long, deep kiss. "I suppose you want to stay in all weekend? You told me you had plans for us."

Jesus Christ, yes. Although, it wasn't all about sex. I'd had the most vivid dreams of talking about houses, arguing over whose turn it was to do the dishes, synching work schedules, grocery shopping, and...well, twin girls.

In short... "Yeah. Plans for a lifetime."

But hold on. It's not over yet.

OUT for the holidays
CARA DEE

"I'm just going to write something quick to give the readers a glimpse into their future." –Silly Cara

That little epilogue wasn't enough for me. I wanted more than just to tie up loose ends, but when I started writing the original epilogue, a few pages quickly turned into 20,000 words. I don't want to delete any of it. I want a sweet, dirty, funny, and Christmassy sequel with just a bit of drama.

If you want to read more about Zach and Henry and their friends and family, <u>Out for the Holidays: An Out Novella</u> will be published on December 12th, 2017.

Between the home Zach and Henry have created in Camassia Cove, the hectic life in Los Angeles, and a photo shoot in Mexico, they juggle two teenagers, responsibilities, a so-called friend who won't take no for an answer, two elder Benningtons who won't go

A NOTE FROM THE AUTHOR

down without a fight, a tipsy Nan and Martin, and a cat that still needs to shed a couple pounds.

Zach and Henry just wanted a quiet Christmas with their loved ones.

Yeah, that's out.

MORE FROM CARA DEE

In Camassia Cove, everyone has a story to share
Dominic
Adrian
Meghan
Chloe
Adam

Though each Camassia Cove novel is a standalone within the series, the characters tend to make appearances in other titles. Cara freely admits she's addicted to revisiting the men and women who yammer in her head. If you enjoyed *Out*, you might like the following.

Noah (Noah & Julian's story.)
Home (Dominic & Adrian's story.)
Out: Out for the Holidays

MORE FROM CARA DEE

Check out Cara Dee's entire collection at www.caradeewrites.com and don't forget to sign up for her newsletter so you don't miss any new releases, updates on book signings, giveaways, and much more.

ABOUT CARA

I'm often stoically silent or, if the topic interests me, a chronic rambler. In other words, I can discuss writing forever and ever. Fiction, in particular. The love story—while a huge draw and constantly present—is secondary for me, because there's so much more to writing romance fiction than just making two (or more) people fall in love and have hot sex.

There's a world to build, characters to develop, interests to create, and a topic or two to research thoroughly. Every book is a challenge for me, an opportunity to learn something new, and a puzzle to piece together.

I want my characters to come to life, and the only way I know to do that is to give them substance—passions, history, goals, quirks, and strong opinions—and to let them evolve. Additionally, I want my men and women to be relatable. That means allowing room for everyday problems and, for lack of a better word, flaws. My characters will never be perfect.

Wait...this was supposed to be about me, not my writing.

I'm a writey person who loves to write. Always wanderlusting, twitterpating, kinking, and geeking. There's time for hockey and cupcakes, too. But mostly, I just love to write.

~Cara.

Made in the USA
Middletown, DE
22 January 2018